THE
FORGOTTEN
GIRLS

THE FORGOTTEN GIRLS

SARA BLAEDEL

Translated by

SIGNE RØD GOLLY

GRAND CENTRAL
PUBLISHING

NEW YORK   BOSTON

Copyright © 2015 by Sara Blaedel
Translated by Signe Rød Golly; translation copyright © 2015 by Sara Blaedel

Grand Central Publishing
Hachette Book Group
1290 Avenue of the Americas
New York, NY 10104
www.HachetteBookGroup.com

Printed in the United States of America

RRD-C

First edition: February 2015
10 9 8 7 6 5 4 3 2 1

Grand Central Publishing is a division of Hachette Book Group, Inc.
The Grand Central Publishing name and logo is a trademark of Hachette Book Group, Inc.

The Hachette Speakers Bureau provides a wide range of authors for speaking events. To find out more, go to www.hachettespeakersbureau.com or call (866) 376-6591.

The publisher is not responsible for websites (or their content) that are not owned by the publisher.

Library of Congress Cataloging-in-Publication Data

Blaedel, Sara.
  [Glemte piger. English]
  The forgotten girls / Sara Blaedel ; translated by Signe Rod Golly. — First edition.
    pages cm
  ISBN 978-1-4555-8152-8 (hardcover) — ISBN 978-1-4789-8329-3 (audio download) — ISBN 978-1-4555-8150-4 (ebook) 1. Policewomen—Fiction. 2. Detectives—Denmark—Fiction. 3. Murder—Investigation—Fiction. 4. Missing persons—Fiction. I. Golly, Signe Rod, translator. II. Title.
  PT8177.12.L33G5413 2014
  839.813'8—dc23
                                                                    2014010802

My own dear mother
I long for you
If only you knew
How they mistreat me
Confined to bed
Bound by belt and gloves
Dear mother
I long for you

—*Solborgs bog* by
Solborg Ruth Kristensen

THE FORGOTTEN GIRLS

PROLOGUE

*G*ONE IS *coming, Gone is coming!* The words pounded in her ears as the rocks and branches of the forest floor tore her feet and shins. Her head was whirling, and fear made her heart constrict.

She was headed for the only light she could see. Like an opening in the dark, the gleam of white pulled her deeper into the woods. Confused and scared, she stumbled through the trees, gasping for air.

Her fear of the dark was like a choke hold around her neck. It had been that way ever since she was ordered as a young child to turn off the light and go to sleep. Or Gone would come and take her.

Gone, Gone, Gone—the words sounded rhythmically, and she was too slow to prevent a branch from flicking across her cheek.

Holding her breath, she stopped and stood as if frozen,

completely surrounded by the saturated darkness from the trees that towered around her. Her legs were shaking from exhaustion. Frightened by the sound of her own crying, she slowly stepped forward, her eyes fixed on the light ahead. It blinded her when she looked straight at it.

She didn't know how she had gotten lost. The door had been ajar, and they hadn't noticed her standing in the doorway. She had been overcome with joy when she felt the sun warming her and beckoning her, but that was hours ago and now everything had turned cold and unsettling.

At one point hunger made her give up, and she sat down. Twilight fell while confusing fragments of images tumbled through her head until finally, unable to settle down, not knowing how long she had been sitting, she got back up. She wasn't used to interrupted routines, and being alone was not good—especially not for the person left behind.

She increased her speed, getting closer to the white light. It was pulling her in like an irresistible force, and she shut out the pain and the sounds—a skill she had mastered by now. She had never learned to handle the fear, however. She needed to escape the dark, or Gone would come and take her.

She was getting close; only a little farther ahead through the last trees. Her heart slowed as she caught a glimpse of a moonlit lake. Just as she was about to slow down, the ground suddenly disappeared from under her feet.

I

FOUR DAYS. That was how much time had passed since the woman's body had been discovered in the woods, and the police had yet to identify her. They didn't have the slightest clue to go on, and Louise Rick was frustrated as she pulled in and parked by the Department of Forensic Medicine late Monday morning.

The autopsy had started at 10 a.m., and it had been a bit later when the head of the Search Department, Ragner Rønholt, walked into the office and asked her to drive over and assist her colleague Eik Nordstrøm. Shortly before, Forensic Medicine had announced the decision to upgrade the autopsy to include homicide tests for DNA.

It was Louise's second week as technical manager of the Special Search Agency, a newly established unit of the department. Each year, sixteen to seventeen hundred people were reported missing in Denmark. Many turned up again and some were found dead, but according to the assessment of the National Police, there was a crime behind one out of five of the unsolved missing person reports.

Her department was tasked with investigating these cases.

Louise got out and locked the car. She didn't quite understand why they needed her at the autopsy when Eik Nordstrøm was already there. He had been off on vacation the past four weeks, so he was the only person in the department that she hadn't yet met.

It was Louise who had gone through the list of missing persons on Friday afternoon and discovered that none of the missing women matched the description of the woman found in the woods. Perhaps Rønholt felt that she ought to be present for the examination of the deceased as well. Or it could simply be because she had come from the Homicide Department and had more experience dealing with autopsies than her new colleagues. The move was an unusual step down, to be sure, driven by an excruciating decision Louise had felt compelled to reach. She'd make the best of it, but she wasn't thrilled to be here.

It actually felt nice to be tasked with something she knew how to navigate after a week of unfamiliar territory. Louise hadn't foreseen the hopeless feeling when starting a new job of forgetting people's names and not knowing where to find the copier. She had spent the first week organizing the "Rathole." *Heck of a name*, she thought, hoping that it wouldn't stick—she was already growing a bit weary of her colleagues' witty comments about the unused rooms at the end of the hall. The two-person office was above the kitchen and had been empty since Pest Control had dealt with a considerable rat infestation last spring. But the rats were gone now and no one had seen them since, her new boss assured her.

Ragner Rønholt had done his part to get the new department in order, purchasing new office chairs and bulletin boards along with a number of plants. The chief superintendent had a personal preference for orchids and apparently felt that some greenery was what was needed to bring life into the unused office. That was all very well, Louise thought. But what really mattered to her was the fact that she sensed his commitment. Ragner Rønholt was clearly determined to get this new sub-unit up and running. They had been granted one year to prove that there was a need for the special unit, and Louise had everything to gain. If this new job did not become permanent, she risked ending up a local detective somewhere in the district.

"You decide who you want on the team," Rønholt had generously told her when he introduced her to the idea of heading the Special Search Agency.

Since then she had considered at length who might be suitable prospects, and the final candidates on her list were all people with whom she had worked before. Experienced and competent.

First on the list was Søren Velin from the Mobile Task Force. He was used to working all over the country and had good contacts at many local police stations. But he liked his current position, so Louise didn't know how easily he would transfer; the question also remained whether Rønholt would match his current salary.

Then there was Sejr Gylling from the Fraud Department. He was great at thinking outside the box. But he was an albino, sensitive to bright daylight, and she was not sure that she could stand always working behind closed curtains.

Finally there was Lars Jørgensen, her most recent partner in the Homicide Department. They knew each other inside and out, and she felt comfortable working with him. There was also no question that this type of work would suit his temperament as well as his status as a single dad to two boys from Bolivia.

So there were several promising candidates. Louise just hadn't decided yet which one she should try to reel in first.

Outside the door to the autopsy unit, she spotted Åse from the Center of Forensic Services. The slender woman was crouched next to her briefcase but stood up, smiling, as Louise approached.

"We snapped a couple of photos for you before we really got started," she told Louise after they said hello. "Just of the face, in case you decide to ask the public for help in identifying her."

"Yes, it looks like that might become necessary," Louise conceded, even though pictures like that always caused a stir. Some people felt showing the faces of the deceased was too morbid.

The forensic officer gestured toward the autopsy rooms, her green eyes serious.

"The woman in there won't be hard to recognize. That is, if she has any next of kin," she said. "The entire right side of her face is covered by a big scar, presumably from a burn wound, which continues down onto her shoulder. So if she hasn't already been reported missing, a picture is probably your best chance of discovering her identity."

Louise nodded but didn't have a chance to answer because just then Flemming Larsen walked up along with two lab technicians. The tall medical examiner beamed when he spotted Louise.

"Well, I'll be—I guess we haven't seen the last of you after all!" he said, hugging her. "I was worried that it was me you were trying to get away from when you suddenly changed departments."

"You didn't really think that," she retorted, smiling and shaking her head.

Louise had known Flemming Larsen for the eight years she worked in the Homicide Department. She had been happy with her job and counted on staying there until her retirement, but with Willumsen gone and Michael Stig appointed new group leader, she had needed no time to think it over before accepting Rønholt's offer.

"Is Eik Nordstrøm in there?" Louise asked, tipping her chin toward the doors to the autopsy rooms.

"Eik who?" Flemming looked at her with confusion.

"Eik Nordstrøm from the Search Department."

"Never heard of him," Flemming said. "But let's head in there. We've completed the external part of the autopsy so I can give you a quick summary."

Louise was puzzled by the absence of her colleague. She held the door open for Åse before walking into the sluice room, where rubber boots and coats were lined up.

"What do we know about this woman?" she asked as she put on a lab coat and hairnet.

"So far, not much, except that it was a forest worker who found her on Thursday morning by Avnsø Lake on mid-Zealand," Flemming answered, handing her a green surgical mask. "According to the coroner's examination, she died sometime between Wednesday and early Thursday morning.

"The police think she fell or slipped maybe fifteen feet down a steep slope and landed badly," he continued. "The coroner's examination was carried out in Holbæk on Friday, and the medical officer and the local police decided to get an autopsy done—because she died alone, of course, but also because we have no idea who this woman is. I decided to upgrade the autopsy so we'll get the DNA."

Louise nodded in agreement. DNA and dental records were always the first steps toward an identification. It would have been nice if Eik Nordstrøm had bothered to show up, she thought, so one of them could follow up with the dentist right away.

"I can say almost for sure that this is no ordinary woman we're dealing with," Flemming went on, explaining that this was clear from both the clothes she had been wearing before they began and the condition of the body. "Or at least it's not a woman who has lived an ordinary life," he corrected.

"We've run her fingerprints through the system but with no matches," Åse added. "I'm thinking she might be a foreigner."

Flemming Larsen agreed that this was a possibility.

"It's certainly clear that she has not participated in any kind of social life for many years," he elaborated. "You'll see what I mean."

The medical examiner led the way down the white-tiled hallway with autopsy bays side by side to their right. In each, medical examiners stood bent over steel tables with dead human bodies. Louise quickly averted her eyes when she caught a glance of an infant's body on one.

"When we scanned the deceased's head before starting the autopsy, deep furrows in her brain were clearly evident," Flemming elaborated. "Simply put, she had a large cavity system, so there can't have been much going on in there."

"Do you mean to say that she was mentally handicapped?" Louise asked.

"She certainly wasn't the next Einstein."

2

THE HOMICIDE ROOM was at the end of the hallway. This rearmost autopsy room was twice the size of the other bays to allow room for police and forensic officers, but the room was set up the same as the others: with a steel table, a wide sink, and bright lamps.

Louise took out her Dictaphone and placed it where it could record Flemming's examination of the body. The entire process was photographed by Åse, who was compiling the materials for investigation at the Center of Forensic Services. The samples that Flemming collected in the process would be passed on to the forensic geneticists upstairs.

While Louise wouldn't exactly say the woman lying on the table in the middle of the room was dirty, neither would she say she was well groomed. Her hair was overgrown and tangled and her nails long and jagged. Most striking was the large scar that covered one cheek and pulled down the eye a little, giving her face a sad expression.

"The dentist was astounded, to put it mildly, when he finished his examination," Åse said as she lifted her camera. "He said it's extremely rare for him to see a set of teeth in such a state of neglect. They're ruined from cavities and very crooked."

Flemming nodded. "She has apparently never had any kind of orthodontics, and there's severe periodontal disease in the upper part of the mouth," he said. "She already lost several teeth."

Louise grabbed a tall stool, which she moved closer as Flemming started the internal examination. The organs had been removed and transferred to a steel tray next to the sink.

"We're dealing with a full-grown woman but I'm having difficulty assessing her age." He bent over the body. "As far as the distinctive scar is concerned, I feel certain that it has never been treated. It's a violent injury from some time back. It may also have been a corrosive burn," he added, pensively. "There hasn't been any grafting, and it must have hurt like hell when it happened."

Louise nodded. That had been her initial thought as well.

"She also has an old scar that could easily date all the way back to her childhood. At one point in time she broke a bone in her left forearm, which wasn't treated."

The medical examiner looked up at them as he drew his first conclusion.

"All of this tells me that she has been profoundly neglected throughout her life and that she was probably quite isolated."

Louise looked at the ruined soles of the woman's feet and the cuts on her ankles. They clearly showed that she had gone barefoot for a long way.

Flemming turned his eyes back to the woman's body once more and continued the autopsy in silence for a short while until he noted that in falling down the slope, the deceased had broken seven ribs on her left side.

"There's about five pints of blood in the left pulmonary cavity," he announced without looking up. "And the lung is collapsed."

After rinsing the internal organs and examining them one by one, he straightened up and told Åse that he was finished.

"Aside from the broken ribs and the blood in the pulmonary cavity there's no indication of violence," he said, rolling off his skintight gloves and throwing them in the trash. "My immediate guess would be that she died of her internal bleeding."

He paused and thought for a moment before adding: "One detail that may be of interest is that I'm quite convinced the woman had intercourse shortly before her death."

Louise looked at him in surprise.

"I believe there are remnants of semen in the vagina and on the inside of both thighs," he explained, "but I need to get that confirmed, of course, so I'll have to wait to get the test results back before I can say for certain. That could take about a week."

She nodded. It very well could when there was no indication that the death was the result of a crime. She got up and walked back to look at the woman's disfigured face.

"If I'm right, it could mean that perhaps she wasn't that lonely after all." Flemming walked over to call the technicians, letting them know he had finished.

"But still lonely enough that no one has found reason to report her missing despite the fact that she's been dead almost a week," Louise said.

She waited while Åse put away her equipment and then they said good-bye to Flemming, who had moved to the computer in the corner to dictate the details to his report.

They left the autopsy room with a nod at the two forensic technicians, who had to close up the body before it was taken back to the cold-storage room in the basement.

3

Angry, Louise phoned Ragner Rønholt, her fingers punching the keys. "There was no Eik Nordstrøm when I got to the Department of Forensic Medicine," she began when Rønholt answered. "I don't know how you usually do things but it's a complete waste of the medical examiner's time when the police aren't there from the beginning. He had to repeat to me what they'd found out from the external part of the autopsy."

"Oh, what the hell," Rønholt grumbled. "He didn't show up?"

"At least not where the rest of us were," Louise answered, adding that she was heading back now.

"Hold on a minute," her boss said. "Just stay there. I'll call you right back."

After he hung up, she took the stairs down to the foyer and stood for a bit, waiting for his call. Finally she lost patience and walked across the street to the car.

She had just slid into the driver's seat when Rønholt's name started flashing on her phone.

"Did you leave?"

"I'm about to," she answered, making no attempt to hide her annoyance that he had kept her waiting.

"Could you do me a favor and pick up Eik at Ulla's out in Sydhavnen?" he asked. "Looks like he's having a bit of trouble getting back into the swing of things after his vacation."

Louise sighed and asked for the address. She ignored Rønholt's thanks as she entered the street name in her GPS.

She hadn't signed on for this. She was not some eager-to-please rookie; nor was she comfortable being asked to retrieve her drunken partner from some seedy pub.

Number 67. Louise couldn't find the place, only 65 and 69. Between them was a run-down closed bar, the door hidden behind rusty grating.

Just as she started walking back to her car, a beer truck pulled up at the curb, horn honking. Louise turned to watch the driver, who had already jumped out of the driver's cab and started lowering the wide tailgate.

She could have sworn that the bar with the peeling Carlsberg ad in the window had been sapped of life for years, but now a stocky, heavyset woman with jet-black hair appeared in the door, struggling to unlock the two padlocks on the rusty grating.

"Excuse me," Louise began once the woman had removed them. "Do you know if number sixty-seven is in the backyard?"

The woman hauled the grating inside the door, stepping aside as the truckers started hauling in boxes.

"This is sixty-seven," she answered, a stale smell of old smoke and spilled beer drifting out from behind her.

"I'm here to pick up Eik Nordstrøm at Ulla's. Do you know her?"

The middle-aged woman looked at Louise for a moment then gestured toward the room behind her.

"I'm Ulla. Ulla's is my bar, and he's in there."

The men were replacing the beer casks as Louise was ushered toward the back of the room, where two gaming machines hung on the wall. The carpet under her feet was sticky in several places, and full ashtrays were still sitting on the tables. Ulla was working on cleaning up after the night's drinking.

Nordstrøm was sprawled across four chairs that had been pushed together in a row against the wall. Someone had covered him with a small fleece blanket. He was snoring softly with his mouth open, and his greasy, longish hair covered his forehead and fell on his nose.

"Someone's here for you, hon," Ulla called, placing her hand on his black leather jacket as she started to shake him.

Louise took a few steps back, cursing Rønholt. "Never mind."

She was about to leave when Ulla stopped her. "Just give him two minutes and he'll be ready."

Louise stood and watched as Ulla walked behind the counter and got out a shot glass and a bottle of liquor, which she brought over and put down on the table before she started shaking Eik again.

He grunted loudly as he finally sat up with much difficulty and accepted the glass that Ulla handed him. He closed his eyes and tipped his head back, pouring the small drink down his throat and quickly accepting another.

Then he redirected his eyes and tried to focus on Louise.

"Who the hell are you?" he asked, his voice sounding as if it were coming through an old, rusty pipe.

"Rønholt asked me to pick you up," she answered. "Your vacation's over."

"Tell him to go to hell," he grumbled as he lit a cigarette from a flattened pack on the table.

Louise watched him for a moment before she turned around and left. Outside, the truckers were about to close the truck's tailgate, and Ulla started replacing the grating.

"Wait!" a voice jarred from inside.

He came stumbling out into the street, blinking in the bright sunlight while he ran his hands through his hair. For a moment it looked as if he was going to lose his balance, but then he started to follow her as she walked toward the car.

"Do I know you?" he asked, tossing his cigarette on the curb.

Louise shook her head and introduced herself. "You were supposed to be at the Department of Forensic Medicine three hours ago, so I filled in for you."

She opened the passenger door and maneuvered him into the car. She had barely walked around to the other side to get in before he leaned his head back and fell asleep.

The ride back to the Search Department was accompanied by a gentle snoring but Louise shut it out, instead focusing on the unidentified woman. There had been something vulnerable, almost childish, about the part of her face that wasn't disfigured by the large scar. She must have been pretty once. But the question remained—when?

Louise left Eik Nordstrøm in the parking lot. He was still sitting in the car, eyes closed, when she slammed the door shut behind her. Then she walked to her office, keeping her eyes fixed on the grayish linoleum floor so as not to show the anger that was simmering in her head.

She dropped her bag on the floor and closed the door. The walls were still bare but Louise noticed that venetian blinds had been installed while she was out.

The sun shone brightly into the room so she walked over to adjust the blinds before sitting down at her desk and turning on her computer. She found the file containing résumés along with her own notes on the three people she thought would be well suited to lead the department with her while she considered if perhaps Henny Heilmann might also be a candidate.

Her previous group leader, who had been assigned to Radio Communication, had a long career in the Homicide Department behind her. She was one of the most experienced investigators Louise knew, but perhaps she did not have what it took to return to the fold, she thought, acknowledging that Heilmann was a wild card. She would either be incredibly committed and efficient, as in the old days, or it would be hard to get her back up to speed.

Someone pounded on the door. When it was flung open a second later Eik Nordstrøm barged in with a couple of boxes stacked on top of an office chair, which he was pushing in front of himself with one foot.

"All right, there's a chair in here already," he noted and stopped in the doorway.

"What's going on?" Louise exclaimed, quickly gathering up her notes while noticing that he had put some water in his hair and combed it back. She was guessing that he'd had a clean T-shirt at the office and had done a quick rinse-off in the locker room.

"I'm moving in," he said, nodding in the direction of the empty seat on the opposite side of the window. "I always wanted a female partner."

Louise got up, dumbfounded.

"You and I won't be working directly together," she shot back at him. "The Special Search Agency is more like a parallel unit to yours."

"Yes," he agreed as he unloaded the boxes on the desk. "And that agency is going to be you and me. I was just told to pack up my things and move in here with you."

"Then there's been a misunderstanding. Who told you that?"

Eik had tossed his leather jacket on the floor and started to unpack the two boxes.

"Rønholt. He put me on the case involving the woman from the woods."

Louise stared at him in disbelief.

"Sure, but you don't have to be in here to work on that case, right?" she tried.

"Yeah, 'cause I'll be working with you," he said and coughed as if his lungs hadn't quite gotten their day started yet.

She stood quietly for a moment, letting his words sink in. Then she grabbed the file from the desk and pushed past him as he started to maneuver the surplus chair out again.

"Is Rønholt in there?" she asked when she stood in front of her boss's secretary. Hanne Munk had also worked in the Homicide Department some years ago, but only briefly. Her big red hair, multicolored clothing, and spiritual tendencies had not exactly been Detective Superintendent Willumsen's cup of tea, so within a few months he had managed to scare her away.

"You can't go in right now!" she said. "Ragner is preparing for a meeting with the national commissioner."

"I need to speak with him. It'll take two minutes." Louise continued through the front office.

Hanne leaped up and got to the door before Louise could raise her arm to knock.

"You can't just barge in and interrupt." She blocked the way, giving Louise an angry stare. "And he won't have any more time for the rest of the day. But of course you're welcome to schedule a meeting later this week."

"Oh, would you stop it!" Louise said. She stayed right in Hanne's face with no intention of giving in.

Just then the door opened and Ragner Rønholt nearly tripped over his secretary, who was still blocking the threshold.

"Well, hello there," he said, grabbing Hanne's shoulders to regain his balance while smiling at Louise. "I'm glad you were able to get Eik up and about. He's a good guy once he gets out of vacation mode."

"Yeah, about that…" Louise slipped past Hanne while pulling Rønholt back into his office and closing the door behind them. "Our deal was crystal clear: I get to pick the other person who'll work in the new department."

She handed her papers to him.

"Here's a list of the people I consider qualified."

As he accepted the file, Louise remembered the small notes she had made, which were meant for her eyes only, and pulled the papers back out of his hands.

"No one ever said that you could just unload some drunk on me."

"Who said anything about unloading anyone?" Rønholt sounded defensive, a deep crease indented across his forehead. "Eik is my best guy, and I'm sure that the combination of the two of you could be world-class."

World-class? Louise was dumbfounded at both his choice of words and how effortlessly he'd dumped the colleague on her.

"He was sleeping it off in a bar. Once he finally came around, he downed two shots before he even got on his feet. That is not world-class. Forget it. I want Lars Jørgensen. I'm sure he could be transferred over here quickly."

Rønholt had moved behind his desk. He looked at her. "You're right that Eik is fighting some demons, which at times are stronger than him. But sometimes people's weaknesses can also turn out to be their strengths," he said. "Lars Jørgensen is a possibility. But give Eik a chance. For a start, I suggest that he and you find the woman's identity, investigate if there are any next of kin who need to be notified, and then we'll get this case closed."

It was not the reaction Louise had expected. She took a deep breath and exhaled. This wasn't over yet.

He looked at his watch and grabbed his coat from the rack. "I'm running a bit late. Tonight's bridge night and I'm in charge of the cheese platter, so I won't be able to make it back after my meeting."

Louise followed him out but paused by the door. Eik Nordstrøm was standing in the front office, chatting with Hanne, who was nodding and smiling at every word he said.

"So how about we figure out the identity of our Jane Doe?" Louise asked. "If you're not too busy?"

She marched through the front office, well aware of the sour tone in her voice. She heard Eik whisper something in Hanne's ear that made her giggle before he tore himself away to catch up with Louise in the hallway.

"You want a cup of coffee?" he asked, turning to walk into the kitchen.

"No thanks, I drink tea." Louise stopped in surprise by the door to the Rathole. The office was transformed. It suddenly looked like someone had moved in. Maybe those music posters in snap frames weren't exactly to her taste, but at least it looked inhabited.

"Well, I'll be..." she exclaimed.

"I can chuck it all back if it bothers you," she heard from behind her where Eik was watching her, a cup of coffee and two cheese sandwiches in hand.

"No, it's fine," she answered quickly. Truth be told, she was happy to leave the decorating to someone else. It was nice to have some things in the room, but she had no personal interest in the details.

She walked over to her desk, put her stuff down, and dropped into her chair.

4

I PUT A black marker on the case so the woman is now cate-
gorized as deceased in Interpol's register," Louise said. She
looked at Eik, who was digging into his second sandwich. "But
before we release the photo to the media, maybe we should
send it to the police districts and to Interpol?"

She waited, unsure of the proper procedure. The case had
been transferred to the Search Department once it became
apparent to the Holbæk police that they were unable to identify
the woman on their own.

"Not that it'll do the other districts much good when we
don't have a name to put on it," she added.

He shook his head while he quickly finished chewing. "We'll
only be wasting time if we sit around and wait for someone to
recognize her by chance. When it comes to unidentified bodies,
we usually start by focusing on the area where they were found."

"All right," Louise said. "It was a forest worker who found

her on Thursday morning by Avnsø Lake on central Zealand. Does that ring a bell with you?" He shook his head as she rattled off locations: "Hvalsø, Skov Hastrup, Særløse, Ny Tolstrup. There's a refugee center out there."

"Is it down by Køge?" he asked, shaking the crumbs off his black T-shirt.

"No, it's not near Køge." She sighed. "It's between Roskilde and Holbæk. The forest worker was cleaning up along the lakeside when he spotted her. He doesn't know anything about the deceased and hasn't noticed any signs of anyone living in the woods."

She recounted information from the autopsy but fell silent when he held up his hand to stop her. "I need a refill." He picked up his mug and left. On his return, he asked, "Do we know if the local police searched the area around the slope where she fell?"

"The report from the police department in Holbæk says there were clear skid marks in the wet soil at the top," Louise confirmed. "There had been light rain overnight but they didn't find any footprints apart from hers."

"Maybe she lived in the woods," he suggested. "Could she be homeless?"

Louise put down the brief police report as someone knocked on the door. Hanne poked her head in; the corners of her mouth turned down, and reminded Louise that she still had not put her name on her cubbyhole. "It'd be nice if things didn't end up on my desk. They're piling up!"

"Did something arrive for me?" Louise asked. It could be mail forwarded from the Homicide Department. The head of the Negotiation Group had agreed Louise would be spared any new assignments while she worked on getting the new unit up and running, so she wasn't really expecting anything.

"There's an invitation to the summer barbecue and the phone directory that I printed for you."

"And you didn't bring it along when you were stopping by anyway?"

"I can't run around delivering mail to everyone in the department," Hanne replied pointedly.

"Oh, but you usually don't have a problem with that," Eik chipped in, winking at her.

"You're a different story," Hanne cooed.

Louise stared at the door for a few seconds after Hanne closed it behind her. Then she shook her head.

"She's not used to competition," Eik said, leaning back in his chair to fish a wrinkled pack of cigarettes out of his pocket. "Hanne is the queen of the department, the one we all court." He pulled a flattened smoke from the pack and put it in his mouth while he looked around for a light.

"There's no smoking in here," Louise said as he was about to light the cigarette, having found a lighter in the desk drawer.

He cocked a brow and eyed her for a moment before tossing the lighter back down.

Louise put the police report on the desk.

"As far as the lists of missing persons go," she continued, "I only went back a month at first. But that just gave us the woman from up in northern Jutland and a young guy from Næstved. So I went back a year, but in that time there were no women within the age group. Finally I went back five years."

Louise had the lists from the police in a stack in front of her.

"No one fits the description. The big scar would, without a doubt, be listed under distinctive features. So she's not listed as missing."

Eik still dangled the cigarette from his lips and seemed restless.

"Give me the lists and I'll take a look at them," he said, already on his way out the door, lighter in hand.

"Just go smoke your damn cigarette so you can focus and we can move on," she burst out irritably and sat down to wait.

Seven minutes later he returned. "Send me that picture of the woman's face, would you?"

After examining the photograph he declared, "If she's Danish, someone must recognize her. That scar is so striking that there'd be no mistaking it if you'd seen her before."

Louise nodded.

"Do you want me to write a description and send the picture to the press? I've got a list of the contacts we use for missing person alerts."

"Please do," she exclaimed, happy to see him finally come alive a little. She looked at the clock. "I have an appointment down in Roskilde so I'll be leaving a bit early today."

She was still trying to get used to the fact that her dear friend Camilla Lind had moved into her future in-laws' large manor house in Boserup just outside Roskilde. After his brother died and their sister left her position as chief executive of the family business, Camilla's boyfriend, Frederik, had decided to leave the United States and move back to Denmark to take over management of Termo-Lux.

Camilla ending up as "lady of the manor" was something Louise had not seen coming. She knew that her friend's small apartment right by the Frederiksberg Swimming Baths was on the market, and Markus had changed schools about a month ago because Frederik Sachs-Smith had gotten him into some private school in Roskilde. It had all happened so quickly, and now they were getting married, too. Louise had stopped by a craft store to pick up more pearls for the invitations. Camilla insisted on making them herself; Louise knew how important all this was to her old friend and confidante, so she promised to bring them down after work, even though she found the whole thing to be a waste of time.

She sighed at the thought, already weary of being dragged into the wedding preparations. It was as if her friend had gone into romantic overdrive.

"Done!" Eik Nordstrøm broke the silence a little later. "The description and photo have been sent out with a notice to contact the Special Search Agency if you recognize the woman or have any idea who she might be."

He looked expectantly at Louise.

"Great," she complimented. "Have you seen the pictures they took where they found her?"

He shook his head.

Louise brought them up on her screen and sent them to him.

His furrowed face turned serious as he leaned forward, intently studying the photographs. "My mom had flowered smocks like that. They closed with a bunch of hooks in front, too," he said. "I think it was the sixties but you would think they hadn't invented the zipper yet. I didn't know they still existed."

Louise contemplated the picture and nodded. From the clothes it did look as if time must have stood still for her.

"How 'bout we drive down and speak to the guy who found her ourselves?" he went on. "We can put a little pressure on him."

"I already made plans to do that first thing tomorrow," Louise said. She briefly wondered whether her temporary partner intended to show up on his own the next day or if she was going to have to pick him up again.

"You go ahead and go to Roskilde," he said, shutting down his computer and putting on his leather jacket. "I can talk to him. I have nothing else to do now anyway."

Louise took her eyes off the screen and watched him as he dug the last cigarette out of the pack, which he crumpled up and tossed into the wastebasket.

"It's not exactly a high-priority case that calls for overtime," she objected. She guessed that he was the type of person who would come in late and then turn around and add extra hours to his time sheet if he ended up staying past 4 p.m. That wasn't going to fly with her. "You don't even know where Avnsø Lake is!"

"I've got GPS."

"Sure, you'll find your way to the woods but then that's as far as you'll get. There's no coverage once you drive in there."

She was usually the one to insist on getting things done, she reflected. And she wondered if this could be a sign of her getting old and complacent. *No way*, she decided, picking up her bag. She may have just turned forty, but she wasn't ready to be "fat and finished," as the old Danish saying went. "All right, fine; we'll go now."

On their way out they stopped by Hanne's office. Louise left it to Eik to pick up the key for one of the department's two cars. When they got downstairs, though, she held out her hand.

"I'm driving," she informed him.

5

THEY DROVE TOGETHER in silence. Louise turned her head several times to see if Eik had fallen asleep but he sat attentively, his broad hands folded in his lap, and watched as she turned left and passed a closed-down lumber mill with broken windows. The abandoned wooden structures had an air of ghost-like emptiness.

Right on the woods' edge sat a thatched-roof farmhouse with three wings almost obscured by the dense treetops. It was enclosed by a white fence and large gate. Louise slowed a little as they passed. The old gamekeeper's house had been her dream home for years.

"There's a camping cabin all the way up by the meadow where the slope descends to the lake," she explained as they drove down Bukkeskov Road. "But if we drive up to the cabin, we'll have to park quite a way from where she fell so I'm going to continue to Avnsø Lake, and then we can walk along the path. It's faster."

"Sounds like you're pretty familiar with these parts," he observed, looking at her with curiosity.

"I'm from here," she admitted, struggling to avoid the biggest potholes in the road. "Well, not from right here but from Lerbjerg over on the other side of the woods. I spent most of my childhood on these roads. When we got a bit older, we'd get together by the lake and make bonfires."

She refrained from letting him in on the fact that the gatherings had usually involved plenty of beer as well as joints being passed around. Not that she had smoked any herself, but she would lie in the grass with the others and gaze up at the stars.

"Do you still come here?"

"My parents live here," she answered briefly. "But it's been years since I've been to the lake."

Lies! Louise often went there when she needed to gather her thoughts. To her, Avnsø Lake had always been the most beautiful and peaceful place on earth. She loved sitting against a tree at sunset, watching as the light made the pitch-black surface look as if it were filled with flames. It was the ultimate meditation.

Of course, there were painful memories, too. And a nightmare she'd worked hard to put behind her. But that was none of his business. Just like the fact that she had brought her foster son, Jonas, along the last time she went. In fact, none of what she did was any of Eik's business.

"There," she said, pulling over. "We'll park up here."

She could see the light reflecting off the water at the foot of the hill; a narrow path ran straight to it. This was where they used to ride their bikes when she was a child. It was also a good bridle path, especially when it was time to ride back up at a gallop.

She pointed ahead to show him that they could also walk down a little farther and take the forest road, which was slightly less steep.

"Is there good fishing out here?" he asked after he got out of the car.

Louise nodded and suddenly remembered catching some small roach fish with a homemade fishing pole one time. She seemed to also recall something about pikes or perch. "There's a path down by the water so you can walk all the way around the lake." She pointed at the thicket to their right. "We need to get to that side."

They had to walk a quarter of the way around the lake to get to the place where the forest worker had found the woman.

"Shhh." Eik suddenly hushed and put a hand on Louise's arm.

She stopped talking and heard a child crying. The sound was heartbreaking as it reached them through the trees.

"People come out here for picnics," she explained, lowering her voice. "There are picnic tables down there."

Many people came to Avnsø Lake when the weather was nice. When Louise went to school in Hvalsø, they had come on several field trips out here as well. The girls would sit in the meadow tying garlands while the boys carved their initials in tree trunks or swung out over the lake from a rope that hung from one of the large trees. At least that's how she remembered it.

Her thoughts were abruptly interrupted by the sound of the child, who was now crying so hard that she worried for a moment if he or she could even breathe.

"Why isn't anyone comforting the kid?" Eik grumbled. He

was already heading down the steep path, grabbing onto a few of the shrubby branches to keep from slipping.

She locked the car and followed him.

ON THE LEVEL stretch by the lakeside where the swing had hung from the tall tree for as long as Louise could remember, she spotted three small children. The child who was crying was a boy in a striped windbreaker and jeans. He sat on the ground, sobbing so violently that his entire face was beet red, his eyes squeezed tightly shut. Next to him, a second, blond boy lay on his stomach. He was dragging himself across the ground like a caterpillar while emitting a series of loud, unhappy sounds that threatened to turn into crying.

Louise stopped and looked at the last child—a girl wearing loose red clothing. She was sitting dangerously close to the water, her fingers in her mouth and dirt all over her face.

Two, three years old at most, Louise guessed. Who left small children alone in the woods this close to a lake? She quickened her pace as the girl got up and toddled all the way to the water, where she dropped to the ground, leaning forward as if she wanted to catch the slight ripples lapping the edge.

Before Louise was able to get there, Eik was beside the girl, quickly picking her up and carrying her to the bench by the swing.

"Hello?" Louise called out, looking around. But clearly there were no adults nearby.

Eik had walked back and was crouched down next to the boy, who was still crying, his small body convulsing. Gently he lifted the child up in his arms and rocked him.

"There must be someone here!" she exclaimed, her eyes searching the area.

Eik had brought all three children to safety by the bench. He was now walking around with the crying boy in his arms while the others crawled on the ground.

"Hello!" Louise called again. "Will you stay with them while I go look?"

Without waiting for his answer she started running toward the boathouse, then followed the path along the lakeside. On several occasions she had to duck beneath branches that reached over the narrow trail. Anger was pounding in her temples. She could easily picture it: a couple of young people more interested in each other than in looking after the children they had brought along on their outing. She had done a bit of babysitting herself when she was in school and had also brought along a boyfriend once or twice, and it was easy to forget about the children when they were just sitting around playing.

"Hello?" she called out once more as she stopped by a shed being used to store a boat. There was a large padlock on the door, and the place was deserted.

She paused for a moment to look around. She could still hear the boy crying, but not as desperately. Louise continued to the forest road that most people used to get to the lake, gasping for breath as she reached the top, but once again finding no one.

When she returned, Eik was sitting on the ground with the three children. The crying boy was almost asleep in his arms, and the two others were scratching in the dirt with small sticks.

"I'll try going the other way around," she said, pointing behind them. Not a wind stirred the treetops. Louise listened for a moment then ran in the opposite direction.

It wasn't really a path. The trail had just been walked so many times that the dirt had been stamped down. Stumps protruded in several places, threatening to trip anyone who wasn't careful.

"Hello!" she called but fell silent when she spotted a child's stroller a few yards ahead. It had been knocked over and was blocking the path. From a distance she could tell that it was one of those dark-blue, multiseated institutional strollers—the kind kept in nurseries and day care centers.

"Shit." Briefly she was stricken with fear that a fourth child might still be in the stroller, because it was completely quiet.

Louise jumped over a tree trunk and ran to the stroller, the bottom of which was facing her. Relief washed over her when she found that it was empty. A diaper bag had been pushed down into the fourth seat along with a white cloth diaper. A clear plastic bag with a couple of water bottles and a pack of rice crackers had been flung from the cargo net and lay on the ground a short distance away. As if the stroller had been moving when it overturned.

With an increasing sense of unease, Louise once again ran her eyes over the area while calling out a few more times before walking back to Eik. "Their stroller is over there," she told him, pointing toward the path.

The crying boy was now completely asleep in his lap while the other two had started to whimper.

"Can you go get it so we can put them in?" he asked. She nodded and looked up through the sparse trees, fully aware that nobody would voluntarily leave three small children at the edge of a lake. She felt the adrenaline starting to flow.

Then she went back for the stroller.

Louise was bending down to grab the frame when she spotted her. On the ground between two dense bushes, the naked leg of a woman was visible with bloody scratches from the thorns.

Louise let go of the stroller and ran to the thicket. "Hello," she called, this time more quietly. "Hello!" She squatted down and protected her hand with the sleeve of her jacket as

33

she reached through the thorns to lift the branches aside. The woman's pelvis was exposed and her lifeless body lay in a contorted position.

"There's a woman over here on the ground," she yelled loudly without considering whether the children would sense that something was amiss. Then she got out her cell phone and called for an ambulance.

The dispatcher at the emergency call center hesitantly admitted he was unfamiliar with the area. "The easiest way to find it is coming into Bistrup Forest from the road in Hvalsø," she explained. "Then they just need to go straight past the forester's house. I'll walk up to the road so I can guide them the last bit of the way."

Louise couldn't see the woman's face, so she walked around to the other side of the bushes. The branches tore at her pants as she pushed through the scrub.

The woman's forehead was badly battered. It almost looked as if her head may have been knocked against a tree, she thought, looking at the woman's eyes, which stared blindly up toward the treetops above the dense bushes.

Louise didn't need to check the pulse to know that the woman was no longer alive. She looked at her face. She was probably around her own age, she guessed, and heavyset. Her hair had been pulled up in a ponytail but only a little of it was still contained by the elastic band. Louise looked at a strand that had come loose.

Which seemed to indicate that perhaps the woman had tried to escape and then the perpetrator had grabbed her long brown hair and pulled her back. The injuries to the woman's face were so brutal that Louise immediately thought there must have been rage involved. This victim had been beaten to a pulp.

Louise took a few steps back then stopped for a moment and looked around. What first struck her was that someone had tried to hide the woman in the scrub, but she was puzzled by how sloppily it was done. If anyone walking on the forest road looked down, they could have easily spotted her.

A shoe and a pair of pants lay on the ground some distance away. Louise walked over and bent down over the light-washed jeans. The button was torn out, the zipper ripped apart. The perpetrator had simply torn the pants off the woman without bothering to open them first.

Then some dark shadows on the green forest floor nearby caught her eye, but she couldn't tell if they were blood. It appeared that the assault had taken place between the trees.

Louise, worried that the dispatcher might not have understood her directions, considered calling again as she walked back to Eik and the children.

"She's dead," she said. "We'll have to leave the stroller until the police get here."

"Yes." All three children had fallen asleep and were settled next to each other on the ground. One was sucking his thumb. "Was it a crime?" he asked, standing up.

Louise nodded.

"If she's a child care provider, I suppose it won't take long before some of the parents notice their children are missing," he guessed.

She'd had the same thought herself. The deceased woman would not be difficult to identify. Presumably, she lived nearby or she wouldn't be walking down to the lake with the children.

"I'm going up to the crossroads to wait for the police and the ambulance," she said, then hesitated. "Or do you want to go meet them?"

He quickly shook his head. "I can't find my damn way

around here," he said, getting his cigarettes out of his coat pocket.

Louise started up the steep path. Her legs felt heavy; she was panting over the last part of the slope. She took a right onto the forest road and found after the first turn that the stretch to the intersection and the small triangle where the roads parted was farther than she remembered. She half-regretted not driving.

When she finally got to the main forest road, she sat down on a tree stump by the side of the road to write a text message to Camilla. She had her doubts that she was going to have time to drop off the pearls her friend was waiting for.

6

Sirens sounded through the quiet of the woods long before the emergency responders came into view. Louise assumed that it was mostly to give her notice that they were getting close so she would be ready to show the way.

She got up from the stump and waved as the ambulance appeared over the hill a moment later. "Go straight about half a mile and then take a left," she instructed them.

Louise was about to walk back when a police car pulled up, stopping next to her. She took a step back in surprise when she noticed Mik Rasmussen behind the wheel. She hadn't seen him in a long time—not, in fact, since he had ended their relationship.

He had screamed, calling her names, bringing up past issues both slight and egregious, accusing her of all kinds of terrible things because she couldn't, or wouldn't, commit.

She was going to die alone and he didn't even really feel

sorry for her, he had yelled. The words had kept resurfacing every time she thought of him, so gradually she had forced herself to stop.

There was no doubt in Louise's mind that he had meant every word, and on those rare occasions when she opened up that place inside herself where she was most vulnerable, she could sense her own fear that he might turn out to be right. Still, it was the result of her decision, years earlier, that she wasn't going to make promises to any romantic partner. That she wasn't going to rely on anyone so heavily that she could get so deeply hurt again.

They had met in 2007 while she was "on loan" to the Mobile Task Force to assist the Holbæk Police Department in solving a case. They had shared an office, and at first she had seen the lanky local deputy as more awkward than charming. But then he had invited her to go kayaking and she had gratefully accepted the chance at a little diversion from the case as well as the station hotel in which she and her task force colleagues had been accommodated. They'd ended up drinking Irish coffee at his place. One evening led to another, and they saw each other for two years. He called it a relationship but to her it wasn't quite as serious.

"Hi," she said, pushing away her thoughts. She gave a quick nod to the female colleague sitting next to him. She noticed that her own voice was a few degrees too cool and professional as she shared with them that the slain woman was possibly a child care provider or nursery teacher who had taken the children out for a walk.

"And the kids—are they still down there?" Mik asked, pointing ahead toward the lake.

"They're sleeping but my colleague is with them." Louise added that they were probably both thirsty and hungry.

Deep in thought, she stood for a moment and watched the car and then the forensic officers' blue van drive by.

EIK WAS SITTING on the bench, talking to a male colleague from Holbæk, when Louise returned. The children were still sleeping on the ground. The area to his right was being cordoned off, and another police car came down the forest road.

"We heard the kids," Eik explained. There was dirt on his pants, and his T-shirt was still wet on the shoulder where the boy had cried. "It was probably five, ten minutes before Louise found her." He turned to her. "Isn't that about right?"

Louise nodded and watched as Mik walked back from where the body was. She noticed that the stroller had been picked up.

"Her name is Karin Lund," he told them as he got to the bench, the woman's wallet in hand. "She lives on Stokkebo Road. Does that ring a bell?" He looked at Louise.

She thought for a moment then shook her head. Another road led to the camping cabin—that might be it, but she wasn't sure.

"My guess is that you need to continue straight on from here and then stay left when the road forks," she explained as she pointed up behind them. "There's a big parking lot at the end of the forest road that runs over there. Stokkebo Road could be the gravel road that continues out of the woods."

She couldn't recall any other entrances into the woods within such a short distance.

"There are some houses there at least," she added.

The forensic officers had begun searching the area around the body for evidence. The stroller had been pushed away from the path a little. For a moment Louise was struck by the intense concentration that always descended over a new crime scene. Everyone was working on their assignment, and nothing could be overlooked.

Today she just wasn't part of the team.

"We need to take the kids back to the address," Mik said to his female colleague.

His leadership and way of assigning tasks seemed relaxed and natural. Though this was the first time Louise was working with him as he headed an investigation, Jonas had recently told her that Mik had been promoted. They still kept in touch. And shared Dina.

The yellow Lab was actually Mik's dog, but after Jonas lost his father and moved in with Louise, Mik had offered him the puppy. And she knew that very few twelve-year-olds would be able to turn down an offer like that. Nonetheless, she'd been furious. Because they had failed to consult her, and she had no plans whatsoever of being tied down by a dog needing food and walks at regular intervals throughout the day.

Now Mik walked over and stood beside her. "I was a bit puzzled when I saw that the dispatcher had put you down as the person who found her."

"I should have notified you guys that we were driving down here," she apologized. It was standard procedure to check in when conducting investigations in other police districts even when they were the ones who had asked for assistance. "There was an accident out here last week," she went on, telling him that they had come to see the place where the woman had fallen to her death. "And then we're going to talk to the guy who found her."

He told her that he was the one who had passed on the case to them.

"Could the two cases be connected?" Louise asked.

Mik shook his head. "There's no indication that the woman from last week was the victim of a crime. We brought the dogs out here to search the area but they didn't come up with a thing. Of course we shouldn't rule out anything but the autopsy shows that she died from the injuries she sustained in the fall, and her footprints were the only ones by the edge. Did you find out her identity?"

"Not yet, but we're working on it."

She was happy to see him but could tell that whatever had existed between them was now gone. In exchange, no anger remained, either; only the camaraderie and the professional relationship, which suited her just fine. It suddenly seemed very natural to be standing there, talking as colleagues. Louise smiled at him.

"It's good to see you," she whispered before anyone else could overhear. Eik had left the children in the care of the female officer and was now leaning against a tree, smoking a cigarette.

"Have you settled into your new position?" he asked.

She automatically started to nod but then caught herself. "Not really," she admitted. "But I'm sure it's just teething troubles."

She sometimes experienced pangs—she'd miss Mik, then snap out of it quickly, realizing it had needed to end and she was far better off without him. Given the familial ties that had grown between them, she'd felt a void after the breakup. Of course she had Jonas and Melvin—their retired neighbor in the downstairs apartment, who loved to spoil them a little and cook dinner when Louise did not make it home in time. But that still left the nights. And Louise just had to accept the fact that she was the kind of person willing to give up sex if it meant also giving up the pressure of having to be something for someone else.

"Do you need us for anything else?" she asked, signaling to Eik that they ought to be moving on. "We haven't been to the slope yet and we still need to speak with the forest worker."

"Not at the moment, I don't think," Mik answered. "I don't suppose you saw anything when you drove in here?"

Louise shook her head. "Not until we found the kids."

The little ones were being placed in the backseat of the police car. The girl whimpered, the volume rising when the officer tried to buckle the seat belt around her slight body. The other two seemed to have gone into hibernation—they let themselves be buckled in without any objections.

"We'll take the back way," Louise decided, pointing toward the slope and the lakeside below. She stood for a moment and watched the police car drive away. She actually felt more like sticking around to follow the work.

"Coming," Eik answered, making sure that his cigarette was out before shoving the butt in his pocket.

7

THE PATH LEADING to the slope where the unidentified woman had been found was not easily passable. It was muddy and slippery, and they needed to cross the creek to get to the other side.

"There's usually a couple of tree trunks up ahead to cross on," Louise remembered, signaling Eik to follow her through the trees.

She assumed that they would learn the most by going to the top of the slope. There was little to gain from seeing the place where the woman had landed.

"Do people hang out all the way around the lake?" Eik asked, gasping for breath behind her.

"No, mostly by the swing. And of course some go to the area below the meadow by the camping cabin."

"So if she was homeless and had her camp somewhere

nearby, it's possible that nobody would have seen it," he concluded just as he tripped on a stump.

"Only if it was right around here," Louise agreed and balanced her way across the creek on a narrow tree trunk.

THE SLOPE WAS steep, and the drop was about sixteen to twenty feet, Louise estimated as she contemplated the spot where the woman had fallen to her death. Neither path nor trail led down from there. From where they stood, it mostly looked as if the ground just disappeared in a free fall down through the wide tree trunks.

"Seems like it must have happened after dark," Louise said. "Otherwise the woman would have surely noticed the steep drop."

"What the hell was she doing up here?" Eik mumbled and walked all the way to the edge. "It's not exactly a place you just happen to pass by."

Above the slope, the entire area was shaded by the tall trees.

"Could she have been lost?" he suggested, looking around. He had taken off his leather jacket and carried it over his shoulder with one finger. "Perhaps if she came from that camping cabin you keep talking about?"

Louise nodded. "It would be difficult to find your way in the dark," she said. There was nothing to take bearings of unless light shone through the windows of the cabin.

"Can we find out whether it was rented out last week?"

Louise shrugged. "Maybe the forest worker knows. Let's ask him."

They began walking back but stayed at the top this time to avoid the creek.

"The cabin's back there," she said, pointing to the left. She noticed that the fire pit by the lake was still there. It had even been spruced up with stumps to sit on. As she recalled, they used to sit on the ground.

Together they continued across a small, grassy hilltop, and from there they could see the green wooden cabin. It wasn't as small as she recalled, but of course it could have been expanded within the past twenty years.

"It would make sense if she'd been walking from here." Eik looked back in the direction they'd come from.

Louise nodded. It was possible if the woman had used the cabin for shelter when it wasn't rented out.

In front of the cabin was a large, gravel yard and to the left was a lawn, which needed to be mowed. There were two large swing sets, and Louise spotted a couple of benches in the tall grass. There hadn't been people here for the past few days, she noted, because the grass had not been trampled down anywhere.

They walked over to the house and looked through the windows. A typical school camp place, Eik noted. Bunk beds and the tables had been pushed together in the dining room. Along the walls, chairs were stacked high. There was no sign of anything resembling a homeless woman's possessions in either the common room or any of the multiple bedrooms in the building's two long wings.

"What do we know about the forest worker?" Louise asked after she had turned the car around and Eik had gotten the police report out of the glove compartment.

"We know his name is Thomsen," he read, "and he lives in Skov Hastrup. Are you familiar with that place, too?"

Louise nodded, once again concentrating on the potholes. She blinked and proceeded slowly to keep stone chips from hitting the car. The sun was bright through the leafy treetops and blinded them like photography flashes cut off by the moving leaves.

She was about to speed up as they emerged from the forest, but just then she spotted a large man standing with a rake in the yard outside the old gamekeeper's house, waiting for them to pass by. Instead Louise eased off the gas and waved.

The man waved back eagerly like an excited child.

Louise took her time before speeding up and drove past the driveway with one hand still raised as a greeting.

"Old boyfriend of yours?" Eik laughed and joined in waving to the man, whose grin grew even bigger.

"You could say that." Louise told Eik that the man in the lumberjack shirt had been in a work accident. "He was working at a construction site and had just removed his hard hat to put on a sweater when an iron pipe fell from the scaffold. He and his wife moved out here shortly after the accident, and she's been taking care of him since. Jørgen is always there, waving whenever someone drives by."

Eik stopped laughing and looked in the side-view mirror at the man with the rake, who still had his arm raised.

It was less than two miles to Skov Hastrup, a tiny village shaped like a crescent behind the main road to Hvalsø.

"Tell me the forest worker's name again," she asked, signaling to turn.

"Ole Thomsen," he read off and coughed once more as if his lungs were trying to escape from the deep.

Big Thomsen, Louise thought, nodding to herself. She could certainly picture him. More brawn than brains. As she recalled, he had worked in the gravel pit, so it was no stretch of the imagination to think that he would have made the transfer to the woods.

"He lives somewhere called Glentesø Road," Eik went on once he had caught his breath.

She pulled away from the main road and drove down a narrow road with wide shoulders.

"It could be the next farm down there," Eik suggested, pointing ahead at a turn in the road.

Louise slowed before turning into the courtyard, where she parked behind a beat-up Toyota Land Cruiser.

She had just turned off the engine when the kitchen door swung open, allowing her a clear view. Big Thomsen had barely changed. He was still tall and muscular, but his dark hair was shorter than the last time she had seen him, and he was balding above his temples. The new haircut was probably meant to disguise his receding hairline, Louise thought as she got out of the car.

She let Eik take the lead and stayed in the background as he introduced himself and explained that he was aware Ole Thomsen had already made his statement to the Holbæk Police Department; they had just a few follow-up questions.

"Do you mind if I use the Dictaphone?" Eik asked and pulled the small voice recorder from his pocket.

Big Thomsen nodded expectantly. He leaned back a little, arms folded across his chest, so he was looking down at them slightly. At first glance there was nothing to suggest that he recognized Louise, she noted with a sense of relief. Not even when she reached out her hand and introduced herself. He just accepted it, his wholesale lack of interest or curiosity palpable.

"Well...I guess there isn't much more to tell, though," he drawled, biting his lip as if thinking were a strenuous exercise. "She was just lying there, dead." He shrugged.

"And you didn't recognize her?" Eik asked.

"I hadn't seen her before."

"You didn't see her walking around the area?"

"Never."

"Could she have been staying in the cabin up there?" Eik suggested.

"I sure as hell don't think so!" Big Thomsen firmly exclaimed. "That's Boner's area...you know, Bo Knudsen from out by Særløse. He keeps an eye on things; keeps away kids and stuff like that so they don't run around throwing rocks through the windows and tearing the place apart. He's up there daily when no one is staying there."

"And was the cabin rented out last week?"

Big Thomsen exhaled heavily and squinted a little before shaking his head. "I don't think so. But next week there's some people coming down from Hillerød. They come down every year, and there's one of the counselors in particular who's worth keeping an eye on." He sent a knowing wink in Eik's direction. "We always kind of pay attention to who's around in the woods."

Eik asked whether he had a phone number for Bo Knudsen.

Louise remembered Boner. He was a small guy who had been a few grades ahead of her. His parents had a large farm, and there were days when he didn't have a chance to change out of his boiler suit after helping out with the cows in the morning before school.

Ole Thomsen got his cell phone out of his chest pocket and focused intently on pressing the buttons with hands much too big for the task.

"Why don't you call and ask him yourselves," he grumbled after giving them the number.

Yeah, I'm thinking we will, Louise thought irritably.

"Could the woman have set up camp somewhere in the woods?" Eik continued, unaffected.

Ole Thomsen dismissed him: "We'd have seen her. It's not like we're just idle while doing our job out there. They also made us responsible for wounded and dead animals after they cut funding for the gamekeeper."

He inhaled and was about to go on when Louise interrupted.

"That was all, I think." She thanked him and turned around to walk back to the car.

"You're welcome." Big Thomsen added, "Anything to help!"

Louise sensed that he stayed and watched them walk away.

"Say...aren't you the one from Lerbjerg?" he called as she was about to open the car door. "You were Klaus's girlfriend back then?"

She froze. And stood there, her back still to him, while struggling to compose herself before slowly turning around.

"I thought I recognized your name," he enthused. "Just had to get it all lit up on the old scoreboard, you know? Do you still keep in touch with his parents?"

Tense, and worried her voice would betray her, Louise gave a small shake of the head before quickly getting in the car.

"What was that about?" Eik asked after they had been driving for a bit.

Louise ignored his curious look and stifled a sneeze.

"Careful with that," he said. "If you sneeze too hard, you could break a rib or herniate a disc, but if you try to hold it in you could burst a blood vessel in your head or your neck. And die."

"Thanks for the warning," Louise snapped. She hated sneezing while driving, but it wasn't because she was worried about bursting a blood vessel. It was more about the split second of losing control while the car was going.

49

They drove for a little while before he broke the silence again.

"You know Ole Thomsen," he concluded once they had passed through the last turns in the road and she sped back up a little.

"Knew," she specified dismissively.

"When exactly did you live down here?" he asked, this time turning to look at her.

Louise sighed but then gave in. "We moved down here the summer before fifth grade," she said. "And I was twenty when I moved away."

"But you still have friends who live down here?"

"No," she replied quickly.

She had just turned onto the tree-lined avenue in Lejre when he picked up the subject again. "But you had a boyfriend!"

"Yes, but that was a long time ago."

Annoyed with his continued questioning, Louise hit the gas. She knew, of course, that it wasn't going to stop him, but at least she would be busy keeping the car on the road.

"Was his name Klaus?" Eik tried but she ignored him, suddenly remembering one late evening when she and her brother had been riding in the backseat of their parents' old Simca. There had been an accident here on the avenue, in this exact spot. A car had collided head-on with one of the tall trees. She didn't see much before her mother told them to get on the floor of the car and warned them not to look out the window.

This was long before cell phones so their dad had run to the nearest farm to call for help, and as Louise lay wedged on the floor of the car, she had heard the screams: loud and filled with pain and shock. She never found out how many people had been in the crashed car or whether they all survived. But her brief glimpse of the wreck had stuck with her.

"Did he stand you up?" Eik asked while he fiddled with the two worn strings around his right wrist. One yellow and one green.

"You seem to know these roads so well, considering how long it's been since you were here," Eik continued, seemingly intent upon pushing her to open up.

Louise visibly tightened but didn't answer him. She continued straight instead of getting on the freeway ramp.

"What?" he asked.

"I'm going to Roskilde," Louise said, assuming that he had sobered up enough to drive by now. "That way I can still keep my appointment."

"So where do you want to get out?"

"It really doesn't matter," Louise replied and meant it. "How about right here?" She started to pull over.

"No, stop it. Just drive to your appointment and then I'll take over from there," he argued, waving her back onto the road.

Louise turned and looked at him.

"Then I'm going to need you to shut up," she said. "Because otherwise, frankly, I'd rather walk."

"Okay. Calm down." He put his hands up disarmingly and cocked his head a little so his long bangs slipped down over his nose. "I will."

Louise turned back out on the road with a tense smile, practically fuming with irritation.

THE IMPRESSIVE ESTATE that had become Camilla's new home was majestic and beautiful, with windows as tall as French doors. A wide stone staircase led down from the front door with elegant pots of flowers on both sides. The courtyard in front of the house had a round lawn with a small fountain in the middle, and everything was covered with small pebbles, which crunched under the tires as Louise pulled up by the front door.

She noticed the unimpressed look in Eik's eyes as he glanced up at the house while getting the pack of cigarettes out of his pocket once again. Smoking wasn't permitted in any of the department's vehicles, but after she got out he jumped behind the wheel, rolled down the window, and flouted the rule.

"See you tomorrow," he said and gave her a quick nod before he turned the car around and drove off.

8

W HAT WAS THAT about the kids you guys found?" asked
Camilla, who hadn't seemed overly surprised when her
friend showed up after all.

"The girl was just playing as if nothing had happened,"
Louise told her. "First we heard the little boy, completely beside
himself and dissolved in tears, and then we found the others."
She shook her head a little. "I wonder how long they'd been
left to themselves," she mumbled. She was having a hard time
getting the children out of her head. They had been so close
when the woman was beaten and killed.

"Heineken," she answered when Camilla asked what she
would like to drink and listed off her options. She would not
have minded a cigarette, to be honest, if it weren't for the fact
that she had quit long ago. Besides, she had been inhaling Eik's
secondhand smoke all day. She wasn't sure if this was due to

seeing Mik again or the encounter with Ole Thomsen. Maybe it was just because the day had been so crappy from start to finish, she thought. It seemed like days had passed since she had picked up Eik Nordstrøm at the bar in Sydhavnen.

"I saw Big Thomsen today," she said after Camilla opened her beer. "Do you remember him?"

Camilla shook her head without taking the time to think, but then again she had always been better at putting things behind her than Louise had. "I have no idea who that is." She put a glass on the table.

"Yes, you do," Louise insisted and started laughing. "You slept with him!"

"I did?" her friend asked, surprised. From the look on her face, the discussion didn't seem to be ringing any bells.

"That time when you visited me in Hvalsø for the Whitsun celebration," Louise reminded her. "At the very least, you went home with him."

When they'd first met each other, Camilla lived in Roskilde, too, and it had been difficult to convince her to come to Hvalsø even though the two towns were only one train stop apart.

"Well, I don't remember any of that," her friend insisted.

"Back then he had an apartment in the basement of his parents' house with a corner bar and a big stereo. His dad was the chief of police in Roskilde. You remember him; you just don't want to."

"Wait," Camilla said, her eyes moving back and forth as she seemed to shift the pieces in her head. "Oh, that guy! How's he doing?" she asked, her attention obviously elsewhere. Then she looked out the window and excused herself. "You'll have to keep yourself entertained for a minute. I think the workers are about to leave even though we had a deal that they were going to keep at it until they finished the back room."

Louise was left to drink her beer alone. Through the open doors, she could hear her friend having a loud discussion with someone. She returned to the kitchen soon after, her eyes dark with anger.

"I told him that they don't need to bother coming back," she groaned. "They're not finished even though they promised, and they have the nerve to just pick up and go."

She banged the table angrily with her hand. "It's Lars Hemmingsen—do you know him? Didn't he used to hang out with Ole Thomsen and those guys back then?"

Louise didn't remember him off the top of her head, but Ole Thomsen did always have a group of followers.

"They'll get it done," Louise soothed, not sure why this all came as a surprise to Camilla. Everyone knew that contractors never finished on time.

"The painters are coming tomorrow," her friend added indignantly. "But I guess there's no point now since those bastards didn't finish plastering the walls. And you know what?"

Louise dutifully shook her head and listened.

"That Hemmingsen guy asked if we could pay them under the table!"

"Oh?" Louise asked, confused.

"But Frederik said he wanted an invoice. Obviously that's why they're dragging it out—so they can charge us for more hours."

Camilla had decided to have the wedding at home. She wanted to hold the ceremony in the park behind the house where the grounds sloped down toward Roskilde Fjord; the reception would be inside in the spacious rooms. From what Louise had gathered, Frederik would prefer to have the ceremony at Roskilde Cathedral and then celebrate with a nice dinner at a restaurant, but Camilla refused.

"I ran into Mik out by Avnsø Lake," Louise said and poured the rest of the beer into her glass. "It was kind of weird seeing him again."

"What was he doing out there?"

"He's head of the investigation."

"The investigation of what?"

"The homicide of the woman."

Camilla wasn't listening at all. If this had been in her old days as a journalist, she would have gobbled up every detail, pressing for more.

"Was he doing okay?"

Camilla stood by the window, her back turned, watching the workers load their equipment into their vehicles.

Louise shrugged. "I didn't ask."

"You were so stupid to screw that up," Camilla scolded and turned toward her. "Things could have worked out really well for the two of you."

Once again she turned her attention to the workers. Louise emptied her glass in one long swallow to avoid having to reply and stood up, annoyed. Camilla was in a whole other world, and she didn't have the energy to be part of it.

Just then the door opened and Markus walked in, closely followed by two friends. "Mom, can we go to the movies?" he asked. "And can you give us a ride?"

Camilla said a quick hello to her son's friends and nodded. "As long as you don't have any homework."

Only then did Markus notice Louise, and he walked over and gave her a hug. It was quicker than they used to be, she noted, remembering that he would be turning fourteen on his next birthday. So perhaps it wasn't so strange, especially with his friends watching.

Louise had not seen much of Camilla's son since he changed

schools, and even though Jonas and Markus had been friends since the first grade, and promised each other to keep in touch, Jonas had only been to visit him once. Luckily, Markus appeared to have settled in well in his new class.

"Can you drop me off at the station?" Louise asked. She got out the bag of decorations from the craft store and put it on the table. She had no idea why Camilla wanted to mess around with making the invitations herself when she had the entire bottom floor to remodel.

"Did you make any plans with Mik then?" Camilla asked as they sat in the car, the boys making a racket in the back.

"He was in the middle of a homicide investigation," Louise repeated. "The woman's body was still there. To be honest, we didn't talk much."

"But now you have a reason to call him," her friend went on, oblivious to her feelings. "You know, there's nothing like some good sex to lift your spirits."

"Please stop," Louise pleaded, picking up her bag from the floor so she would be ready to jump out in front of the station.

"Take care."

She gave Camilla a quick peck on the cheek before she got out and waved to the boys from the sidewalk.

WHEN LOUISE GOT home, Jonas was in his room, playing the guitar. She could hear the music through his closed door, and after taking off her shoes and saying hi to Dina she walked over and knocked to let him know that she was home.

"Hey," he said, looking up.

"Do we know if Melvin's having dinner with us tonight?" she asked. She hadn't had a chance to call their downstairs neighbor as she'd said she would. On weekdays they ate together if neither of them had other plans. The deal was that they would take turns preparing the meal, but in reality Melvin did most of the cooking.

"He's with Grete. They were going to her friend's place by the community garden in Dragør. He said we could come along if we want."

"I really don't feel like it," Louise burst out.

Over the past few months Melvin had been seeing Grete Milling quite often. The two of them had met while Louise was investigating the disappearance of Grete's grown-up daughter in the Costa del Sol. Her daughter had been murdered, but the two retirees had subsequently stayed in touch, and Louise was pleased that they were enjoying each other's company. It eased her guilty conscience a little on those occasions when she lacked the energy to be social.

"Fine by me," Jonas said. "I'd rather finish this one anyway so I can put it up on YouTube."

Her birthday present to her son had been a software program that allowed him to upload his original music to his computer and put together his own mixes. He spent several hours every day writing and editing, which was just fine by Louise. She was glad that her teenager was not zoning out in front of video games full of mindless violence or spending entire evenings commenting on his friends' status updates on Facebook.

"Should we just have sandwiches or do you want me to go to the store?" she asked on her way to the kitchen.

"Sandwiches," Jonas answered from his room, where he was once again bent over his guitar.

9

"GOOD MORNING," EIK greeted Louise as she stopped in the doorway to their office just before 8 a.m. He had his feet on the desk, her large tea mug full of black coffee in his hand, and the morning paper in his lap.

He was wearing black again. Louise figured it was probably just his standard wardrobe.

"Good morning," she mumbled and put her bag down on the floor next to the desk.

"You want some?" he asked, pushing a bakery bag toward her.

Louise shook her head. "No thanks, but I would like my tea mug."

He looked at her with obvious confusion until she pointed to his coffee.

"Oh," he said. "There weren't any thermoses out there so I just grabbed the one that would hold the most. You can have it when I'm done, okay?"

She sighed and went to fill her electric kettle and find a mug.

"The woman *was* a child care provider, just thirty-four years old," Eik went on with a gesture toward the paper. "But other than that, your friend up there in Holbæk isn't letting much out of the bag. Did he put a lid on it, or what's going on?"

Louise shrugged. "I have no idea. I didn't talk to them," she answered. She was annoyed that she had only been able to find a small white cafeteria cup for her tea. "Can't we just stay focused on the one we need to identify?"

Eik nodded. He folded the paper and tossed it on the floor.

"She's not showing up on the Danish lists of missing persons, so how about searching the international records? See if there's been any description through the years that matches the scar on her face?" Louise asked, secretly pleased that he couldn't reach his computer without taking his feet off the desk.

"Which time period are we looking at?" he replied, moving Louise's mug to the window next to his dirty cup from the day before.

If this is a woman who went into hiding, we'll start by going back twenty years, she decided. "Start by searching for women born between 1960 and 1975, and see who's been reported missing in that age group since 1990."

Louise recalled the smooth skin on the uninjured side of the woman's face and her almost childlike expression and briefly wondered if perhaps the woman was actually younger.

It was quiet in the office while Eik logged on to Interpol's headquarters in Lyon.

"I sent them the picture yesterday," he said after a little while, "and I think they would have reacted to her distinctive scar if she'd been in their register. But I'll look through the list myself now."

"Good." Louise didn't have enough experience in the new department to know whether Interpol headquarters would notify them if there was a match in the international register of missing persons.

She opened up the national register and entered "1990" in the search field. She pulled up a list of reports and cancellations. The names were still listed in the register even if they had turned up again or been reported as deceased, in which case a cancellation code had been added.

She entered the year of birth in the advanced search field and checked the box on the right to indicate female.

The first case that caught her eye was a woman born in 1964 who went missing on March 3, 1990. But reading farther down on the page, Louise saw that the case had a black marker: The woman had been found dead four months later. The next photograph she focused on was of a small, stocky woman with long, dark hair like a tangled halo around her head. The woman was from Kolding and shared certain similarities with the deceased, but she did not have a scar.

Louise figured it might be possible that the woman had been reported missing and then subsequently been in an accident, so that the scar wouldn't be mentioned in the report. But Flemming had said it was an old injury, she reminded herself; she dismissed the Kolding case.

Lower down on the page, her eyes lingered on the town name of Hvalsø. Louise leaned forward and activated the case from 1991. It had been neither canceled nor affixed with a black marker, so the girl had never been found.

She stared at the name for a little while, her eyes squinting, and realization began to dawn. She remembered the case, even though she had moved away from the town by then. Lotte

Svendsen was the girl's name, and she had been twenty-three years old when she went missing. She had been a few grades ahead of Louise, who had only recognized her from her picture.

Lotte Svendsen had been reported missing in connection with the town's annual Whitsun celebration. It was the night between Saturday and Sunday when there had been a party at the sports center. Louise suddenly realized that she had never cared to know how the case turned out. Those were the years when she had put Hvalsø behind her. *So the girl never turned back up.*

But Lotte Svendsen fit the description of their Jane Doe in no way. The next couple of women in the age group had all been found and canceled in the system. And then there was one more that same year, but Louise quickly determined that she was not the woman they were looking for, as she was tall and fair. She only dwelled on the case because this one had never been closed, either. The woman was nineteen and had been living with her parents in Espergærde. She had disappeared while visiting a friend who went to boarding school in Ny Tolstrup.

This case was one Louise had never heard of, probably because she had spent so little time at her parents' place in the years after she left town.

The cases had long been deleted from the electronic system and were now only stored in the basic archive, which didn't hold much information. All she found was that the second case had been placed with the old Search Department three weeks after the young woman's disappearance. Back then it had also been noted that there might be a connection to the missing person case from Hvalsø. The two towns were only about five miles apart, and both places bordered on the woods in which the girls, according to witness statements, had disappeared. Otherwise, there were no links between the two girls, and the lead was a dead end.

*   *   *

HANNE OPENED THE door without knocking to remind them of the department meeting at ten.

"Did you put the cake in the kitchen?" she asked, looking at Louise.

"The cake?" Louise answered, puzzled.

"Yeah—we take turns bringing cake," Hanne said. "Did you think it turned up by itself?"

Louise had only attended the weekly department meeting once and had given no thought at all to how the snacks ended up on the table. "No, I didn't realize it was my turn."

"It's on the cake list," Hanne informed her and let her know that it was posted on the notice board in the lunchroom.

Nobody had bothered to tell Louise about any cake list. She suspected the "someone" who should have told her was Hanne.

"I'll run down to the bakery," Eik cut in. "Just tell them I'll be back in a few minutes."

The meeting was scheduled to begin in five minutes but he had already put on his jacket and was heading out the door.

"No, don't," Hanne said, quickly heading him off. "I've got a box of cookies as backup. We'll have those today."

Eik gave her a big smile. "Honey, I'm all out of smokes, so I've got to go down there anyway," he said, patting her cheek.

Louise sighed wearily as she got up to go to Rønholt's office. The hallway walls were painted a pale green, and apparently someone had a penchant for cartoons, because black-and-white drawings of all the well-known cartoon characters were displayed in varnished wood frames the whole way. Only now did Louise discover that a new one had been added right across from her door: Remy, the kitchen rat from the movie *Ratatouille*.

SARA BLAEDEL

Oh, funny! she thought, sarcastically at first but then she couldn't help but smile. She didn't recall the names of the three investigators down the hall. They were all guys, and the artist had to be one of them, she guessed.

"You like it?" Eik asked from behind her.

"Like it?" Louise asked. "I don't think the point was for me to like it. Isn't it just meant to remind me that I'm the one who got the office that was infested?"

"I don't think so," he said as they walked down the hallway together. "Olle is the one who drew it, and I'm guessing it's his housewarming gift to you. He's really talented, and he's made a drawing like that for everyone in the department. I got Goofy."

He pointed toward his old office, where the picture hung right next to the door.

"Olle's been in the department the longest," he continued, "even though Hanne claims he could actually make a living selling his pictures. But he only paints on the weekends and when he takes time off for his overtime."

Louise couldn't quite imagine who would actually pay money for the cartoon characters in the glossy frames, but perhaps that was just because she was not the target audience.

"Well, then I'd better hurry up and go thank him," she said. She was still smiling when Hanne suddenly came rushing toward them.

"I've just put a phone call through to you," she said. "It's a lady who recognizes the woman you've been trying to identify."

10

I T's BEEN so long now," the woman on the phone began after Louise picked up the line.

"But you recognize the person in the photograph?" Louise asked quickly, to help her get started.

"Yes, I'm sure I do," she said. "I once knew a little girl whose face became disfigured like that. I think I also recognize the features on the other side of her face."

"Then I'm glad you called." Louise asked the woman for her name and phone number.

"Agnete Eskildsen," she said, adding that she lived on Hallenslev Street in Gørlev.

"And you've crossed paths with the woman we're looking for?"

"Yes. Absolutely. Her name is Lisemette."

Louise asked Agnete Eskildsen to tell her what she knew.

"Well, back then she was just a little girl," she started. "I've just been trying to count the years. Lisemette must have come to Eliselund around 1965. I remember because I myself was on D back then, and that was the section for the little ones. The children were around three years old."

"Eliselund?" Louise interrupted as she noted that the deceased would have been born around 1962. "What's that?"

"Why, it was a home for the retarded," Agnete Eskildsen explained. "They're called mentally disabled now, of course, but that's what they were called back then. It's just outside Ringsted. I worked there as a care assistant."

She seemed to be thinking.

"I can't remember exactly anymore what the area is called, but there's a pretty big lake that the institution was facing. You should be able to find it if you have a map."

"So she'd been put in a home for the mentally handicapped," Louise confirmed. That was consistent with the results of the brain scan that Flemming had done. "Do you remember anything about her parents? Were they locals?"

"I'm afraid I don't recall."

"We would really like to find her next of kin," Louise explained to emphasize the importance of the woman thinking carefully.

The line was quiet, and Louise assumed that Agnete Eskildsen was probing her memory. But when the woman finally spoke again, her tone was a little sharper.

"I'm sure you understand," she said, "that many children like that did not have any contact with their parents once they'd been handed over to us. Several of them never saw their parents again so we didn't necessarily know the names of their relatives. They were called 'forgotten children.'"

"But surely their families didn't write them off just because they'd been put in an institution?" Louise objected.

"Quite a few did." Agnete Eskildsen explained that many parents preferred to hide or even forget the fact that they had a "flawed" child. "They didn't want to visit the home. But there were also times when the parents were advised to break their contact with the child because their visitation led to nothing but trouble. The children became agitated and upset when their mothers and fathers left, so it was best for everyone if there was no contact."

"I see," Louise said, trying to swallow her disgust. What Agnete Eskildsen was telling her sounded completely inhumane. She knew it happened every day—she'd seen enough horror on the job—but could hardly accept the idea that any parent would abandon a child merely because he or she did not live up to expectations.

Breaking the silence, the woman seemed defensive as she went on. "I know it sounds terrible now, but that's just how it was back then."

"Yes, right. So the girl had no contact with her parents?" Louise asked, her composure regained.

"I'm not sure exactly," Agnete Eskildsen admitted. "But as I recall, she never had any visitors. I could be wrong."

She fell silent for a moment.

"Do you remember her last name?" Louise asked.

"No, sorry."

"But someone must have known the names of her parents?" Louise tried, thinking of the Care Division or the facility supervisor.

"Yes," Agnete Eskildsen conceded. "It was in the records, of course, but that wasn't something the staff paid much attention to."

"So there are records?"

"Sure, those kinds of things are always archived, but I

don't know if the old files are still accessible. Back in my day, they were stored in the basement. We had records dating all the way back to 1860, when the first patients were admitted to Eliselund. Several of the really old case files are probably exhibited in the museum now."

"The museum?" Louise repeated.

"Yes," the woman replied as if annoyed that Louise knew nothing of the place at all. "When the Division for the Care of the Mentally Retarded ceased to exist in 1980, much of Eliselund closed down. Only the main building is still in use today, and it's been set up as a day treatment center for the mentally disabled. Many of the other buildings ended up empty, but I read somewhere that the old washhouse has been converted to a museum with some of the devices that were used in the place through the years. I remember there was a Utica crib, and I'm sure that's been brought over. Of course it's been a long time now since the mad ones got locked up like that, thank God."

"I'm not really sure what a Utica crib is," Louise admitted.

"It's a wooden box, maybe ten square feet, that was used to confine people. You always kept the worst ones locked up to have some peace. We used straitjackets and belts as well but at our place at least they were indoors in winter. The Utica cribs were outside or in the barn."

"But you think I'll be able to find the old records down there?" Louise asked, shaken by the casual tone with which Agnete Eskildsen spoke.

"Someone at the day center will probably be able to help," she suggested. "I'm thinking you'll find someone there in the main building all week. But what do I know? It's been more than forty years since I stepped foot in the place. I just felt like I had to reach out when I saw that picture of little Lisemette."

After thanking Agnete Eskildsen once more for reacting to the police alert, Louise looked up Eliselund online.

Day Center Eliselund, West Zealand County, it said, followed by a phone number. Louise dialed and waited while a mechanical voice offered choices: the business hours of the day center, how to contact a client, and which number to press to get in touch with the main office. She selected the last option and her call was picked up right away by a Lillian Johansen.

"Records like that are very sensitive, of course, so we can't just hand them over," the woman said curtly after Louise explained who she was and why she was calling.

"We're not asking you to hand over the files," Louise quickly pointed out. "We'd just like to see them—"

"All records are protected by the Privacy Act," the woman cut in.

Louise tried again. She had just been so excited about possibly moving a step closer to an identification, and now this petty official was going to stand in her way.

"We're trying to identify a dead woman. We received a tip from someone who recognizes her, who told us that the deceased lived at Eliselund as a child," Louise elaborated. "All I'm asking is if someone from your staff will go and see if her file is still there and give us a civil registration number or the names of the woman's parents so we can get in touch with her next of kin."

"I'm afraid that's not possible," the woman stated bluntly.

"I guess I'll have to get a warrant then." Louise sighed, aware that she had missed her opportunity to talk her way through the bureaucratic wall. "But maybe you can tell me if the old records are still kept on site?"

"Yes, of course. It's not like we throw anything away," the woman answered pointedly.

Following this minimal opening, Louise quickly assessed that it would be worth it to give it another try, now that she had confirmed that the records were accessible.

"But then I'd just like to ask you," she tried again, "if someone could please go down to the archives and check the old patient records to see if a girl lived there by the name of Lisemette. She was born around 1962."

"Anyone could call and ask for something like that," was her reply, and Louise was about to lose what was left of her patience when the woman added that the police might bother to show up in person for starters. "Then you can explain to us exactly who it is you're looking for."

"I'm coming down," Louise quickly decided. "Would there happen to be anybody I can talk to who worked at Eliselund in the mid-sixties?"

"No, but we've got the yearbooks. They have the names and pictures of everyone who lived here during that period."

LOUISE QUICKLY WROTE down the address and ended the conversation.

"Let's go," she said as Eik came through the door, holding a pastry in his hand. "In all likelihood, the woman's name is Lisemette and she was placed in a home for the mentally disabled outside of Ringsted as a child. It's closed down now but they've got all the records. If you've got nothing else, I think we should drive down and have a look at the yearbooks to see if we can find out if it's her. Maybe then we can find her next of kin as well."

11

THE WARM MAY sun had turned the roadsides lush and green, and the yellow dandelions had finished flowering and transformed into fuzzy gray spheres. Every corner was drenched in idyll as they rounded a turn in the road lined by a couple of thatched timber-frame houses and horses grazing right by the road. Ahead of them was a tree-lined avenue, more than a mile long and winding through fields running down toward Haraldsted Lake. The drive from the main road had almost made Louise forget their reason for being there. The sky was clear and the area was divinely beautiful. The road curved one last time before it descended toward the water, bringing Eliselund into view.

The closed-down white buildings of the institution stood out like abandoned giants. The large structures formed a square around a courtyard in the center with several smaller buildings behind them. It must have all been enclosed by a tall wall, Louise thought, stopping on the hilltop to take in the old home. The remains of the peeling brickwork still bounded the area.

Cars were parked on one side of the courtyard, and from the hilltop it was easy to see which building housed the day center. The main building was freshly limed and the plinth glistened black, in sharp contrast with the rest of the buildings, which appeared to be abandoned.

Louise drove slowly down the hill.

"At least she grew up in beautiful surroundings," Eik noted as they continued through a gate that reminded Louise of Vestre Prison. It was the same kind of impressive red-brick arch; less pronounced, but knowing what had once been here it was nonetheless reminiscent of entering a prison.

"Yes," she conceded as she pulled in to park alongside the wall across from the main entrance. "It looks like the residents must have been completely isolated from the rest of the community, though."

Eik nodded. "I suppose they were locked up in this area," he said, looking around as they stood in the courtyard.

The place had a depressing effect, as if the past still clung to the battered walls of the abandoned buildings.

There was no doorbell by the entrance to the day center so they let themselves in and immediately heard people talking.

Louise walked in a bit farther to look around. They had entered a long hall with framed photographs of the place as it looked in the past. On the opposite wall was a row of portraits with small brass signs underneath: the consulting doctors for the institution through the years.

"Are you looking for someone?" a voice sounded suddenly from above.

Louise hadn't noticed the stairs to the left of the front door.

"Yes," she answered and waited as an elderly lady with straight gray hair and a welcoming smile descended the stairs. Definitely not the unnecessarily difficult woman on the phone. *A good start*, Louise thought.

Eik stepped forward to shake her hand while he explained who they were, and that they had called, were told the archives and records were kept either on-site or in the museum, and that they could come in to discuss gaining access.

"We would really like to see your old yearbooks." Louise took over, explaining that they had an unidentified woman who now turned out to have possibly stayed at Eliselund as a child.

"I saw the notice in the paper," she said. "Do you think she might have been a patient here?"

"We were contacted by someone who used to work here at Eliselund." Louise told her that the former care assistant thought she recognized the distinctive scar. "We would really like to get in touch with the deceased's next of kin. We were hoping that you might help us find her civil registration number so we can locate her family."

The woman seemed to give their request some thought before weighing in. "I believe the yearbooks were mostly used to document full occupancy to the Care Division. They don't say anything about the family relationships of the patients. That's only in the patient records."

"And they're in the museum?" Louise asked.

The lady smiled and shook her head. "Only the patient records for the groups from the middle of the last century are displayed over there. The rest of them are archived in the basement."

Louise sighed. "I wonder if you'd be kind enough to take a moment and check whether the file we're looking for can be procured?" she asked. "I have a first name and a year."

The woman waved them along. "I can't see that it would be a problem if you want to just go down to the basement yourselves and look through the records from that year. As long as you don't remove them."

"That would be very helpful."

"After all, it's almost unbearable to think that the next of kin should find out about the death from the media," the woman continued.

Louise was well aware that you could not hand over confidential information even to the police, but in this case she did not see how it could do much harm, and was pleased to have found someone open to reason. And pleasant to deal with, as well.

"Follow me," the woman said, walking to the stairs, which continued down to the basement. "It's a bit chilly down there and if you don't have enough light to read in the archives, just go ahead and bring the files up here."

Louise had no intention of bringing anything back upstairs for fear of running into the shrew, who might throw a wrench in the works before they had a chance to obtain the information they needed.

"I'm sure it'll be fine and we'll be out of your hair soon," she said quickly. To her satisfaction she saw that Eik had already pulled a notepad from the inside pocket of his leather jacket.

A row of wooden doors with heavy iron fittings ran the length of the wide basement hallway on both sides, and the ceiling was high enough for them to walk upright without difficulty—even Eik, who had to be around six feet. The air smelled damp and musty, and it didn't look as if the basement was used for anything but storage. Passing by the open rooms, they saw several beds with buckles and straps as well as an old dentist's chair, which had been fitted to immobilize the patient's arms and legs.

"I know—it gives you the chills just thinking about the torment that's been suffered in that chair," the woman said, having turned around. "I've been told that the dentist who looked after the residents' teeth here didn't use any anesthetic. Instead he just tied down his patients before he got started."

Louise shook her head.

They took a right at the end of the hallway and continued down yet another long corridor.

"The archives are down there at the end. It's actually several rooms that have been combined into one," the woman informed them. She explained that this part of the basement had at one point been used as a separate sick ward "for those patients who couldn't be controlled without tying and who needed to be in isolation for a short time to avoid contagion."

Louise shuddered and thought for a moment that she could still sense a little of the spirit from that time. But most likely it was only because the moisture made the air stagnant, she thought.

"Here." The woman opened a door and showed them into a large room with shelves from floor to ceiling. "You'll find the years marked under the volumes."

She had turned on the ceiling light and was pointing to some white labels affixed to the front side of the shelves.

"The old institution had a bed capacity of three hundred, but additional beds were often set up so there'd be upward of four hundred patients at a time," she told them. "As you can see, a lot of destinies have passed through here over the years."

Louise looked around. All along one wall, patient records were crammed together so tightly that she could barely make out the dusty green backs of the individual files. They all ranged from 1930 to 1960. On the next shelves, the records had been placed in beige files and spanned the next decade until

1970. Louise walked over to a slightly smaller bookcase behind the door and found that it was for the residents who were born in the last ten years of the institution, from 1970 to 1980. Some of them must have still been quite young when Eliselund closed down, she thought.

"Here it is," Eik said, pointing to an index tab projecting between the beige files. "Nineteen sixty-two."

Louise walked over and stood next to him to see. He had started pulling out files one by one in order to read the white label on each front page.

"Wouldn't it be easier if you take them out?" she suggested. "Let me take some of them and then we can quickly look through them all."

He pulled a stack of files from the shelf; there were about twenty from that year. Louise took half of them and brought them over to where the light shone from a naked bulb hanging from the ceiling. She squatted down with the files on her lap. There were both men and women, all of them born in 1962. Erik, Lise, Mik, Søren, Hanne, Lone, Mette, Vibeke, Ole, Hans-Henrik…

She put the pile down on the floor so she wouldn't get them mixed up. Eik brought the rest of the files over and squatted next to her.

"Apparently the residents came from all across Zealand," he noted as he quickly leafed through his pile, which had almost all boys.

There was no Lisemette in the records that Louise had, either.

"Agnete Eskildsen wasn't a hundred percent sure of the birth year," she said. "Let's get the year before and after."

"I'll take the early ones," Eik suggested.

Louise wasn't listening. She had picked up an old black-and-white photograph that had slipped out of one of the files when she got up. She walked over to the light and looked at the young girl's face and naked torso. All of one side was peeling and nearly raw. In the few spots where the skin remained, it was heavily blistered. The girl lay with her eyes closed in a hospital bed, a white pillow under her head.

Eik had brought another volume from the shelf and was about to open the first file.

"I think she's here." Louise replaced the stack of patient records on the floor in order to find the one to which the photo belonged. "I just need to find her."

She put the file for Erik aside and opened Lise's record. "Look!"

There were more photographs of the disfigured girl, including some in which the wound had started to heal. The damage to the tissue was so severe that it looked white and thick in several places. The skin stretching from the cheekbone and out toward her temple in particular was still rough and swollen with scabs. The shoulder was badly damaged as well.

"Lise Andersen, born August six, 1962," Louise read off, picking up the file. It didn't say much about the scar except that the accident had happened in 1970. So the girl had been around eight years old, Louise concluded, quickly scanning the pages. In the back of the file, two forms from the home's sick ward were attached.

Louise removed the paper clip and saw that Lise Andersen had had surgery to treat an umbilical hernia when she was five. The year after the accident, she had sustained a fracture to her left arm. Both were completely consistent with Flemming's observations during the autopsy.

"It's her." She replaced the clip before handing the medical record to Eik. "Her civil registration number is at the top right corner. Write that down, would you?"

Quickly she leafed through the final pages to find the girl's basic information and learned that her parents had lived in Borup when the girl was admitted to the institution.

"She has a sister," she read aloud and stood up to get closer to the light. "A twin sister named Mette."

Eik put the medical record back into the file on the floor and came over to read together with her. He positioned himself so closely behind Louise that she could feel the heat from his body in the cold basement.

"I saw the sister's name in the pile I went through."

"*Did* you find it?" she asked to make him back off a little.

"Lisemette," he said as he found the record in the pile. "Lise and Mette—there were two of them! Then I'll write down her civil registration number as well—"

"She's dead," Louise cut in, astonished. "Lise Andersen died February twenty-seven, 1980."

"Nineteen eighty?" Eik repeated uncomprehendingly and brought over the sister's file. "What do you mean?"

"There's a death certificate in the back of the file, and according to that she died thirty-one years ago, six months shy of her eighteenth birthday."

Louise knelt down and spread out the few pictures from the file on the floor.

The girl had dark hair, and the prominent scar covered the exact same area as on the body she had seen at the Department of Forensic Medicine. She also thought she recognized the uninjured side of the face. The same delicate features.

"But that makes no sense," she said, bewildered, and asked to see the sister's file.

Eik leaned in to read along.

"Mette Andersen," she read. The two sisters were admitted to the institution together. Louise turned to the back of the file, letting the records slip out and fall to the floor as she pulled out one more death certificate.

"They died on the same day," she noted with puzzlement and accepted Eik's outreached hand as she went to stand back up. "February twenty-seven, 1980."

Eik looked as if he had completely checked out.

"Not only did they die on the same day," Louise continued, "they died at almost the same time, nine fifty-six a.m. and nine fifty-seven a.m."

"So the woman with the scar is long dead?" he asked, confused.

"Looks like it," Louise said. "But we know that she couldn't have been because she's still in cold storage at the Department of Forensic Medicine."

She quickly leafed through the files, stripping them of whatever looked useful at first glance. She replaced the rest so the files were not left empty.

"We'd better leave something in there in case we need to get a warrant in order to gain official access to the information," she said, sticking the papers and death certificates in her bag. "Let's get out of here." She helped Eik put the records back on the shelf.

"But how could she already be dead?" he tried again.

Louise shook her head. She didn't have an answer.

"Any luck?" a voice sounded behind them.

Louise could tell that Eik was in a rush to leave so she stopped and turned around to avoid giving the impression that they were running away.

"It was a big help," she said, thanking the woman and smiling. "Now we've got a few things to go on."

"So was it her?" the gray-haired lady asked, her hand on the light switch to keep the light from going out.

"We think so," Louise said. "And now we're going to contact her family."

She started walking down the hall to signal that they needed to get going.

"Well, good luck," the woman called out behind them. "I'll keep the light on until you've made it upstairs."

RIGHT UNTIL THE end, Louise had feared running into the cranky hag she had spoken to over the phone, so once they were safely in the car she felt like it had been a bit too easy. As they drove over the hill, thoughts were buzzing in her head; she couldn't decide in what order to proceed.

"I'll call Hanne and have her check the twins in the Civil Registration System," Eik said, breaking the silence. He already had his phone to his ear and the notepad on his lap. "If she was declared dead at age seventeen like it says, it would be in the official register as well."

Louise nodded, concentrating on the narrow country road while feeling completely convinced that the woman she had seen on the autopsy table was Lise Andersen. It was perfectly plausible that the dead woman was forty-nine years old, she thought, and asked Eik to locate Lise's parents. Surely they would know if they had buried their two daughters.

"Did we bring the photos of our Jane Doe?" she asked as they were parked at a rest stop outside Ringsted waiting for Hanne to call them back and tell them whether the twins' parents were still alive and, if so, where they lived.

Eik laboriously pulled two folded-up sheets of paper from his back pocket. "I printed them out before we left. Maybe you should call the guys at the Center of Forensic Services and the Department of Forensic Medicine and give them her civil registration number," he suggested. "They should be able to find medical or dental records once they have something to go by. That is, if they still exist."

He pulled out his pack of cigarettes and was about to roll down the window.

"All the way out," Louise demanded, and told him that she would make the call. "But I'm not sure if that stuff is saved that long after someone is dead. In 1980 there were no computer archives, of course, so it seems like they should have been in the records we found if they still exist."

"Were they?" he asked through the open car door.

Louise shrugged. "I actually didn't notice, and I don't think we should go back until we know if it's necessary."

The opening notes of Pink Floyd's *The Wall* sounded when Hanne called back.

Louise watched Eik with curiosity as he wrote something down, asking Rønholt's secretary to repeat the last part.

"Thanks, gorgeous," he flattered before tossing the cell phone onto the front seat. "They're both reported as dead in the national register."

"What about their parents—are they still alive?"

Eik looked at the notes he had taken while talking. "The father is. Viggo Andersen lives in Dåstrup, which according to your good friend Hanne is just outside Viby Sjælland."

"We'll go talk to him," Louise decided, already setting up the GPS.

"Hell no," he objected. "We're not going to see a father who lost both of his daughters more than thirty years ago and ask him to confirm that they're dead."

His hand darted to the leather string he wore around his

neck and he started tugging at the yellowed shark's tooth that hung from it.

"Of course we are," she decided. "And that father did not lose his daughters thirty years ago. One of them is in the basement of the Department of Forensic Medicine right now. We need to speak with him."

"We don't know for certain whether our Jane Doe is identical with one of those twins," he insisted. "We only have our information from one person, who knew her a long time ago, and from guesswork based on a patient record. To me, that's not enough to make an identification."

Louise turned toward him irritably.

"But it is to me," she insisted, feeling convinced that she was right. "She has the same scar on her face, the same fracture on her left arm, and she's had surgery to treat an umbilical hernia. That can't all be a coincidence. Of course it's the same person, and the father needs to identify her. And besides, he might know where she's been hiding for the past thirty years."

12

T HE PLACE WAS a yellow-washed, three-winged farm with a thatched roof and a well-kept garden with large rhododendrons in bloom. From the road, Louise had spotted a man walking around the yard with a wheelbarrow and thought from his age that he might be the father. They pulled into the courtyard and parked next to an old-fashioned well pump. Everything was so well maintained that it was obvious that someone with plenty of time looked after the property.

"I'm sure he'll be thrilled to have the wound of his daughters' deaths reopened," Eik grumbled, having otherwise stayed quiet for most of the drive. He let Louise lead the way to the yard through a narrow passage between the main building and one of the wings, and she realized that he was simply uneasy about the situation.

"Don't you think he'd be more upset if he wasn't informed of the fact that his daughter is at the Department of Forensic Medicine waiting to be buried?" she whispered over her shoulder.

"I suppose you're right. Let's get this over with."

Just then the elderly man came walking toward them. He had put down his wheelbarrow and placed his rake atop a pile of freshly cut grass.

"Can I help you?" he asked in a welcoming voice.

Louise put out her hand. "My name is Louise Rick and this is my colleague Eik Nordstrøm. We're from the Search Department with the National Police. Are you Viggo Andersen?"

"Yes." The man looked at them with curiosity.

"We'd like to ask you a few questions if that's okay."

"Ask away," he said readily.

"Can we step inside?" Eik suggested, tipping his chin toward the house.

"Of course," Viggo Andersen said and gestured for them to follow. After opening the kitchen door, he held back a German pointer. "He's harmless but he just gets so excited around strangers."

"That's all right," Eik said and scratched the dog behind the ears. Louise was able to make do with just a quick pat for the pointer, who was wagging his tail and attempting to show his excitement by jumping up.

Eik kept a firm grip on his collar while the older man showed the way through the kitchen and into the living room.

"Did someone go missing?" he asked after putting the dog in the scullery and offering them a seat at the dining table.

"Yes, but a long time ago," Louise answered, looking around the charming living room.

"Can I offer you anything?"

"No, thank you," Eik quickly replied. Louise shook her head as well.

"We have a couple of questions about your daughter Lise," she began once the father was seated opposite them.

Viggo Andersen looked at her in surprise.

"About Lise?" he repeated. A furrowed net of wrinkles slipped across his forehead, and his look turned to puzzlement. "What do you need to know after all these years?"

Louise decided that she might as well cut right to the chase.

"We have reason to believe that your daughter did not die at Eliselund in 1980, and we have some questions and a photograph we'd like to show you."

She could tell from the look Eik shot in her direction that he was not crazy about the "we." He clearly wanted her to speak for herself.

"What do you mean she didn't die?" Viggo Andersen asked, clearly confused.

Louise took a deep breath and asked Eik to show him the picture he had brought.

"Last week a woman was found dead in a forest here on central Zealand. She had a very distinctive scar, which is identical to the one your daughter had on the right side of her face and on her shoulder."

Viggo Andersen sat motionless and listened.

"There were details discovered during the autopsy that also suggest this might be the same person: a broken bone in her forearm and a surgical scar from an umbilical hernia. Mr. Andersen, we understand this is quite a lot to take in after all these years, but we believe that the woman who was found in the woods is likely your daughter."

The father turned pale while Louise spoke. He seemed to be in shock as he leaned forward and tried to make sense of it all.

"But...how could this be?" he stammered, shaking his

head. "This can't be right. You must be mistaken. I was notified back then and the girls' belongings were sent home to me. Everything fit in just a couple of shoe boxes; that's all they had."

Eik smoothed the two sheets of paper on the table and pushed them forward a little.

"The letter said it was pneumonia that claimed their lives," the father continued and swallowed with difficulty. "So why would you be coming around now telling me this?"

Louise dreaded this part of the job. Though they were going purely on instinct at this point, this man seemed to be truly stunned—completely caught off-guard. But they needed to lay hands on what he knew and could contribute to their investigation. They had to push, no matter how painful it might be. And she had to maintain a professional composure, even if she seemed cold and unfeeling.

"It does seem strange," Louise conceded. She asked him to look at the photograph. "I know it's been years and your daughter's all grown up," she added before asking if the dead woman in the photograph might be Lise Andersen.

The elderly man accepted the copies and leaned in, his reaction evident on his face. He pressed his lips together to suppress it but then started nodding, a look of puzzlement in his eyes.

"You recognize the scar?" Louise concluded.

"The truth is," he began a little hesitantly, "that I only saw my daughter once after the terrible accident that disfigured her face. So it's not so much the scar that I notice. I no longer recall the details, only that it marred her delicate features. But their mother's beautiful cheekbones, which she passed on to the girls, are something I'll never forget. The twins may not have been as bright as other kids but they were more beautiful than all of them combined."

He smiled as if forgetting for a moment the reason why

he had been asked to talk about his deceased daughter. But then it came back to him. The transformation from the tender moment, triggered by the memory, was clear.

He looked at Louise with so much sadness in his eyes that she struggled to meet his gaze.

"There's no doubt that that's my little Lisemette; I'm sure of that even after all these years," he said. "But how? How can this be happening?"

He shook his head in confusion and stroked his chin.

"I didn't take good enough care of them," he said almost inaudibly. "I let my girls down."

"Let's turn back the clock a little," Eik suggested. "Your daughters arrived at Eliselund when they were three years old, and you haven't been in contact with them since?"

The man wrung his hands awkwardly for a moment and then nodded.

"Their mother died when the girls were just five days old," he started and softly cleared his throat. "She wanted to have a home delivery instead of at the hospital in Køge. But we didn't know there were two of them."

His chin quivered, but then he braced himself and went on.

"The doctors said afterward that the problem was that the placenta detached. I'd just gone to get an extra pillow when green amniotic fluid suddenly came gushing out," he recalled. "The midwife was there the whole time and reassured us until she realized that there were two of them and they wouldn't turn."

He fell silent for a moment.

"She was the one who sent for the ambulance. She told us she couldn't handle a double breech delivery by herself. But it took far too long before we made it to the hospital. They didn't get enough oxygen before they were delivered," he told them.

"So their brains were damaged during the delivery?" Louise asked.

He nodded. "Mette got it worse because she was the last one out," he said and blinked back a tear as he told them that the girls' mother had died while they were still in the hospital. "So even though the doctors had told me, it took some time before I really realized how seriously the little ones had been damaged at birth."

"But you were able to bring them home?" Louise asked quietly. She felt horrible about raking up such crushing memories.

"Yes, I brought them home with me after we buried their mother. In the beginning I got all the help I could ask for from the county, and when the girls were fussy I could usually calm them down just by singing to them."

He got a warm look in his eyes, but a moment later it was extinguished.

"But it was hard for me to make the hours add up," he admitted and looked down at the table as the difficult time he had put behind him caught up with him. "I had to work."

He looked up at them as if he felt the need to explain his actions.

"I had to—there was the house and the fields. And I had no help. So I didn't have much time to spend with the girls. I could see that, too. So the month when my girls turned three, I was summoned to the health visitor's office," he said, adding that she had usually come to their house.

He paused.

"And then the girls were put in the home," Eik said, coming to his assistance.

"That's how it turned out, yes." Viggo Andersen pursed his lips as if the words were reluctant to be spoken.

"They advised me to forget about the girls and move on

with my life. The health visitor made it sound so easy; as if that's just what you did when your kids turned out to be different from the rest. 'Just forget about them and move on with your life. We'll take good care of them.'"

He pulled a large cloth handkerchief from his pants pocket and blew his nose.

"I didn't want to turn my back on my girls just because they needed more care than other kids, but she told me about a small home in Roskilde with twenty-two mentally handicapped children and said that only three of them got visitors. The remaining nineteen never saw their parents. So that's how she convinced me that this was how it was normally done."

"So you had them placed at Eliselund and broke off contact with them?" Eik asked.

"No, not at first," he defended himself. "I visited them twice, but they cried so hard when I had to leave that the staff asked me to stay away. They didn't think the girls gained anything from the visits if they became so distressed when I left. They had a hard time calming them back down and also felt that the girls would only miss me more if I continued to come."

He sat staring blindly ahead for a moment.

"I still sent presents for Christmas and their birthday, but I never got any response. And around the time of their confirmation, I sent money. I figured that perhaps they could throw them a small party but I don't know if they did."

He heaved a sigh and shook his head as if struggling to comprehend how he could have taken the advice of the staff.

"The supervisor encouraged me to start a new family and put the girls and their late mother behind me. He didn't think it served any purpose to maintain a contact that wasn't benefiting anyone. A few years later I remarried, which did bring a lot of happiness into my life."

"So was that the last time you saw your daughters?" Eik asked.

Viggo Andersen shook his head.

"I was contacted right after the accident happened. They told me it was Lise's sister who'd picked up the pot of boiling water and dropped it on her. Mette couldn't do much on her own, and her motor skills weren't great, so I was shocked that they'd even let her near boiling water. I drove down there that same evening but when I got to the sick ward, neither of the girls recognized me anymore."

He clenched his teeth.

"And after that I never saw them again."

He looked at them, a weary expression in his eyes. Obviously, what he had just told them took a lot out of him and now that the story was told, his body fell into a slump.

Louise felt awful for the old man, but tried to stay focused. She moved her eyes to a row of family photos hung side by side on the wall. She saw the twins' father with his arm around a tall, gray-haired woman. Next to them were two couples who looked to be in their thirties. One was maybe a bit younger, she thought, assuming that they were new children and children-in-law.

"By then, I was a long way into my new life," Viggo Andersen said as he followed Louise's gaze. "That photo's from when I turned seventy."

"But in 1980 you were notified that both of your daughters had passed away?" she said, looking at him.

He nodded.

"Did you go to the funeral?" Eik asked.

"No." The man shook his head. "That had already been taken care of when I received the boxes with what few belongings they had. They asked me if I wanted their clothes, too, but I declined."

"Who notified you of the deaths?" Louise asked, although it might be difficult to recall after so many years.

"The folks down at Eliselund, of course," he said promptly. "They called from the office one day. My wife was the one who answered the phone, and she walked all the way out to the field to tell me. A few days later they sent something more official, too. But I'm afraid I don't have those old documents anymore."

"Please, don't worry," Louise said quickly while trying to curb the uneasy feeling prickling under her skin. If one death certificate was forged, the other one could be as well.

"I was told that all the practicalities had already been taken care of by the undertaker who usually dealt with the residents there," he said. "But it wasn't my impression that they got their own grave because they never asked me to pay for anything. I guess there was a communal grave that belonged to the place for the ones whose families didn't bring them home."

"So you never saw for yourself that your daughters were buried," Louise pressed him, hating having to ask, and ignoring the piercing look from her partner.

"No," Viggo Andersen admitted, "I didn't."

He asked if he could see the picture of his daughter again. Eik handed it to him and said he was welcome to keep it, although the quality wasn't the best.

"Thank you," he said, tenderly stroking the creased paper.

"So then she wasn't put in the ground at all?" he quietly concluded after a moment, looking at Louise for confirmation.

She shook her head.

"We think your daughter was alive until last Thursday. Unfortunately, Mr. Andersen, we don't know where she's been staying or why she vanished from the system all those years ago—or how it was even possible."

She had briefly considered showing him the death certificate in her bag, but now felt it unnecessary.

"Then she's going to be laid to rest next to her mother," he said. A small smile played at the corner of his mouth before he suddenly turned serious once again. "But what about my Mette, then, what became of her? Is she not dead, either?"

He looked at them with concern.

Louise gazed at the floor, unsure how to reply.

"She couldn't possibly make it on her own; especially not without her sister. She became so agitated without Lise."

The father nodded to himself. "I have to find her," he mumbled. "I need to know if she's still alive, too."

VIGGO ANDERSEN WALKED them to the front door and opened it so they could avoid the dog.

"We're so sorry for coming here and opening old wounds," Louise said as they stood in the courtyard.

"Don't be," he replied, shaking his head. "I'm glad you came. Maybe now I can make up for some of what I've done. It's always been hard for me to accept that I let them talk me into letting down my girls."

He shook his head a little.

"They were always called Lisemette," he said with a small smile. "The two of them belonged together even though they had different dispositions. Lise was the courageous one; the one to take the lead and take care of her sister. Mette was less independent but, like I said, she was in a worse state."

He chuckled quietly.

"But there was never any doubt about her feelings when she flung her arms around you and held on."

Then he caught himself and looked down.

"Could they have been alive all these years while I walked around believing they were dead?" he said as they reached the car. "Where have they been? What happened? It just seems incomprehensible..."

Louise took his hand.

"I know; it does. This has to be so difficult. We need to ask you to go to the Department of Forensic Medicine to identify your daughter," she said. "So we can confirm that it is, in fact, her."

"Of course," he said quickly. "And maybe I can arrange the funeral?"

"I certainly don't see a problem with that." Louise smiled before saying good-bye and getting in the car.

13

THEY WERE BOTH quiet as they drove back on the freeway, until Louise's cell phone started ringing.

"No, don't bring raw food," she said after putting the headset on. Camilla was in Copenhagen and had dropped Markus off at home with Jonas. Now she was offering to take care of dinner. "Melvin is making rissoles; I'm sure you're welcome to join us."

Louise felt like she needed to shake off the visit to Lisemette's father before she got back to Frederiksberg if there was to be any chance of her being enjoyable company.

"And who's Melvin, then?" Eik asked.

Louise turned off Kalvebod Quay and drove past the central post office without answering.

"I was just under the impression that you lived alone with your foster son," he mumbled and got out his pack of cigarettes so he could sneak a few puffs.

She parked by the curb, trying to refrain from reacting to the fact that he had obviously been checking up on her. She definitely had not told him any of that herself.

"Melvin is our downstairs neighbor," she answered, getting out of the car. "He's seventy-five, and today is his turn to cook."

"You live in a commune?" he asked with respect in his voice as he tucked his lighter in his pocket.

She laughed and shook her head. "Not at all. We just help each other out to make things run more smoothly. Melvin lends a hand with the practical stuff, and Jonas and I help him keep the loneliness at bay."

"Well, no wonder there's no room for a man in your life."

Louise stopped. "What makes you say that?"

"What?"

"That there's no room for a man in my life? Do people talk about that?"

He shook his head innocently.

"Who said that?" she demanded to know. "Was it Hanne?"

"Oh, stop it, it wasn't meant as an insult," he shouted after her as Louise turned her back on him and walked away. She hated being exposed and questioned; hated that Eik knew her private business after only a couple of days.

IT WAS LATE, so instead of going back up to the office, she walked over to her bicycle while she called the Department of Forensic Medicine to ask if they had set up an appointment with Lise Andersen's father.

"Actually, he's already on his way," Flemming Larsen informed her. He also reported that one of her colleagues from the Search Department had tried to track down the woman's dental records now that they had her civil registration number. "No luck, though," he lamented. "In fact, they haven't found anything. It would have been a different story had she been registered as dead within the last ten or fifteen years. Then there'd have been a better chance of the information still being there."

"I'm pretty sure he'll be able to identify her," Louise said. She asked Flemming to call her once Viggo Andersen had been to see his daughter.

"I'll accompany him to the viewing room myself," the medical examiner said. "If he's the least bit unsure, I'll be able to tell and then I'll be sure to react."

Louise thanked him and got on her bike to go home.

MELVIN HAD MADE scalloped peas and carrots fresh from Grete Milling's greenhouse. Louise smiled at him, appreciating the fact that he went all-out when he was in charge of dinner.

"If only I had a greenhouse like that," he sighed and put the last rissoles in the pan.

"Maybe you could apply for permission to put one up in the yard," Camilla suggested as she handed him a glass of white wine from a bottle she had brought. "It's pretty big."

"But that's not the same," Melvin mumbled while flipping the breaded meat.

"Or you could have your own vegetable garden at my place," Camilla offered. "There's plenty of room, that's for sure. But I'm not going to take care of it for you."

"That's the whole point of it, though," he retorted, "unwinding and caring for the things that grow. Nancy was always so good at that."

Since meeting Grete Milling, he had been mentioning his

late wife less frequently but when he did, his voice always filled with love even though it had felt like forever since they had lived together. For the last several years of her life, Nancy had been in a coma at a nursing home, but Melvin had gone every day to see her.

"Will you tell the boys that dinner's ready?" he asked, nodding toward the closed door to Jonas's room.

Louise walked over and knocked. They had been in there since she got home, and Melvin had only seen them when they came out to ask if there were any more Popsicles in the freezer.

There was a draft from the open window. Louise was a bit puzzled. "Are you guys smoking in here?" She walked over to close it.

Markus was sitting on the bed and shook his head indignantly, offended that she would even ask.

Jonas was practically touching his nose to the screen as if on another planet and he clearly was not paying attention.

"Yeaaah!" he suddenly shouted, jumping up. "Ten thousand hits! Ten thousand people have listened to my new song!"

He pounded Louise on the shoulder and high-fived his friend on the bed.

Markus got up, and Louise joined them in looking at the YouTube page where Jonas had uploaded some of his own music.

"But they don't even know you, so how do they find you?" she asked, shaking her head.

"Jonas has a crazy-high rating," Markus said approvingly.

"It's because the link to the song gets passed around," Jonas explained. "People who like it share it, and that's how it spreads."

"Holy crap, it keeps going up," Markus pointed out and sat down in front of the screen. "There's two more now."

"Are you guys coming?" Melvin called from the kitchen.

"I put the song on Facebook, too, and yesterday I had over two hundred comments and they were from people from all over the world," Jonas explained once they were all seated around the table.

Louise smiled, pleased that Jonas was so absorbed in something that clearly made him happy. There had been a period when he'd been having problems with the other boys at school, who teased him because he'd lost both of his parents. Louise had found it difficult to deal with the cruelty of the kids' teasing, and Jonas had tried to spare her by keeping it to himself until he ended up in the emergency room with a split eyebrow after a fight in the schoolyard.

"Maybe you could play something at my wedding," Camilla said with a smile.

Louise appreciated Camilla's generosity, even if her friend was mostly being polite. She looked forward to being the proud mama when Jonas performed a song or two on the big day.

"Do you think they're smoking?" Louise asked after dinner when the boys had once again closed the door behind them. She looked at Camilla.

"Are you nuts? They're way too young," her friend dismissed. "They're barely teenagers."

Louise laughed. "What does that have to do with anything?"

"Isn't that usually when they start doing things like that?"

"I don't think 'usually' plays much of a part when you're that age," Melvin chipped in, sneaking another half rissole onto his plate. "The whole smoking and drinking thing seems like it just starts when you're ready. I was twelve when I lit up my first cigarette."

"Well, that makes you an excellent role model then," Louise said, hoping that her neighbor hadn't been entertaining Jonas with too many stories of his youth.

"How's THE REMODELING coming along?" Louise asked once they had cleared the table and were having coffee. Before Melvin went back downstairs, he had left a handful of Quality Street chocolates on the table and extended an invitation from Grete Milling to Louise and Jonas to come along to Dragør that Sunday.

Camilla shrugged and grabbed a piece of chocolate.

"Frederik wasn't exactly happy to hear that I'd fired the workers. He'd prefer everything to run smoothly of course, but I'm simply not going to put up with people blowing off a deal," she huffed. "Just because they think they've got you cornered and you need the job finished no matter how they behave."

"Have you found someone else to take over?"

Camilla shook her head.

"The ones we talked to have an eight-week waiting list—minimum."

"So I guess you'll have to rehire the other ones so they can finish," Louise said with a small smile.

"Are you crazy? No way! I won't let them set foot in my house again," Camilla sputtered. "If we can't find anyone else to do the work, I'll put up a tent in the yard. Or hire some Polacks. They don't spend half their working hours reading the paper and drinking Coke, either."

Louise couldn't help but laugh. "That'll look great on the front page when it's revealed that the Sachs-Smith family uses underpaid labor."

"We don't have to underpay them just because they're

foreigners," her friend snapped irritably. Then she cracked a smile herself when she said that she was actually considering overpaying them.

She picked out another chocolate wrapped in glittery red foil.

"But it's all a mess," she admitted, folding the foil into a tiny square. "The contractor—the guy from Hvalsø—came up the same evening that I'd fired them to hand over a huge bill, which also included all of the work they hadn't done. I guess he had no problem finding the time for that," she said, shaking her head.

Camilla finished her coffee and got up to gather up her things. She called for Markus and told him it was time to go.

"I'm in the bathroom," he called back.

"You could just postpone the wedding. That way you'd have more time to get everything in place," Louise suggested.

"We could, but I don't want to. If I'm getting married, it has to be this summer. I'm crazy about him. I've never felt such a sense of belonging with someone as I do with him," she declared. "We're going to have a big, amazing summer wedding, dancing around barefoot in the yard and spending our wedding night on a mattress beneath the apple trees with candlelight and plenty of champagne."

In the beginning Louise had considered the relationship between her friend and Frederik Sachs-Smith a passing fling, but it seemed that Camilla had found the love of her life. It would be interesting to see how two such different lives could be combined, she thought. Her friend, the journalist, who had lived in a two-bedroom apartment in the city and had always taken care of herself and devoted herself to her own interests. And the rich guy who had sat on the deck by his pool in California, writing his film scripts and never wanting for anything.

In addition to the family money from Termo-Lux, he had built a considerable fortune by investing wisely, and he had been a bachelor until Camilla entered the picture.

Markus's shouting roused Louise from her thoughts. She could only hope her friend knew exactly what she was doing.

Are you coming?" Markus demanded of his mother from the entrance hall.

14

"CONGRATULATIONS," RAGNER RØNHOLT exclaimed from the doorway the following morning. "Good job with the identification. Now we can close the case."

He smiled approvingly at Louise and went on: "I've gotten ahold of Lars Jørgensen's résumé, and I intend to have him over for a talk later this week."

Louise put her hand up to make her boss stop.

"We're not ready to close the case," she corrected him. "Lise Andersen has been missing for thirty-one years without anyone knowing it. The case has only just been opened."

"But now that she's been found and identified, her past is no longer relevant to us," he maintained.

She looked at him in surprise while he ran his hand over his well-groomed beard.

"What do you mean?" she asked. "If this special unit is to be justified, it is relevant to find out what's happened in this woman's life since a false death certificate was issued in 1980."

Eik walked through the door, eyes squinting and hair unruly, and she gave him a quick nod.

"Weren't we supposed to look at the cases that can't be classified as standard disappearance cases?"

"Exactly," Rønholt said. "Your job is to focus on missing person cases where we suspect that a crime is involved. And this woman is no longer missing."

"Maybe so," she replied. "But I want to know what happened to Lisemette. How can there be a death certificate when she only just died last week? That seems suspicious to me."

"And how come nobody's missed her since the accident in the woods?" Eik cut in. "We know that she'd been sexually intimate with a man just before she died. Someone knows about her."

"The case is closed," Rønholt insisted, and Louise felt flushed with anger as he went on: "Make sure it gets archived correctly in the system that's been set up for the new department."

As he was about to leave, she stood up.

"We can't file it until we know what happened to the twin sisters," she tried. "What about the other one; where is she? Her death certificate may have been forged as well."

"We have other cases piling up," was his reply. "And one case closed means one less in the pile."

LOUISE SLAMMED THE door behind him and walked over to the window. She crossed her arms. If it turned out that she had quit the Homicide Department for a job that was only about closing and archiving cases, it would be the mistake of a lifetime. The anger felt like a stab in her chest, and she paused for a moment before she was able to turn around and sit down again.

"That's his weakness," Eik said after she sat down. "Rønholt tends to be a bit rigid once the workload starts to grow, and he wants to please management by showing results."

"I couldn't care less about who he's trying to please," Louise said sourly. "It's bad practice to close a case before it's finished. If that's how it's going to be then I won't be at the helm."

"I agree." He put his feet up on the desk. "I suggest we get Viggo Andersen to file a missing person report for Mette. Then we have a case and we can continue."

Louise looked at him with surprise and nodded approvingly. But then she hesitated. "Can you file a missing person report when there's a death certificate?"

Eik folded his hands behind his head. "If we can show the probability that she didn't pass away back then, either, then I should think so."

Her face turned pensive. "The undertaker..." she said. "The undertaker who arranged the funerals at Eliselund. I'll call Viggo Andersen and suggest that he have a talk with him."

15

I'D LIKE TO file a missing person report for my other daughter," Lisemette's father began as he called back just after lunch. "I've spoken with both the son who took over the funeral home that was in charge of all funerals from Eliselund and with his father, who owned the business back in 1980. The father retired that same year. He still has all his old appointment books and he's willing to swear that he didn't bury any of my girls. The only person he buried from Eliselund that year before handing over the business to his son was a man who was so overweight that he wouldn't fit in a standard coffin. That turned into a big mess because they couldn't agree on who should pay for the custom coffin. Also, he's absolutely certain that he never buried a pair of twin girls at the same time."

Louise smiled at Eik.

"I also told him that I didn't understand how they could

make out death certificates for people who didn't die," Viggo Andersen went on.

"What did he have to say to that?" she asked with curiosity and got out a pen.

"He suggested that I check with the parish office to find out if the death was recorded in the parish register."

"And it wasn't?" Louise guessed, holding her breath.

Viggo Andersen told her that the woman at the parish office had checked through the register from 1980 twice. "Neither of the girls had been entered. In fact, no one their age was even buried that year," the father finished, his voice sounding pained. "But now I've identified Lise myself so there's no doubt that she didn't die back then. I just simply can't understand how this happened. Why was I told something like that? It's just incomprehensible . . . And what became of Mette? We have to find out if she's alive, too."

Louise understood his urgency. She knew it had to be completely surreal for him to see his daughter after believing for so many years that she was dead. She had been a little girl the last time they had been together.

"Now we'll write up an official missing person report for your daughter," she promised, "and then we'll continue our search. Thank you so much for all you've done."

"I should be thanking you," he said and asked Louise to keep him informed.

She brought her scribbled notes down the hall to Rønholt's office.

"I just got a call from Viggo Andersen. He's filing a missing person report for the other twin," she told him from the doorway. The front office was empty, and her boss was watering his plants.

Rønholt put down the pitcher. "Now you're being stubborn," he said irritably.

"Neither of the girls was ever buried and their deaths were never recorded in the parish register," Louise calmly explained. "There's every reason to believe that Mette's still alive."

"Well, Jesus, then go find her!"

"WE'RE PROCEEDING," LOUISE said when she returned from Rønholt's office. She started to unfold a map on the desk. "If we can find out where Lise stayed for the thirty-plus years she was outside the system, then maybe we'll find Mette."

"There must be a limit to how far she could have walked through the woods barefoot," Eik said, leaning in over the map while searching for Avnsø Lake. He smelled of cigarettes and leather, and Louise moved over a little to allow him a better view.

She drew an X on the map where Lise was found. "What do you think?" she asked. "Does two, three miles from where we found her sound realistic?"

Eik nodded. Louise placed her pencil on the map and drew a circle to indicate the radius.

"Are there any houses within that area?" he asked.

Louise considered his question. Actually all the houses she knew of in the forest qualified. The circle encompassed both the forester's house in one direction and the Snipe House out toward Skjoldnæsholm; then of course there were the houses in Lerbjerg from the Tollhouse to Crane House.

"Yes, there are several," she said. "I think the most interesting houses are the ones inside the forest. I guess there are five or six of them. Let's start with those, and then we can move on to the couple of houses on the street where the child care provider lived."

When Louise returned from the copy room with more

pictures of Lise, Eik stood holding a cup of coffee. He asked if she wanted one for the drive, too. She was about to say no then caught herself. It wouldn't hurt to be a little more approachable.

"Yes, please," she said and smiled at him.

THEY DROVE INTO the woods on the same road as last time, but instead of turning off toward Avnsø Lake they continued straight ahead. An old timber-frame house lay almost entirely hidden among the tall trees.

"Does anyone live in there?" Eik exclaimed in surprise as they got out.

A couple of dogs barked and threw themselves at the gate before they reached it.

"There, there..." Louise tried to calm them down without much luck, and she startled when something suddenly jangled right by her ear.

Eik had pulled the string of a large ship's bell that hung from the fencepost by the gate. "I guess you're supposed to ring the bell," he said and pulled it one more time.

"Coming." They heard a deep voice from a black wooden shed next to the house. A small man in blue overalls appeared with an ax in his hand. "Shut up now!" he yelled at the dogs before walking toward them.

"Hey, Verner." Louise smiled as he looked at her with surprise.

"Is that you?" he exclaimed. "Last time I saw you, you had braids and were riding bareback on a Norwegian pony."

He was missing two teeth next to his right-side front tooth, which left a black gap in his mouth when he smiled. Verner Post was the epitome of good nature and had lived in the Snipe House for as long as Louise had been coming to the woods. He often visited her parents and helped her father fell trees, and he brought up the horse and the braids every time he saw her. She thought there were certain things you just never outgrew.

She led the way through the gate after he opened it. The dogs had lain down in the shade by the house wall and barely bothered to raise their heads as they walked by.

"A woman was found out by Avnsø Lake last week," Louise started after introducing Eik.

"Yes, terrible story with those little ones." He told her that one of the children was Lene's grandchild. "Lene from the doctor's office—you know her, right?"

Louise nodded. She remembered the medical secretary well, but she didn't know her daughter or the grandchild.

"That's actually not the woman we're here to talk about though." She got the pictures of Lise Andersen's face with closed eyes out of her bag. She told him about the accident by the slope but left out the rest of the woman's story.

"We believe she may have lived out here in the woods or somewhere nearby. The woman looked quite ragged when we found her so she might have been homeless."

Verner Post had looped his thumbs through the straps of his overalls. "They do come around from time to time." He let the drifters sleep in the shed when the weather acted up, he continued. "They always know where to find shelter and a bottle of beer. Not too many people around here that are happy to put them up. But I don't think I've seen that one there. The only woman who shows up with that crowd sometimes is the Tiger Princess, but she hasn't come around since her husband died."

He squinted a little as he tried to remember.

"I believe he was the one who got hit by a car when he was walking along the main road with his pram."

The thought that Lise might have taken to the road hadn't

occurred to Louise. There weren't many vagabonds left, but of course it was worth following up on.

"She would never have survived a life like that," Eik cut in, reminding her that Lise had been severely handicapped.

"You're probably right," Louise agreed. Although many of those who walked the country roads had drowned most of their brain cells in alcohol, they were nonetheless people who were able to take care of themselves.

"Could she have been staying with someone out here?" Eik suggested in an attempt to get Verner Post thinking along other lines.

The small man stared straight ahead for a moment while thinking. Then he shook his head. "It's mostly people from the city moving into the houses out here these days. It all seems so idyllic to them," he said sarcastically and shook his head.

"Are any of the houses empty?" Eik asked.

Louise was relieved to let him do the talking. She felt a little awkward questioning people she knew.

Verner Post frowned a little and rubbed his chin as he pondered the question. "Pasture House," he suggested. "It's been empty for a long time, but it's farther away from here, of course."

He looked at Louise. "You know, out toward Ny Tolstrup."

She nodded.

"Actually someone just moved in," he added. "I think I saw a car parked there last time I passed by. But you should ask Bodil. She lives closer."

At the mention of the name, Louise and Eik looked at each other. She nodded again and signaled to her partner. It was enough; there was nothing more to talk about.

"Tell my folks hi," she said. It had been over a month since she had seen her parents. "You'll probably see them before I do."

*   *   *

"Pasture House," Eik said as he tossed his leather jacket into the backseat before getting in the car. "You know the way."

Louise nodded. One of her friends from school had lived there for a while. "It's not far from the gamekeeper's house if you go through the woods," she explained, and added that talking to Bodil was an excellent idea. "She's the one who's married to Jørgen—the guy who waved to us. They've lived in the woods a long time and know the area. She worked at Avnstrup Sanatorium, which was a care unit under Saint Hans Hospital before it closed down. When I was a kid, we used to ride our bikes to buy candy at Tutten—the kiosk at Avnstrup—and we were always scared shitless because some of the patients would say weird things when we ran into them."

She suddenly realized that she was making small talk about things that were none of his business.

"It was originally an old tuberculosis hospital," she finished, diverting the conversation from her childhood.

"What did you look like back then?" Eik asked curiously. "A skirt and long, dark braids?"

"I wore torn jeans and had a crew cut," she said, even though it wasn't true. She had in fact had long braids. Braids, dirty jeans, and cuts or scratches all over, and she spent most of her time on the back of her horse, but that was none of his business.

The large white gate to the courtyard in front of the gamekeeper's house was open. Even though the gravel was newly raked, Louise pulled all the way up and parked next to the front door.

She had only just turned off the engine when Bodil appeared in the doorway. She clearly didn't recognize Louise at first but as soon as she had introduced herself, they were invited in.

"I'm just having lunch," she said. "Jørgen went to take a nap." She showed them into the entrance hall.

"This will just take a moment," Louise said quickly. "We don't want to interrupt while you're eating."

"Pish-posh—there's coffee in the pot," Bodil said and shook her head at Louise.

Louise remembered that her parents had attended the brunch party when Bodil turned seventy but she couldn't recall if that was one or two years ago. They took off their shoes and followed her into the cozy, low-ceilinged living room.

"I'm out here. Do you guys want a cup?"

They followed her through a small hallway and into a large kitchen.

"He's been so tired all day. I hope he's not getting sick," Bodil chattered while pouring their coffee. "Men are always such babies whenever they catch the slightest thing."

She winked at Eik and put the pot back on the burner.

Louise had taken out the photograph of Lise. She handed it to Bodil across the table and asked if she had noticed the woman walking around the woods.

The elderly woman took the picture and studied it carefully before putting it back down.

"Is she dead?" she asked, looking up.

Louise nodded. "She was found by Avnsø Lake last week."

Bodil slowly put the picture down and shook her head. "It was terrible what happened to our neighbors over on Stokkebo Road."

Louise knew that around these parts, people considered anyone who lived within a mile or two a neighbor.

"How did she die?"

"She fell down the slope behind the camping cabin," she answered.

It was obvious from Bodil's expression that the killing of the child care provider had, understandably, sent waves of fear through the small community.

Bodil picked the photograph back up and looked at it before handing it back to Louise.

"This one wasn't a crime," Eik interjected. "The woman died as the result of an accident and we're just trying to find out whether she lived in the area since she was found in the woods."

"You didn't see anyone driving into the woods last week?" Louise suggested.

Bodil shook her head. "But then of course Jørgen is more the one to pay attention to things like that. Lately he's been very preoccupied with a white van that's started coming to the parking lot. But it's mostly because they don't greet him even though they come here often."

She shook her head a little.

"That kind of thing really hurts him," she elaborated in Eik's direction.

"What kind of van is it?" he asked with interest.

Bodil shook her head again. "I don't know, but then I'm not so good at cars," she admitted. "I'll just go see if he's awake so I can ask him."

She got up and disappeared into the living room. They heard a door open and close. Louise emptied her cup and placed it in the sink. She had put the photograph back in her bag when Bodil returned.

"It's an old Toyota HiAce with no windows, and the last time he saw it was last Wednesday. He's marked it off in his calendar—he does that when there's something he needs to remember."

The day before Lise was found, Louise thought.

"But apparently it was here the Wednesday before last as well, and the Wednesday before that," Bodil continued. "He doesn't know who they are, though, because as I said they don't say hi."

They thanked Bodil for the coffee, and she walked them out.

"Do you know anything about Pasture House being vacant for an extended period?" Louise asked as they stood in the courtyard.

The curtains were closed in the back rooms, and Louise hoped that Bodil's husband had fallen back asleep.

"Sure, it's probably been a year or two," she said. "Maybe even more. There's been some big dispute out there about something or other. I think it was the ceiling that was about to come crashing down and they couldn't come to an agreement about who should pay for the renovation. It's rented out by the forest administration, you know. But now a new family has moved in so they must have solved the problem."

"But you didn't notice anyone out there before they moved in?"

Bodil shook her head. "No, and I pass by the place a couple of times a week."

They thanked her once more when she told them it was time for her to go make sandwiches to have them ready when Jørgen woke up.

Louise stood for a moment, enjoying the courtyard. There was an old chestnut tree by the gate and a tall poplar that blocked the view of the abandoned lumber mill. Someday when Bodil and her husband weren't around anymore, perhaps it might be an idea to put her own name down for the house. She was reasonably certain that it was managed by the forest administration as well.

THEY DROVE IN silence, a tense feeling of being on their way to something that might answer the question of where Lise had been staying.

"Pasture House is right by the roadside. Someone would probably have noticed if anyone had been staying there. At least in the rooms facing that way," Louise said in an attempt to lower her own expectations.

As she recalled, that only included the living room and one bedroom. The front door and entrance hall also faced the road, but back when she used to go there, they always used the door at the back. There were at least two and maybe three bedrooms. The yard was secluded behind the house and not visible from the road.

The forest road narrowed and turned into two tracks.

"I wonder if you can even drive here," she said, trying to recall if she had ever traveled this way by car. They had usually gone by bike or moped.

"I'll get out and push if we get stuck," Eik promised as Louise slowed down and turned out onto the shoulder so she could drive with all four tires on the grass.

"Deal," she smiled, maneuvering the police car along the narrow track.

As they emerged from the trees, the narrow, thatched house came into view right across from them. It was a single building, and it was indeed so close to the road that passersby could look in the windows. A car was parked in the driveway to the right of the house, and a man was shooing a couple of children into the backseat.

Louise pulled up and parked on the shoulder outside the garden fence.

"May we have a moment of your time?" she asked after the man handed a couple of bags to the children.

"What's this about?" he asked in a reserved tone without moving toward them.

Eik introduced himself and held out his badge. The added authority still seemed to have an effect on some people. "We just have a couple of questions about a woman who suffered an accident in the woods last week," he reassured him and was about to continue when the man cut him off.

"I don't know anything about that."

"We think the woman may have been living somewhere in the area and were just wondering if maybe you'd seen her?" Eik continued, unaffected.

Louise brought out the picture from her bag. The man barely glanced at it before shaking his head. Instead, his eyes stayed on Louise.

"Say—didn't you live with the guy who hung himself?" he asked.

She avoided his gaze.

"They say you guys just moved in and hadn't even unpacked yet," he continued, still staring at her.

Louise spun around without answering and walked back to the car. Once she had slammed the car door, she closed her eyes and briefly leaned her head back on the headrest. In the years since leaving here, she had fought to bury her traumatic loss; to leave it and the whole period behind her. As if she could only move on by denying she'd ever experienced the profound pain.

An instant later Eik tore open the door and got in.

"What the hell was that?" he asked. "Do you want me to handle him?"

"No, no! Please, just forget it." Louise quickly started the car without checking her rearview mirror.

"Do you know him?"

Louise shook her head. She didn't. But he obviously knew who she was. And wanted to provoke her for some reason.

16

Louise was shaken all day. Her focus compromised, she wouldn't have been able to recount what anyone had said if asked to describe the conversations they'd had the rest of the afternoon. After Pasture House, her thoughts had switched off; she was present in body only.

They had stopped by the rest of the houses in the woods as well as the houses on Stokkebo Road. They had skipped the child care provider's widower, however, because a police car had been parked out front. But all they had found out was that nobody knew anything about Lise Andersen or had seen her in the woods. That much was clear to Louise although Eik had done all the talking. She was grateful that he had acted as if nothing had happened and refrained from asking questions about the episode at Pasture House.

She tried to pull herself together. Several people had noticed the white van and believed, like Jørgen did, that it had made regular visits to the forest lately. But nobody had seen anyone around the car or knew whom it belonged to, and when they themselves had turned into the parking lot at the edge of the woods where the van had been parked, the place was deserted. There were a couple of picnic tables and two large trash cans, so people must come out here, Louise thought.

"It's hard to get anything out of this," Eik said after getting out of the car. He lit a cigarette and crumpled up the empty pack, throwing it in a high arch into the trash can.

Louise stayed in the car. She couldn't really psych herself up to join him in searching the parking lot.

"This is fucking useless," he concluded. "How far is it to Avnsø Lake?"

Louise pointed through the windshield but then she got out. She walked to the road, which continued into the woods, and showed him that he needed to continue straight ahead. The road split a bit farther on.

"You'll want to hang a left the first time and then right," she explained but fell silent as she heard a siren.

She walked past the fir trees, which screened one entrance to the parking lot, and looked toward Stokkebo Road, where the sound was originating.

There was more than one emergency vehicle, she noted with a growing sense of unease.

"Now what?" Eik asked and walked over to stand beside her as the sound drew nearer.

Just then three police cars came around the corner. They slowed a little as they entered the woods; even so, their wheels sent a scattering of pebbles onto the side of the road. A moment later five more cars from the canine unit sped by.

Louise jogged toward their own car, and Eik dropped his cigarette and jumped in as even more canine unit vehicles went by.

"What the hell's going on?" Louise yelled. She backed up the car so fast that the wheels spun out before she put it in gear and stepped on the gas to keep up. She made it onto the forest road just as the last vehicle disappeared at the fork in the road.

"Turn on the police radio," she commanded. They usually only had it on when they were on patrol.

"Just drive," he said, drowning out the voice on the radio reading off GPS coordinates to the emergency response.

The police car in front of them stayed left but when they reached Avnsø Lake, it continued at high speed a little farther before turning down a small hill and slowing down.

"That's the road to Hvalsø," she said. She let off the gas when she noticed that the cars had pulled over and were parked behind each other in a long row.

She and Eik stayed in the car; the dog handlers in front had already gotten out of their vehicles. Several cars still had their emergency lights on, but the sirens had been turned off.

It occurred to Louise that the officers probably thought she and Eik were a couple of police reporters who had intercepted the emergency dispatch and latched on, and she was briefly embarrassed by the thought. Then she spotted Mik making his way toward the dog handlers, who had gathered in a group behind the last car.

He was pale, and it looked like he had slept in the clothes he was wearing. They were wrinkled, his shirt untucked. *That's not like him*, she thought, then got out when she realized he was heading their way.

"What's going on?" she asked, but her voice was drowned out when a pair of dogs were let out.

Mik seemed exhausted. He ran his hands through his hair as he walked up to her and sadly shook his head. She could tell his eyes were bloodshot from fatigue, and she felt an urge to pull him close and give him a hug.

"Mik, what is this all about? What's with this huge police presence? Do you have something new on the child care provider?" she pleaded.

Mik nodded heavily and dropped his hands. "It turns out there were four small children on the walk."

He looked at her gravely.

"We found Janus in the lake early this morning. He was the child care provider's own son. Just turned two. He'd probably already drowned by the time you found the other children."

Eyes cast down, he quietly shook his head.

"Oh no. I'm so sorry," Louise whispered.

"We decided to withhold the information about the missing child out of concern for the father, who's gone into shock. But since it became apparent that he was missing, we've been conducting an exhaustive search."

Louise put a hand on Mik's arm.

"How did you find him?" she asked.

"I sent for divers and a boat from the Emergency Management Agency. The bottom of the lake drops very quickly, and they didn't find him on the first try. But then this morning they went back out there. The boy's sweatshirt had caught around the end of a plank on a sunken raft, which held him down."

"And now you're on the scent of the perpetrator?" Louise asked, gesturing at the line of police cars.

Mik shook his head and inhaled deeply as if trying to recharge his energy supplies. "I wish," he said. "We've got nothing on him, but I'm hoping we'll get the DNA results back later today. Otherwise they should be ready by tomorrow."

The forest floor was green but already trampled by the officers flocking the area. He followed her gaze in their direction.

"We've received new information," he said. "A twenty-nine-year-old woman was reported missing after her morning run."

Louise let go of his arm and was about to ask a question when he went on: "Her husband raised the alarm just over an hour ago. The woman left their home in Hvalsø around seven a.m., about the same time that he left for work, and when he came home he began to suspect that she hadn't returned."

Louise saw that the handlers were getting the dogs ready behind them.

"He'd set the table for her breakfast and the things were untouched. Her purse and cell phone were still in the bedroom. Last night she set out the clothes she was going to wear today, and they were still there. The only things missing were her running shoes and workout clothes."

"And she didn't show up for work," Louise guessed.

Mik shook his head.

"The husband called her boss, who confirmed that she hadn't come in and hadn't called in sick. The boss was surprised, but he wanted to hold off a little before calling to check on her."

Mik had tasked two people with investigating whether the couple had been fighting or if there could be any other reason for her staying away.

"The husband flat out denies any problems. He insists that everything was normal."

Mik shrugged and bit his lip, making his crooked front tooth visible.

"He's spoken with her girlfriends, too, to find out if they know anything."

"And she usually runs in the woods?" Louise cut in.

"Three times a week she runs out here to the Troll's Oak," Mik confirmed, swatting an insect off his arm. "After what happened by the lake the other day, I didn't dare hold off on sending out our people. We can't wait until we've uncovered her personal background."

Louise agreed completely. As long as the perpetrator was still on the loose, they needed to make every effort to find the woman.

She saw Eik talking to some colleagues from Holbæk she didn't know. For a moment she stood and watched as he walked over to the canine unit's on-site commander, who was busy organizing the search.

Two more units had arrived, and she assumed more were on their way. It always took a little time to rally the troops for a major search effort. She counted fifteen dogs now. Once the team was ready, they would start making their way through the woods, forming a chain with about twenty yards between each dog.

Louise sensed her fatigue. She felt heavy and sad and was having trouble keeping her thoughts straight. She hated that she'd allowed that man from Pasture House to get under her skin. What did he know about her and her past? Were people still talking after all these years?

Eik walked over to her.

"I'll stay and help with the search," he said, gesturing toward the men he had been talking to. "As soon as everyone's here, we'll get started."

She nodded weakly. She did not have the strength to offer her assistance. She needed to be alone.

"The couple was expecting their first child," he added. "She wasn't that far along but the husband said they'd already painted the nursery."

"I'm glad you're staying." She didn't know what else to say, but he didn't seem to expect an explanation for why she was not joining the search. He simply walked with her to the car and got his jacket out of the backseat.

"I'll see you tomorrow," he said as she got in.

17

CAMILLA STOOD IN the kitchen, arms folded across her chest, and looked out the window. Out in the field, Markus and two of his new friends from school were taking turns riding the new ATV that Frederik had bought for him. She thought the four-wheeler was much too fast for boys their age, but nobody took her seriously when she worried about their safety. Each time they just told her that it was safer than a two-wheel motocross bike—as if that was any comfort. Camilla also did not accept the argument that everything was perfectly all right as long as they only rode it on private property. From what she could tell, an accident could just as well happen in your own field.

While the bike was moving at high speed, Markus stood up from the seat and leaned to the side to make it ride on two wheels before taking a sharp turn to the left. He was breaking every agreement they had about driving slowly and carefully; clearly he'd forgotten that she could see him from the kitchen.

Camilla walked back into the rooms where the walls were still peeling and unfinished. Two of them were completely untreated and there was a sour, musty smell.

She opened up the tall windows facing out toward the courtyard. For the first time, she felt like turning her back on her new life.

The minister had just left, their conversation having turned into an argument when she realized that he had only come to see her to talk her out of getting married in the yard. He had insisted that the only appropriate thing would be to have the actual ceremony in Roskilde Cathedral and suggested that she could then have the wedding reception in her backyard.

He didn't understand that she wanted to keep it informal. Camilla wanted to be surrounded with joy and laughter. She didn't want an organ or the church choir, which made her think of everything that had happened to her future husband's family. And when the minister finally confessed that he would like the media attention that the Sachs-Smith wedding would undoubtedly attract, to also benefit the cathedral, Camilla had definitively decided that he would not be marrying her at all.

"Hey!" Frederik called from the entrance hall. She had called him right after the minister left.

"Hey," she said wearily, turning her back on the bare walls and cardboard-covered floors.

He walked over and kissed her, and she savored the warmth of his body for a moment. "Now we don't have a minister either," she lamented and dropped her hands despairingly.

He held her at arm's length and smiled. "You sure do scare everyone off." He kissed her again, running his hands up her back while gently nibbling at her earlobe. "I can go by the parish office later and have a talk with him. Don't you think we can bring him around?" he whispered as he pulled up her shirt to find her soft skin.

Camilla removed herself from the embrace and took an angry step back. "Like hell you will!" she said, tucking her shirt back in. "I don't want him to come around. I'm the one who's mad!"

"Come on!" said Frederik. "He married my sister. And he buried our mom and my brother, too. He's part of the family."

She could tell he was getting annoyed.

"If you still want to get married in two months, we're going to need him. He already changed his plans for us and squeezed us into his full schedule," Frederik reminded her, "so we can be a bit flexible, too."

"It's not about being flexible. It's a question of having a wedding that reflects who we are," she tried. "You just give in and go along whenever there's the slightest conflict."

"I don't think that's entirely true," he continued calmly. "But there's no reason to make things more difficult than they need to be."

"Difficult!" she burst out. "It's not difficult to get the mayor to marry us instead. We just have to make an appointment. The most important thing is that we feel comfortable and that the day turns out exactly how we want to remember it."

"Of course," he hushed. "But we're not going to go running to the mayor just because you got carried away by your temper and fired our minister."

Camilla was so furious that tears welled up in her eyes as she turned her back to him and walked away.

*　　*　　*

SHE CLOSED THE door behind her and slumped down by her desk. No way was she backing down. Every fiber of her body objected to the idea of a church wedding. That was not at all how she imagined it, and the minister could have just told them from the beginning that it would not be possible. Then she would have looked for another minister. There were plenty of churches in Roskilde. But right now she was mostly angry that she didn't have Frederik's support.

She straightened up and tried to force herself to think of something else. Suddenly she realized that she had thought about little else but the wedding since she and Frederik moved in together. She had left several phone calls from her previous editor at the morning paper unanswered, and she had shown no interest in what Terkel Høyer wanted from her.

She folded her hands under her chin and stared out the window, a feeling of emptiness washing over her. Then she closed her eyes and put her head in her hands. She hadn't even been listening when Louise told her about the missing twin girls. In fact, she hadn't heard much of what her friend said because she had been so preoccupied with her own problems, mostly needing someone to listen.

She sighed heavily. She remembered something about one of them living off the grid until her death last week, and that the whereabouts of the other sister were unknown.

She heard Frederik calling from the living room that he was going back to the office, but she didn't answer although she knew he was probably waiting for her to come out. Instead she tried to think of the deceased twin's name. She opened her laptop, typed "Lisemette Eliselund" in the search field, but quickly saw that there were no results.

Then she logged on to Infomedia and tried searching the newspapers' database, but again—nothing. Well, obviously the articles had not been electronically saved so far back, she thought, but she'd wanted to give it a shot before calling Louise.

Camilla immediately picked up on her friend's sullen tone but asked her anyway if she knew the name of the woman who had reacted to the published photograph of Lisemette.

"Do you know where she lives?" Camilla asked after writing down the name.

"I believe it was somewhere down by Gørlev—but try running a search with her phone number," Louise answered without asking what her friend planned to do with it.

It wasn't like her at all, Camilla thought to herself. Louise was usually all ablaze as soon as she showed any interest in one of her cases. It was only after she hung up that Camilla realized that her friend could have been upset.

She did an address search for Agnete Eskildsen and figured that she could easily sell the story—that is, if she was able to crack it.

"Can Filip stay for dinner?" Markus called up the stairs.

"No," Camilla called back without getting up.

"Why not?"

"Because you and I are going out to eat!"

She suddenly craved time with Markus, just the two of them the way things used to be, and she wanted to get out of there before Frederik got back.

"So can't he come, too?"

"No," she yelled, well aware that her son had grown into enough of a teenager that it could lead to a major argument if he felt offended by her rudeness. "He can stay for dinner tomorrow," she suggested, offering a deal to keep the peace.

"Fine," Markus sulked and slammed the door as he went back outside.

She rested her head in her hands for a moment before getting up and going to survey one of the guest rooms. Then she got her duvet and pillow and made up a bed before returning to the office to set up an appointment with Agnete Eskildsen.

At this moment, family life was getting on her last nerve. They could all bite her.

18

L OUISE CALLED IN sick the next day after tossing and turning most of the night, her head buzzing with bad memories she'd tried so hard to repress and didn't want to deal with now. After maybe an hour of early-morning sleep, she came to in a daze. She couldn't face dealing with Eik; forget about Hanne.

After seeing Jonas off to school, she went back to bed and spent most of the day just staring into the white ceiling of her bedroom while concentrating on chasing off the shadows that filled her with memories and painful thoughts.

She was still in bed later that day when Jonas put his key in the lock to let himself in and dropped his book bag on the floor. She was thankful her son was home, and safe. She always worried about him and felt better knowing he was under her roof. But she was not ready to come out of seclusion just yet. She lay quietly, hiding from reality. She heard Jonas's footsteps and him talking to Dina even though the dog was deaf. She heard him take the leash from the hook in the hallway; shortly after, the door slammed behind them.

Then Louise got up and wrote a note. She took a quick shower, got dressed, and was out the door before Jonas got back. With a slightly guilty conscience, she got in the car.

AN HOUR LATER she was driving down Main Street in Hvalsø. Just before the church, she signaled and turned down the road toward the rectory. Louise parked the car and turned off the engine. She sat with her eyes closed, completely still for a moment before she opened the door and got out.

She barely looked before crossing Main Street. Ever since moving, she had avoided it when visiting her parents. The fear of running into a familiar face was lodged inside her just as it had been when she'd fled town twenty-one years ago.

The bell in the store clanged as she closed the door behind herself. She let the heavy, humid scent of flowers that filled the small room from floor to ceiling wash over her. From the back room she heard the sounds of conversation and a door being opened.

"Coming," a light voice said. Then the woman came into view.

For a moment they paused and stared at each other in silence before Louise regained enough strength to bend down and grab one of the ready-made bouquets from a bucket on the floor.

Vivi had been in Klaus's class and although she had put on the pounds since Louise last saw her, she still looked the same. She was one of the girls who had faithfully hung around Big Thomsen and the rest of that gang throughout their youth, Louise recalled, eyes locked on her debit card, which was already in the machine.

They had not exchanged a single word and they still didn't as Louise accepted the bouquet wrapped in light green paper and exited the store.

She had walked a distance down the sidewalk before she stopped to put her debit card in her wallet and close her purse. Then she crossed the street and walked toward the church.

The gravel on the path crunched under her feet. Louise did not know exactly where Klaus was buried. She had not been there the day of her boyfriend's funeral. Couldn't cope with everybody staring at her and people whispering. All she knew was that his grave was somewhere behind the church. Her younger brother had told her.

Mikkel had been there and placed a single red rose on her behalf. Louise had never asked for any details. She did not want to know how many people had shown up or which songs they had sung. All she heard was that Klaus's younger sister had broken down by the coffin after saying a few words; when Mikkel wanted to recount what she had said, Louise had asked him to stop. The sister had been away at boarding school when it happened but after the funeral she never went back. At least that was what Louise had been told.

As she got to the church, a sense of guilt hung over her once again. She had worked on it and fooled herself into thinking that she had finally managed to put it behind her, but she was never able to rid herself of the shame of the rumor.

Louise bangs for a chopper ride. Her brother was the one who heard it first down by the soccer stadium. At first she had laughed and ignored it. At the time she had been seeing Klaus for almost five years, and he just shook his head and could not even take it seriously. It was only when she started noticing that people whispered about her, at times so loudly that she could not help but hear what they were saying, that it started bothering her. But by then the rumor had taken hold and it didn't matter what she said. No one could answer when she asked them to tell her whom they had seen her ride with. Because the only one she ever rode with was Klaus.

Louise held her breath for a moment, pulling herself together. The path ahead of her ran straight as an arrow between the low evergreen hedges, which framed the grave sites on both sides of the path. He was somewhere down this way.

She took a few steps but felt her aversion and grief rise up like a shield, blocking her movement. She didn't want to go down there. It was no more than ten yards but she simply couldn't.

Back in the small church parking lot, she threw the bouquet in a trash can and hurried away. She walked back to the car, her head bowed and eyes on the pavement, struck by an overwhelming sense of loss. Loss of dignity and loss of love.

Her throat contracted as she ran the last part of the way to the car. She felt as conflicted about this town as ever. It trapped her, yet she couldn't seem to let it go.

19

AGNETE ESKILDSEN GOT a thermos from the kitchen counter and placed it in front of Camilla before turning around to pick up the small plate of cookies next to the coffeemaker.

When Camilla had called and asked if she could stop by, she had told Agnete she was a freelance journalist who wrote for various newspapers and magazines. The older woman had accepted this without further questions.

"I understand you worked as a care assistant at the institution Eliselund down by Ringsted," Camilla began. "And that's how you recognized the girl with the scar?"

The woman nodded, and for a moment it looked as if she were lost in a labyrinth of old memories.

"Yes," she finally replied. "It really was a pity because she was such a pretty little girl."

"So it happened down there?" Camilla burst out. "Do you remember when it happened?"

Agnete Eskildsen nodded again. "It was in 1970," she answered without hesitation. "I know because I quit immediately after. That's why I can say with certainty that it was in July. I preserved berries for the entire first week that I was at home."

Camilla raised an eyebrow, surprised that this was a detail she recalled after so many years.

"During my last year at Eliselund, I was the night nurse in section C. My first husband had fallen ill, so I picked up quite a few night shifts. I spent the days at home with him, and toward the end the only thing I could get him to eat was the stewed fruit I made from our garden," Agnete Eskildsen explained, adding with a little smile that she hadn't been very brave back when she worked nights. "We had to make the rounds every hour, and I didn't like going into the men's dormitory because they'd be in bed with each other and it wasn't a quiet affair."

She briefly lost herself in the memories.

"One night I thought one of the men had a cramp. When I walked into the room, his whole bed was shaking so hard that it had moved away from the wall. I was alone on duty and not really happy about the situation but finally I walked over and lifted up his covers, and then it turns out he was just masturbating. We got exposed to the strangest things," she said, shaking her head once again.

"How old was Lisemette back then?" Camilla asked.

"I'd say she was around eight at the time," the older woman answered hesitantly.

"What do you recall about the two sisters?"

"They were like two peas in a pod," she answered spontaneously.

Camilla nodded encouragingly.

"One functioned better than the other one, of course, but when they were together they just seemed happy," Agnete

Eskildsen remembered. "There was some trouble one time when one of them, the brighter one, had to go to the sick ward for some sort of surgery. Or maybe she'd gotten hurt; I don't quite recall. In any event, they were separated, and it turned into a big mess."

"How so?" Camilla asked with curiosity, pulling her notepad closer.

"The one who got left behind started banging her head against the wall so violently that the caretaker had to take her to the sick ward. They had to give her a sedative and bring in an extra bed. You couldn't separate those two."

Camilla looked at her in surprise. "Surely there must have been other times when they had to be apart? They must have gone to the bathroom occasionally?"

Agnete Eskildsen smiled for the first time since unlocking her memories and shook her head. "Back then they had large toilet rooms, mind you. There were four toilets lined up against each wall so they'd sit in there together. We'd bring twelve of them to the restroom at a time as I recall."

"In the same room?" Camilla burst out.

"Sure. I guess that wouldn't pass today," the older woman said, "but that's how it was done back then."

She smiled a little and told her that there had actually been quite an uproar when the restrooms were converted and partitions put up around the toilets.

"They didn't want us to close the doors," she recalled and explained that the residents didn't care for change.

Camilla tried to picture it: a large, tiled room with toilets all lined up. It brought to mind the mucking ditch in a livestock barn. *No, that wouldn't pass today*, she thought.

"I can't actually think of any other times that the girls were apart," Agnete Eskildsen continued, shaking her head pensively. "When they transferred from the nursery section, they were placed in one of the large dormitories with fifty beds and their two beds were pushed together. That wasn't usually allowed so they did make some concessions. But then again, they were forgotten girls," she added.

"Forgotten girls?" Camilla repeated.

Agnete Eskildsen nodded. "They had no contact with their family or anyone else from the outside. That's how the system worked back then. You weeded out the ones who were defective and hid them away. Visitors were a rare occurrence," she recalled. Several of the mothers were not allowed to visit their children, she went on, because their husbands were annoyed that they would be upset afterward.

"The children?" Camilla asked.

"No, the wives," she quickly replied. "The visit would leave them so distraught that they forbade them from going. So many of the children never had visitors, and yet they stood faithfully by the gate, waiting for someone to come. It was quite heartrending."

"That sounds crazy," Camilla said, shaking her head. "But after the accident when Lise was being treated for her wounds, the two sisters couldn't have stayed together?"

Camilla noticed the expression on the woman's face shifting to something like animosity. It took her by surprise that the night nurse remembered so many details from that time.

"Yes, they stayed together," Agnete Eskildsen finally said. "But that was also the reason they couldn't send her to be treated at the hospital—because they wouldn't allow the sister to come along. So she stayed at Eliselund, and our own consultant doctor treated her even though it wasn't his specialty."

Agnete Eskildsen fell silent for a moment before she added that an extra bed was placed in the sickroom for the sister.

"I imagine they decided that her presence wasn't important since she was feebleminded anyway," she added quietly after a little while.

"But the accident," Camilla said. "What happened?"

"It was just that—an accident." Agnete Eskildsen sighed and looked sadly out the window. "A really bad, no-fault accident."

"How was it no-fault?" Camilla asked.

Agnete Eskildsen folded her hands on the oilcloth in front of her and picked at a fingernail before she reluctantly started to recount the incident.

"We always had to turn up the water heater in the basement the day before the weekly bath day to allow time for the water to heat up. But that day, the thermostat was broken, and that's when it happened."

She looked down at the striped oilcloth.

"The girl was already in the tub when the shower with boiling-hot water got turned on, and her screams carried throughout the large building."

Agnete Eskildsen closed her eyes and stayed that way as she went on: "It was me who turned on the water," she whispered despairingly, "and I'll never forget her scream. I wake up at night because it tears through my dreams. The skin on her face and down across her shoulder was stripped clear off before we could react, and afterward she wouldn't let us touch her. She just lay in the bottom of the tub, burning pink, screaming until the consultant doctor came and gave her an injection."

Camilla had put her pencil down. Now she just sat there in shock, listening.

"We hustled everyone out of the bathroom. It wasn't a pretty sight of course," Agnete Eskildsen continued after a pause. "They had all been lined up and ready, naked as the day."

They both sat in silence, the picture all too clear.

"It was a difficult time afterward," she acknowledged. "Back then we didn't talk about it much when things like that happened. At first I tried to forget but now I've long come to terms with the image of that terrible wound to her face.

"I only stayed till the end of the month. Then I quit and I haven't used my caretaker training since."

"So you don't know what became of the two sisters?" Camilla asked after a minute, picking her pencil back up.

Agnete Eskildsen shook her head. "I have no idea. But you can imagine that it brought up a lot of memories when I suddenly saw her picture in the paper."

Camilla nodded sympathetically.

"The last time I saw Lisemette was when they lifted her little body out of the tub. I wasn't even allowed to visit her in the sick ward, even though I'd bought chocolates for both of them."

It got quiet again, but this time the silence held so much sadness that Camilla felt that she had to get up and let the woman off.

"I put Eliselund behind me," Agnete Eskildsen said as they were standing in the courtyard after Camilla put her purse in the car. "Mr. Nørskov, who was head of the place, retired a few years later, and I'm not shy to admit that I wasn't one to send flowers to his farewell reception after the way he treated me— even though it was the janitor who hadn't serviced the water heater properly."

She fell silent and thought for a moment.

"Toward the end, Parkov was in charge, but I never met her. All I can say for certain about the twin sisters is that they would have, without a doubt, stuck together if at all possible."

*   *   *

HER WORDS STAYED with Camilla as she headed back toward Roskilde. If both sisters were alive when the death certificates were issued, then they must have stayed together. And if Mette was still alive when her sister fell down the slope last week, then where was she now? And how was she managing without her sister?

Camilla's thoughts were mingling too fast for her to keep them all straight. She pulled over, got her iPhone from her purse, and turned on the voice recorder to make sure she wouldn't forget the things that needed further investigation when she got back home. It occurred to her that she hadn't given one thought to Frederik or their wedding plans since the moment she had sat down at Agnete Eskildsen's oilcloth-covered table.

20

THE SMALL COMMUNITY gardens were so tightly spaced that it was practically like having dinner with the neighbors, Louise thought as she got up to clear the patio table. She had to concede, though, that Grete Milling's friend's small, black-painted wooden alcove and the garden had a calming effect on her. She still felt guilty about playing hooky from work and ditching on Jonas, even though he hadn't noticed. She was shocked to discover that the past continued to have such a hold on her.

She put the salad bowl on top of the stack of plates and carried everything into the small kitchen area behind the living room.

Melvin was making coffee the old-fashioned way on the stove, and the two older ladies were rinsing the dishes. Everything was a bit too tight but sufficiently relaxed that it wasn't really an issue, Louise noted, suddenly enjoying having people around to drown out the silence that had overcome her since she fled the cemetery. On her way home in the car, she had felt so empty and ashamed that she couldn't even manage to put some flowers on Klaus's grave.

"You'll have to remind me if you take sugar?" Grete said, looking at her questioningly.

Louise shook her head and replied that just milk would do fine.

She hadn't mentioned her visit to Hvalsø. When Melvin asked if they wanted to go to the community gardens for dinner, all she wanted to do was get back into her bed and pull the covers over her head. But Jonas wanted to go; he'd been there a couple of times and loved it. So, to make her son happy, and keep herself even, Louise decided to join in. Jonas took off right after dinner to see some friends he'd made there the last time.

Melvin handed Louise a blanket and swatted a couple of mosquitoes off his arm. They had agreed that they could sit outside a little longer as long as they bundled up.

"Do you think Jonas is smoking?" she asked after they sat down.

Almost absurdly, she hoped that he would say yes because then she would have a concrete reason to focus her thoughts on something other than herself.

Melvin shook his head and smiled. "Right now that boy has only one thing on his mind," he said, "and that's his music. If he were smoking, he would have been doing it with Markus the other day because that kid smokes like a chimney and has for a while."

Louise looked at him with astonishment. "Why didn't you say something?"

Her downstairs neighbor hesitated for a moment before answering. "I think the kids should be allowed a little privacy," he finally said. "They're about that age when it becomes quite natural to have little secrets."

"But Melvin, you have to tell me when you find out stuff like that!" Louise said. For once she felt resentful of her neighbor.

They heard Jonas and his friends approaching on the garden path, and Melvin lowered his voice.

"Didn't you keep any secrets from your parents when you were that age?" he asked.

About to shake her head, Louise stopped herself. When she was fourteen, she and her friends hid Martinis in the bushes outside the community parties at the local sports center. And then hadn't she lit up her own first cigarette down by the old gravel pit when she was in the sixth grade? As images from her years in Hvalsø flooded her mind, she stood up as if she could shake them off.

"My advice to you is that you give the boy a little space if you want to hold on to him. If things get too suffocating, he'll only pull away and live his own life."

"I'm cold," said Jonas, who returned after saying good-bye to his friends and took a seat next to Melvin.

Louise handed him her blanket and noted that it was getting dark already. They'd better get going. She was still shaken by Melvin's disclosure. She would have to talk to Camilla about it, but she wanted her friend to have the chance to enjoy her wedding first.

Melvin and Grete had promised Grete's girlfriend to return the next day to help her paint the fence facing the path. It was Louise's understanding that it had to be done by June 1 or you would be setting yourself up for conflict with the other garden owners. Melvin had already gotten involved with several of the other members of the garden association and had promised to come help out for the work weekend as well because the common areas needed cleaning up.

He was completely hooked on the whole community garden life, Louise thought, watching him get up and walk over to test the soil of a small raised bed by the hedge along the neighboring lot.

"I think I might have a temperature," Jonas mumbled, feeling his forehead.

Louise looked at him. She worried about him feeling anxious and sick as a reaction to her skipping work and acting depressive.

"You'll have to go downstairs to Melvin's if you're going to stay home from school tomorrow," she said as the four of them walked to the car together.

"Hrhhmm," Melvin cleared his throat. "I kind of figured on borrowing a mattress in Dragør."

Louise smiled; she found it sweet that Melvin still had a hard time saying he planned to spend the night with Grete.

"You know—because we've got an early start out in the garden tomorrow," he tried to explain himself.

"I can take care of myself," Jonas cut in, and Louise thought that it might not even be something that would last until the next day after all. The boys had been running around in short sleeves, and maybe they had just gotten chilled. Maybe it was a case of nerves he could sleep off.

21

B UT LINGER IT did. The following morning, Jonas woke up
with shiny eyes, his skin burning up with fever. Louise
called Hanne to let her know that she would be late because she
had to put Jonas on a train to Hvalsø, where her parents could
pick him up at the station.

"You'll probably need to have someone else take care of
that," Hanne cut in curtly. "Attendance at the monthly managers' meeting is mandatory, and it starts in twenty minutes—
which you would have known if you had been here yesterday
when I handed out the agenda."

Hanne raised her voice a little before playing her trump card:
"And I personally put it on your desk."

"I can't be there in twenty minutes," Louise answered
quickly, not even bothering to comment on the fact that she
had not been informed about these monthly managers' meetings, either.

"You'll have to pass on that message to the national commissioner yourself," Hanne cut in. "That's not part of my job description."

"Don't even worry about it," Louise snapped, straining to contain her anger. Right now she didn't give a damn about Hanne or the national commissioner.

"The meeting runs until noon and after that there's lunch at Restaurant Posten as usual, and I already ordered for you."

"Then you'll have to cancel the order or send Eik in my place," Louise hissed and hung up. She was no longer in a hurry to get to the Rathole and decided that she would drive Jonas to Lerbjerg herself. Then he wouldn't have to rattle around on the train with a fever.

Louise had just seen off her parents and their grandson when Mik called to tell her that the Forensics Department had run the test results from the body of the child care provider through the system.

"No match," he sighed, sounding as tired as he had looked when they ran into each other in the woods. "So now we'll have to go searching."

They had performed an autopsy on the child care provider, and the medical examiner had noted indications that she had put up a hard struggle.

"Large tufts of her hair had been ripped from her head and she had several pronounced hematomas. It seems so brutal that it got me thinking that maybe there was more than one attacker?"

"Did they find semen from anyone else?" she asked with interest.

"No," Mik admitted. "Just from one person, but I find it confusing considering the amount of violence inflicted."

"What about the runner; has she turned up?"

Louise had seen neither the news nor the papers since she left the investigation in the woods. It suddenly occurred to her that she hadn't even spoken with Eik. She was well aware that she owed him an explanation for her absence and an apology for making him attend the meeting this morning.

"No," Mik exclaimed, clearly frustrated. "The forensic officers have combed her regular route and there's indication that she was attacked a couple hundred yards before the Troll's Oak, down by the Deep where the road turns," he explained. "Do you know the place?"

"Yes," Louise mumbled, picturing the road with its steep descent and how you had to stand up and pedal hard to make it back up the hill. Tall pines lined both sides of the road, throwing the wooded area into shade. Someone must have told Mik that they called it the Deep, she thought.

"They found her iPod down there, and bloodstains at the spot, which of course need to be checked for DNA. The ground was torn up from resisting feet," he continued and quickly added: "The forensic officers think she may have dug her heels in and been dragged away from the road. Unfortunately, the tracks weren't deep enough to make imprints from the shoe prints. And there's nothing else to indicate that a crime may have occurred because no one has seen her or heard anything."

"Not even the people who live in Starling House?" Louise asked. "It's not far from there."

Back when she lived out there, an old lady owned the small house in the middle of the woods. It wasn't far from the gamekeeper's house; in fact, it was right between that and Verner Post at the Snipe House. When she and her brother were kids, they used to call it the Gingerbread House. They were convinced that the old lady was a witch because she never left the house, so they imagined that she lived off the children who played in the woods.

Later on, Louise's father told her that the old woman suffered from sclerosis and couldn't get around much the last several years. She used to get her groceries delivered from the store in Hvalsø. So it wasn't that much of a mystery after all, Louise thought. By now the woman had been dead for several years and the house had been thoroughly renovated.

There was nobody home at Starling House when she and Eik stopped by on their tour of the houses around the woods. Louise had noted that a large patio had been added in the back with an outdoor hot tub. A motorcycle was parked in an open shed, too, so clearly someone had taken over the place.

"No," Mik replied. "The wife out there was home and drinking coffee on the back porch when her husband left for work around eight, but she didn't hear anything. But of course by then it may have already happened."

There was silence at the other end of the line for a moment, then he cleared his throat.

"So in other words: We've got nothing. So we have to hurry up and find out whose DNA we've got from the blood. We just sent out a press release asking for the public's assistance in finding any people who regularly visit the woods. Then we'll have to see if they've noticed anything. It's obviously going to scare them, but I don't think we have a choice. As long as the perpetrator is out there, we have to do everything we can to catch him and warn others against walking around alone."

Louise heard his other phone ringing and barely had a chance to say good-bye before he hung up.

She called her mother. She could easily have turned around

and driven the short distance back to her parents' three-winged farm but then she would have to go inside again and she just didn't feel up to it.

"Don't go out in the woods," she warned when her mother picked up the phone. "I don't know what you've heard but it seems that there are now two victims and they have no lead on the perpetrator."

"Sure, but isn't that overreacting a bit?" her mom said, a smile in her voice.

"I don't know about that," Louise replied. "The police are sending out a press release warning women against walking alone in the woods. I just thought I should let you know." She hung up, wondering why she always felt the need to sound so surly when her mother was merely trying to calm a worry.

For a moment she closed her eyes, leaned her head back, and tried to collect herself. She needed to get out of here. The door to her past had been opened and she was unable to control her thoughts so close to where it all happened.

She had put so much energy into denying and rejecting the parts of her past that were too painful to remember that it had never occurred to her how easily they could be roused. She considered, very objectively, what her options were for moving on. To her dismay, there were only two: She either had to hand the case over to Eik, or stuff all her feelings and get on with it. The first would be the ultimate admission of failure, and against everything she stood for. So as she reached Hvalsø and turned right at the roundabout as usual in order to avoid Main Street, Louise realized that she had only one choice.

She drove past the pharmacy and the old stadium, which had given way to a row of town houses. That's where she used to play handball. She thought of Morits, their coach back then, and Arvid, who was the stadium manager and ran the concession stand.

This was where she lived her life. The memories came rushing in, but it all happened so long ago and she had done everything in her power to distance herself from her youth. Maybe that was a mistake. Maybe that was why it hit her so hard now. Because after all, a lot of it had been good. She had kissed in this town, gotten drunk, and gone to plenty of parties.

But she did all of those things with Klaus.

THEY STARTED GOING out when Louise was a freshman. She didn't have to strain to picture his face, his chestnut-brown hair and grayish-blue eyes, which were always warm even though he wore a leather jacket and tried to look tough.

He had been one grade ahead of her through her school years in Hvalsø, and she'd had a secret crush on him since the seventh grade—so much so that she didn't even notice the other boys who tried to catch her attention. And her heart was about to break when he left school after sophomore year to become a butcher in Roskilde because she felt certain that once he went there, he would forget all about her.

But he didn't. He faithfully held on, always asking if she wanted to come along whenever he made plans to go out.

She lost her virginity to Klaus. There had been a bonfire out by Avnsø Lake that evening. They rode their bikes home through the woods, and the next morning she lay in bed with her eyes closed for a long time, trying to determine if she felt different somehow; if maybe she was more grown-up or loved him deeper. And it was probably a little of both.

It wasn't until he got an apprenticeship in Tølløse that he started hanging out with Big Thomsen and his crowd. Klaus was still the same person, but Louise didn't care for the rest of them. They made her feel insecure because she was never sure if they were serious or just playing crude jokes. As she recalled, they always took it right to the line and sometimes they pushed their followers over it. Luckily Klaus didn't adopt the same superior attitude or their relationship would have been over.

Louise wondered what the gang thought of her. She had never really mingled with the group—she mostly stayed with Klaus when there was a party, and otherwise they usually stayed in, spending time in her room or his, unless they were hanging out at the stadium. They got engaged on her eighteenth birthday. He had bought two thin silver rings from the jeweler on Main Street and surprised her when they retired to her bedroom after dinner with her parents.

When his apprenticeship ended, he was able to continue working for the butcher in Tølløse. One evening they had been sitting by Avnsø Lake, thinking about moving in together. As she recalled, it wasn't much more than a month later that Klaus stopped by one afternoon to tell her about the farmhouse in Kisserup. The rent was just 1,625 kroner a month.

The house was vacant when they went to see it, and Louise loved it even though it needed cleaning and paint. An elderly man had lived there for the past several years before going to a nursing home. Later that same day, after signing the lease, they sat on the lawn beneath the large heritage apple tree, dreaming and making plans for the future. She had shaken her head at Klaus when he pointed out that the two smaller bedrooms behind the living room would make good nurseries.

Her only concern was whether Big Thomsen and his gang planned on moving in as well. It was always a great draw when someone got their own place; friends no longer had to hang out at their parents' house and be careful to keep the volume down.

As they sat there in the grass, she had told Klaus that of course he could keep seeing them. She just didn't want to live with them.

WITHOUT GIVING IT much thought, Louise signaled and turned off toward Kisserup and drove past the gravel pit with a knot slowly growing in her stomach. She hadn't been there since that summer. There were more houses now, she noted, slowing down a little. The road to the thicket by the house was just after a row of closely spaced trees, which all but obscured the small sign.

The house was at the end of the road. Louise's palms felt sweaty against the steering wheel as she pulled over and decided to walk the last part of the way. There weren't many houses along the narrow road, and theirs had been a bit farther down than the rest. The trees still hid the house from view like they did back then; it wasn't visible from the road, which turned slightly just before the sloped driveway.

Louise walked along a row of tall trees that followed the field next to the property. She could hear voices. It sounded like children playing with water, whooping and cheering when they got splashed.

She felt cold inside as she stepped between the pines and pushed through the close branches.

The red timber-frame house had a new thatched roof; a large patio had been built in the back. Toys were scattered across the yard and two children squealed with delight as their father turned the water hose in their direction.

Louise slumped down, staying hidden behind the heavy bottom branches of a pine tree. The remains of breakfast were still on the table and a woman sat under a sunshade, nursing an infant. The family was probably enjoying their parental leave with their newest addition.

Louise noticed that they had planted small bushes in the spot where she had planned to put an apple tree. It would have grown big by now, she thought.

She didn't cry as she sat there, breaking inside. It was no longer the kind of sorrow that brought tears. It had settled in a deeper place, and she realized that it had eaten away a bit of her life—or at least the life she had dreamed of having.

THEY HAD MOVED in on a Friday, having spent the previous weeks out there painting. Louise's mother had helped them clean the house, and Klaus borrowed a van from his boss to move their things. They had spent their first night in the house on the living room floor because Klaus had started to unbutton her blouse and then they never really got any farther. At one point during the night, he had dragged in a mattress for them to lie on but they didn't get much sleep. The way she remembered it, they made love until morning.

The following evening she had made plans with Camilla to spend the night at her studio apartment in Roskilde. A rock band was playing at the high school in Himmelev, and Klaus would never let her drag him along to something like that. So she left him with the boxes to unpack and promised to be back Sunday before noon so they could finish settling in.

THE MOTHER WITH the infant stood up. The baby appeared to be sleeping.

Louise watched as she gently laid the little one down in the carry-cot next to her chair before going inside. She returned shortly after with a couple of towels, which she tossed to the two older children. The father had begun rolling up the water hose. The scene of domestic idyll played on as Louise thought back to the day that hers ended.

SHE HAD RIDDEN her bike home from the train station on Sunday morning. She didn't want to call and wake up Klaus to let him know that she was on her way, but she brought freshly baked bread from the bakery on Main Street—both breakfast rolls and pastries.

His motorcycle was parked in front of the house and the living room windows were open so she thought he might have gotten up early to start unpacking.

The door was unlocked but she didn't take any time to puzzle over it. She was so excited to see him, she just walked right in.

He was hanging from a rope over the stairs.

LOUISE CLOSED HER eyes but stood up quickly before the images got too clear. With her arms in front of her, she pushed her way back through the pines and stumbled out into the road.

She froze for a second. For the first time in twenty-one years, she had allowed herself to think back all the way to the moment she stepped inside the house. She would usually force her memories to change course before she got that far. But today she had walked the plank, and as she slowly started to make her way back to the car, she tried to determine whether she felt more broken.

22

I T WAS PAST noon when Louise got to the department, but instead of going straight to her own office, she headed directly for Rønholt's front office. And Hanne.

She had to have a talk with the secretary. If their relationship continued down this road, it would eventually come to a crash, and she knew herself well enough to know that she might end up saying a lot of things that were both rash and filled with anger—admittedly not the smartest thing to do now that she had put herself in a position where she could get the boot on relatively short notice.

She had come to realize that she'd made a mistake in falling for Rønholt's offer and his words of praise. There was no doubt in her mind that Eik had been telling the truth when he said others had been offered the opportunity to head the new special unit but had turned it down because it was a sinking ship. Of course none of them were foolish enough to put their steady and secure jobs on the line for a new unit that was at risk of being short-lived and apparently only served as an office where cases were pushed through in order to be closed and archived as quickly as possible. She was furious with herself now for not making sure that her contract stipulated her right to return to one of the established departments should it become necessary to close down this new unit after the trial period. She had been so eager to get away from the dreaded Michael Stig, who had replaced her old boss, that she acted without thinking.

"Come in!" Hanne's voice sounded chirpy when Louise knocked but her smile faded when she saw who it was. "Well," she said just before Louise stopped her, pulling a chair up to her desk.

"Hanne, what's your problem?" she blurted out. "Why do you act like this with me?"

At first Hanne just stared at Louise as if she hadn't the faintest idea what she might be referring to. Then she gave a small wave as if trying to fan away a smell. But perhaps she was merely trying to hush Louise. Still without saying a word, she reached over and picked up the top item from her letter organizer and handed it to Louise.

She accepted the file but let it drop onto the desk without taking her eyes off Hanne.

"Stop it," she demanded, "and let's just talk about this. We both know I'm not going to quit the department just because you don't like my being here," she continued, growing confused with the look in Hanne's eyes.

"What do you mean?" the secretary asked uncomprehendingly, awkwardly flicking her big red hair a little as if Louise's attack was coming as a complete surprise to her. "Why would you quit?"

"Because you're being so rude, and frankly it seems as if

you'd prefer it if I just went away. But I won't," Louise empha-
sized. "We need to figure out a way to work together, so it's no
use for you to withhold information about important meetings.
Or for you to keep me in the dark about the routines of the
department in general."

There was a moment of silence between them; then Hanne
pointed to the plastic folder on the desk.

"I've got a phone number for you. They got a DNA result
from the woman in the woods, and I promised that you would
call them back."

She said it as if the preceding conversation never happened.

Louise contemplated her for a second. Then she sighed and
picked up the printout from the Forensics Department. She still
hadn't gotten around to putting her name on her cubbyhole.

"Thanks," she said and stood up.

ON HER WAY back to the office, she wondered what in the world
she was going to do about Hanne. In the end she would probably have to speak with Rønholt.

"Hey!" someone called from behind her.

She turned around. When she spotted Olle, she realized
that she never thanked him for the drawing of the kitchen rat.

He was tall and his hair was thinning at the top. Louise
guessed that he was at least fifty, but a look in his warm brown
eyes, which kept smiling as he walked toward her, made his age
difficult to pinpoint.

"Did you like it?" he asked expectantly, like a child who
drew a picture for his parents.

Louise wasn't sure if it was her expression or because she
waited too long to answer, but in any event, he seemed to catch
on to the fact that she probably wasn't a major fan of cartoons.

"I can make something else," he quickly offered. "I just thought I should make you something now that you're going to be working with us."

"No-no," she burst out, embarrassed that he should have to suffer for her irritable mood. "It's really cool and it was so nice of you. I didn't even know you had that kind of talent."

"I've got all kinds of talent," he retorted in a velvety smooth voice, stepping closer and smiling.

Louise was so taken aback at his undisguised flirtation that she couldn't think to do anything but just stand there with a sheepish smile.

"You be sure to let me know if you feel like exploring some of the other ones," he went on as she slowly began to take a few steps backward.

"Olle!"

Eik came out of the cleaning room, tucking his pack of cigarettes in his pocket.

"She's mine."

Louise turned around, feeling relieved that her rescuer wasn't having lunch at Posten with the others. She gave a quick nod to the tall, gangly cartoonist and fled down the hall toward the Rathole.

"DID YOU ATTEND the managers' meeting?" Louise asked as she walked through the door. Then her nose caught a strange smell in the office and she fell silent. Her initial thought was that maybe the rats were back.

Eik had pushed their desks up against the wall to make room on the floor.

"I was busy," he declared without looking at her. His desk was a mess of papers, which lifted as the wind caught them.

"I printed out information on every registered Toyota HiAce that's white with no windows, and I was working on screening out the newer models when they called from the Forensics Department to say that we could come pick up Lise Andersen's clothes."

As Louise walked over to her desk and put down her bag, she realized that the musty smell was coming from the clothes.

He was laying them out on the floor. He had already smoothed out the rust-red, smock-like dress and was now placing a pair of navy-blue ankle socks next to it.

"They're completely worn out." He held out one of them to show her the large holes. "That's why it looked like she'd been walking barefoot."

Louise nodded.

"I'm just trying to see if maybe there's something about her clothes that might give us a clue to go on. But the dress doesn't have a tag, and if you come over here you'll see that the fabric is worn completely shiny. It's old."

But Louise didn't look at the dress. Instead she looked at him as he proceeded to pick up an undershirt from the small cardboard box. Even though Eik was too much in every way, she had to admit that Rønholt was right about him being energetic and good at finding new angles.

"They got a DNA result," Louise told him. She dialed up the DNA section of the Forensics Department.

Eik had finished laying out the clothes and walked over to get the camera from his desk. Then he began to photograph each piece of clothing.

"I guess it's unlikely that we'll be able to trace the dress," he assessed while Louise waited for her call to be transferred.

He had made no comments on the fact that she had come in late, nor her calling in sick the previous day. Perhaps he hadn't even noticed, she thought, and told the man who picked up her call which case she was calling about. "You asked me to call."

To Eik, Louise mouthed *They got a positive DNA match.* The man who had intercourse with Lisemette before she fell to her death was already in the police DNA database.

She was about to ask for the civil registration number when the man added that the person was identified by neither name nor civil registration number. His DNA alone was linked to another case. The perpetrator's identity was unknown.

"But there must be a reference number?" she interjected and jotted it down as he read out the information.

She quickly wrapped up the call and punched in the reference number. Her fingers froze over the keys as she started to read.

"It's him!" she said without taking her eyes off the screen to look at Eik, who was on the floor with the camera.

"Who?" he asked.

"It's the same guy," she said. "The man who killed the child care provider also had intercourse with Lise. And when I was talking to Mik it sounded like he was pretty sure that the perpetrator could also be linked to the missing runner."

Eik left the camera on the floor as he got to his feet and walked over to stand behind her chair.

"But if it's him then why didn't he hurt Lise?" he asked. "There isn't the slightest indication that she was the victim of an assault. Her clothes weren't disheveled, and there were no tears or hematomas on her lower body."

Louise shook her head, momentarily unable to think of an answer.

"Maybe she didn't try to fight it?" she finally suggested, following him with her eyes as he returned to the clothes on the floor.

"You think he took his leisurely time to undo the whole long fastening in her dress? And what about her underwear? None of the things are torn or ripped. I'm not buying that this was rape," he concluded.

"Then what do you think?" Louise asked, growing exasperated as he merely shrugged and reached for the camera.

"I think they knew each other," he said, looking up at her. "And if that's the case, then he might also have access to Mette."

23

"I F WE'RE LOOKING for the same guy, then I've got something you ought to see," Mik said. He explained that he had just returned from the archive in Roskilde, where he had gone to pick up some old cases.

She had called him up to tell him about the latest development, and she could tell that he was walking while they talked. He seemed absentminded, even when she shared the news about the DNA match between the child care provider and Lise Andersen.

"Twenty years ago there were several aggravated assaults in those woods. Two of the women were raped and killed. After the press release that we sent out this morning warning women against walking alone in the woods, we were contacted by a retired schoolteacher from Hvalsø, who told us that one of her graduates was the perpetrator's first victim."

Louise stared straight ahead. She found it difficult to

imagine the same perpetrator being in the area all the way back then. She had no recollection of those cases, but then it was around that same time that she was engrossed in the after-shocks of her own catastrophe and had her hands full just try-ing to keep her life together.

"They never caught the perpetrator," he added.

"But then what about all the years in between?" Louise objected. "If this guy was behind a series of attacks, do you think he just took a break only to pick back up where he left off?" she said.

It made no sense, she thought as she heard a door opening. She assumed that Mik had arrived back at his office.

"Obviously we need to investigate whether he might be behind other crimes in the intervening years," he conceded. "But if that's the case then it definitely wasn't a series of attacks like the ones that took place back then."

"No, of course not," Louise mumbled. Then the police districts would clearly have been aware that the cases were linked.

"His DNA was collected in connection with the old assaults but they never found the person behind the DNA profile," he told her. "That was also before DNA was recognized as evi-dence so they may not have even been able to convict him even if he had been identified—there is no other evidence."

"And it was before the profiles started to get entered in the system automatically," Louise said while still searching her memory. Surely she had heard about it, she thought, but she'd probably just repressed the story along with everything else.

"Right now, the forensic geneticists are working on finding out whether the old cases can be linked to the murder of the child care provider. We'll get the results later today."

"Would it be possible for me to read the case files?" Louise asked. If they were able to link them to the child care provider, they would also be linked to Lisemette.

"You're welcome to it," Mik answered. "But you have to come up here. I can't send them to you because we're going to need them ourselves."

"Of course," she quickly cut in. "I'll head out as soon as I get a bite to eat."

Louise suddenly noticed that she was hungry. She hadn't eaten since they sat outside in the community garden the night before. Now hunger was gnawing at her along with adrenaline, which was well on its way to firing up every fiber of her body.

"Can't we just pick up a sandwich on the way?" Eik suggested as they walked down the hall together shortly after. "And today I'm driving."

She followed him without objection to a beat-up Jeep Cherokee—black, like the clothes that Eik always wore. The car reeked of smoke; empty soda bottles littered the floor. Louise got her cell phone from her bag, and while Eik rolled down the window and lit up a cigarette she called her parents to check on Jonas.

"Do you want to stay in Lerbjerg or should I ask if Melvin will be home later today?" she asked. She told him that she was on her way to Holbæk but could probably stop by on the way back.

Louise looked questioningly at Eik to confirm that he would be okay with taking a detour on their way home. He nodded briefly and emitted some deep grunts as he tapped the wheel to the beat of a Nick Cave song playing from the car stereo.

"I'd rather stay here," Jonas sniffled and stifled a yawn.

"I'll call you tonight then," she promised. "Feel better."

*   *   *

LOUISE PUT A bag on Mik's desk with a chicken-and-bacon sandwich and a Schweppes Ginger Ale.

"You've got a good memory." He smiled and took a gulp before showing them to an office down the hall where the case files were stacked up.

The first case occurred in the month of May. According to the old summary, Diana Sørensen had just gotten out of school to study for her finals when she was attacked in the woods. The girl explained that she was getting off her bike to walk up a hill when a man grabbed hold of her.

"He came out from behind a tree as if he had been waiting for me," the girl had said.

There weren't that many people coming through the woods, Louise thought, so it seemed illogical that he would have actually stood there waiting for the schoolgirl to pass by. More likely he'd followed her without her noticing. The girl had broken her right collarbone and her shoulder was dislocated from the fall, she read, inferring that the man must have yanked on her hard when he knocked her off her bike.

Diana Sørensen had been unable to describe her assailant. The police report noted that the victim was presumably unconscious during part of the incident, and it was added in parenthesis that she had been a virgin at the time of the attack.

Aside from the sounds, the man had been quiet during that part of the rape, the young girl recalled, and she never saw him as anything but just a large shadow.

"It looked as if the sun had disappeared; suddenly everything was just dark," she had explained. Once the perpetrator had thrown her to the ground facedown, he had ripped off her tight jeans.

"He breathed in such a strange way," she had described, and the officer had asked her to explain what it was about the rapist's breathing that frightened her.

"He sounded like an animal," the report said, and Diana Sørensen had elaborated on her statement by explaining that his breathing always seemed to have the same pulse: "Like a fan or a horse wheezing."

"The young girl describes the perpetrator as a monster, a cross between man and beast," Louise said, looking over at Eik, who was intently chewing on a match while reading. "But she couldn't say what he looked like."

He didn't seem to be listening at all, she thought. He had a deep wrinkle across his forehead, and his index finger followed the lines as he worked his way through one of the other old reports. Louise shook her head with irritation and picked up the next case.

Two weeks later, a twenty-two-year-old woman had been raped and killed in the same part of the woods. There were clear indications that she had fought vehemently. The killer's DNA had been scraped out from under her fingernails. According to the forensic report, the young woman had scratched and kicked in her attempt to defend herself until the perpetrator broke her neck, and only then did he consummate the rape.

"Listen to this," Eik interrupted her, spitting out his match into the wastebasket. "If this is the same perpetrator that we're looking for, this says something about his defect of character."

Louise reluctantly took her eyes off the report on the rapist's first casualty.

"Gitte Jensen was walking her dog in the woods and had taken it off the leash even though dogs must be kept on leash. At one point it started barking like crazy and ran off between the trees. She tried calling the dog and was about to go look for him when she heard some strange sounds and twigs snapping on the forest floor. By then the dog had gone quiet, and she ran like hell all the way home, thinking about that rapist that everyone was talking about."

He fell silent for a second as he read on.

"What about the dog?" Louise asked.

"They found it," he replied. "Or rather, what was left of it." He bent over the report and read out: " 'It is presumed that the dog was lifted by its hind legs and hurled around.' "

Eik grimaced and put a new match in his mouth, disgust written on his haggard face.

"You read it." He pushed the report toward her.

Louise pulled it closer while stealing a glance at Eik, whose quiet distress was striking.

The dog's skull was crushed and all of his vertebrae were broken, she read. The police had found bits of fur in the bark of the surrounding trees. Cerebral matter and blood were splattered across a sizable area, and based on that information Louise envisaged that the dog had been hurled around with terrific force.

"How the hell can anyone even swing around a chap like that?" Eik asked after collecting himself a little.

Louise shrugged. The dog was a male weighing upward of ninety pounds. "I guess you can if you're strong enough," she said.

"But it probably tried to bite."

She thought of her dad, who once yanked a large fox out of the chicken coop. He had avoided getting bitten because he held it by its tail and swung it around so it couldn't reach him.

They sat in silence until Louise slid the report back across the table.

"It attacked him," she said.

Eik nodded. "And then he destroyed it."

She felt a tight knot in her stomach. If the twins had been in some sort of contact with this perpetrator, then what had they been subjected to?

"They never caught him," Louise mumbled as she began to lay out the cases on the desk. Diana Sørensen had managed to get herself home after the assault. The doctors subsequently thought that she had probably been lying in the woods for a while before regaining consciousness, and maybe the rapist thought she was dead when he left her. At the back of the file was a map on which the schoolgirl had circled the place where the attack happened.

Louise found Avnsø and turned the map to orient herself.

"The rape happened just on the other side of the large Troll's Oak," she said, looking at Eik. "That's only a few hundred yards from the Deep, which is where Mik believes that the runner was attacked."

She took the map from the next case file. In late summer another woman had been raped and killed not far from there.

"All of the old attacks happened in the same part of the woods," he said, pointing to the place where the dog had been found.

"But nobody lives around there," Louise said with frustration.

"The perpetrator must have thorough knowledge of the woods," Eik said, looking at her. "He knows the forest paths well enough that he's able to take a shortcut to get ahead of his victims once he spots them. Who knows the woods like that?"

He lit a cigarette and walked over to the open window. Louise was about to protest but instead she shrugged and tried to ignore it.

"Lots of people know the woods. Riders, orienteers, forest workers, scouts," she answered. She personally knew every way through there; she had ridden down all the small roads and knew exactly where to cut through the trees to get somewhere as quickly as possible.

Once Eik had finished smoking and closed the window, they laid out all the cases by date.

"The first one happened in May," he summed up. "The last one was in August. And all of them in the early hours of Saturday and Sunday mornings, as far as I can tell."

Louise nodded. "Was there any specific pattern?" she asked. "Or some sort of regularity? Let's have a look." She started writing down the dates on a notepad.

"It was a month between the first one and the second." Eik leaned forward to read the next cases. "But then there were two just one week apart."

"What about the two women who went missing?" Louise suddenly remembered. "That was that same summer."

The year after she'd left town. She had seen the missing person reports back when they were trying to identify Lise Andersen.

"Lotte Svendsen was one of them, and it was just after the Whitsun celebration."

Louise walked over to the computer and ran a search on the year. "There it is. May eighteen. That was the weekend before Diana Sørensen was raped. So maybe she wasn't his first victim after all?"

"What about the other one?" Eik asked. "When did she go missing?"

"I don't remember the date but we've got them both in the system back at the department."

There was a quick knock at the door, then Mik walked in.

"We've gotten a positive result back from Forensics," he said and asked them to gather up the case files and follow him to his office. "The old DNA profiles match our case. It was the same perpetrator in the woods back then."

24

"WHERE ARE YOU?" Camilla asked when Louise finally answered her cell phone. She had been calling pretty much every ten minutes for the past hour even though she had figured out that Louise must have set her phone to silent mode. Anger was still pumping through her body, and her throat was sore from yelling. She couldn't even remember everything she had said. Could she have called off the wedding?

"Can I stay with you for a little while?"

She had packed a large weekend bag and already slammed the door behind herself.

Markus had come home from school in the middle of their fight and when she turned her back to Frederik to go upstairs and pack, she had popped into her son's room and told him to get some clothes together along with his schoolbooks for the rest of the week.

But he wasn't about to go anywhere. He wanted to stay with

Frederik until she came around, and Camilla didn't have the strength to argue with him as well.

So now she had walked out on both of them and wondered if she'd just written herself out of the chapter that was supposed to be the beginning.

"It's only for a few days, until I can find something else," she said, adding that she had to give the couple who was subletting her apartment thirty days' notice.

"Of course," said Louise, and suddenly Camilla couldn't cope with the thought of starting over one more time. Her life was a succession of restarts. When she met Tobias and got pregnant, she had thought that it was going to be forever but it seemed like only a second later that she was left alone with an eighteen-month-old boy. Every attempt at starting a relationship since had capsized.

"We only just left Holbæk to head back to the department so it'll be a little while before I get home," she heard Louise say while she blew her nose.

"No need to rush. I've still got my key," she said and promised to take care of dinner.

LOUISE ASSUMED IT was Camilla calling again as she was about to put her cell phone back in her bag. But this time it was Lisemette's father on the other end of the line.

"We buried Lise today," he told her. "The funeral was beautiful, and of course the weather couldn't have been nicer."

"I'm so sorry," Louise said warmly. She hoped he'd make his peace, and was glad he'd at least gotten lovely weather for the somber event. She'd noticed that the warm May sun had inspired people to put on shorts and T-shirts. After a long winter, they couldn't wait to shed the heavy layers.

"Now she's resting next to her mother, and the minister gave a nice sermon even though the two of them never knew each other. Well, my wife and the kids didn't know her, either..."

"I'm glad it went well," Louise said.

"But now my wife and I were just sitting here talking about Mette," he said. "She would get very anxious if she felt insecure and scared. I can't help wondering if she's just left to her own devices now, sitting out there somewhere feeling miserable and scared. So I wanted to check if maybe there's any news?"

Louise leaned her head back against the soft headrest of the car while she weighed her answer.

"No," she answered honestly. "We don't have anything yet. Right now we're working on finding out where your daughters have been staying all these years."

"I've also been wondering if maybe we could find someone who remembers something from back then," he continued, "but I don't recall the supervisor's name, only that it was a man."

"As soon as we have even the slightest clue to go on, I promise you'll be the very first to know."

"You think she's alive?" he asked, his voice hopeful, and Louise slumped down a little. She thought about the crushed dog and the old homicide cases and couldn't bring herself to tell him about the beast they were hunting in the woods.

"If she's alive, we'll find her," she said grandly, refraining from letting on what she personally believed.

He thanked her so profusely that Louise felt filled with shame at the thought that she might have promised more than she could deliver.

CAMILLA HAD PUT out hummus, ham, sausage, and cheese on the table. It looked like she had cleared out an entire delicatessen, Louise thought.

"The bread's in the oven," Camilla said and sank onto a kitchen chair, taking a large gulp of her wine.

Louise patted Dina and went to pour the dog's food in her bowl before taking a seat across from her friend.

She had a headache, and the Tylenol she'd taken before biking home hadn't kicked in yet. She accepted the glass of wine that her friend handed her and thought that it might be more effective to wash away the thoughts of Klaus and the beast still on the loose.

"I think it's over," Camilla said, putting her glass down. "I'm not so sure that Frederik is the kind of guy who lets you just slam the door in his face."

"You did that?" Louise asked before getting up to find a bread basket when the timer for the bread went off.

"I just got so angry, I couldn't help it. I was minding my own business, having a sandwich in the kitchen. Suddenly he's standing in the doorway, with that look on his face."

She grimaced and picked her glass back up before giving Louise an indignant look. "Do you know what he said to me?"

Louise shook her head dutifully.

"That I'd have to face the fact that it takes a bit of manners to be among the model citizens of Roskilde."

Louise was making herself a plate, but put her fork down and started laughing.

"Frederik seems to think that there are certain rules I have to abide by if we're to keep living at the manor house."

Camilla topped off both of their glasses and grabbed a piece of bread.

"It's not like I don't know how to behave," she said with hurt in her voice. "It's one thing that he got mad about me firing the workers. But they weren't keeping to our agreement! And isn't a minister supposed to marry people the way he promised?"

She put a piece of bread in her mouth and chewed angrily.

"I'm running around to all these lame-ass things," she went on. "The other day, I was squeezed into a corner at some charity auction and could barely stand up when it finally ended because my legs were asleep from boredom. But nobody took any notice."

"Maybe that's not what he meant," Louise suggested. "Maybe he just doesn't need any more problems."

"Problems?" Camilla asked uncomprehendingly. "He doesn't have any damn problems. I end up with all of them!"

"If given a choice, don't you think he would have preferred you and Markus moving to Santa Barbara so he could continue his life over there?" Louise asked.

Camilla shrugged.

"Instead of working his ass off in a family company that he never had any desire to run?"

She fell silent when her friend cast down her eyes.

"Enough about him," Camilla said and told Louise about her visit to the patient care assistant who'd worked at Eliselund. "It was boiling water that ruined her face. Her skin was scalded off. It's unbearable to think of. And Agnete Eskildsen was the one who turned on the tap."

Louise breathed in and exhaled heavily.

"She told me that the supervisor down there told the twins' father a story that it was the girl's sister who had been careless with a kettle of boiling water, but she also said that it was solely to protect the reputation of the institution and not to cover up for her."

"Then it's no wonder she reacted when she saw the photo in the newspaper," Louise said.

Camilla nodded and added that Agnete had told her that the twins were inseparable. "I can barely stand to think where Mette might be now," Camilla exclaimed. "Or what's become of her."

"Did Agnete have any idea about how something like this could have happened?"

"She hasn't been keeping up with what's been going on down there. The director retired and someone new replaced him, but as she said when I was leaving, she turned her back on Eliselund after the accident."

The phone rang in the living room, and Louise got up to answer it. These days, just about the only people who called her home number were her parents and Melvin.

"Why don't you come out here to the gardens for a cup of evening coffee?" Melvin asked when he found out that Camilla was visiting.

"I don't think either one of us is in any condition to drive," Louise admitted, although the idea of sitting in the small garden and letting go of all her thoughts about the case did hold a certain appeal.

"That's too bad. There's something I want to show you." He told her that a garden lot would be going up for sale just a few houses down on the same path as Grete's friend's place. "It's going to be any day now."

"Well, you should buy it!" Louise exclaimed. "Let's buy it together."

She could just picture it: Melvin puttering around an herb garden, digging up new potatoes; her in a hammock while Jonas was cultivating all his new friendships.

"Yes, I'm in," she announced rather giddily just as Melvin added that it couldn't hurt to take a look since he got an inside tip before it really went on the market.

"Wouldn't it be nice to just move out and live in a small house in the community gardens, and not have to deal with work and annoying colleagues?" Louise said when she returned to the kitchen, where Camilla had cleared the table and opened up another bottle of wine even though it was already getting late.

"That would probably be kind of a bummer," her friend

interjected. "Don't they turn off the water and you're not even supposed to live out there in the winter?"

"I have no idea."

Louise hadn't considered the obligations that went with the idea, but she supposed that Melvin would be the one to take care of those things.

"I thought it sounded like you weren't liking your new department so much. Are you having second thoughts?" Camilla asked, opening a sleeve of crackers for the cheese.

Louise stared straight ahead for a second. Was she having second thoughts? Perhaps a little. She was still quite appalled that Rønholt had stabbed them in the back and almost forced them to close the case.

"If he had gotten away with making us close the case about Lisemette, I would have had to put my job on the line for it. I can't just sit around a place where it's all about processing case numbers through the system in order to achieve an impressive percentage of solved ones."

"What about that guy you're working with?" Camilla asked, looking at her curiously.

Louise laughed wearily. "Eik Nordstrøm. On our first day I had to go scoop him up from some dive bar in Sydhavnen. He's a chain smoker who listens to Nick Cave and only wears black."

"Wouldn't it be better for you to bring Lars Jørgensen over?"

They had finished the last bottle, and Louise gratefully left the cleanup to Camilla to get ready for bed.

"No," she said to her own surprise before going to brush her teeth. "I kind of like that he's straightforward. He doesn't do a lot of bullshit and he backed me up when Rønholt was trying to screw us over. It's more Hanne who's being a cow. Eik is all right."

25

W HAT THE HELL are you doing?" Louise yelled when she walked into the office the next morning, her head heavy, and spotted two of the case files from the archives in Roskilde on Eik's desk.

"It's just the ones we didn't finish in Holbæk," he answered innocently.

"You can't just remove the case files! That's Mik's case! How do you plan to explain that you took them?"

"Calm down," he grumbled, straightening up as he opened the top file. "I'll send them back as soon as we're done with them."

"You're not sending them back," Louise cut in, pointing to the phone. "You're going to call up Mik and explain to him that the files are on your desk."

Just then Louise's cell phone started ringing, and she was about to toss it in the drawer when she noticed that it was

Melvin. For a second she started to worry. It wasn't like him to call her during her working hours.

"Yes," she answered briefly, turning her back to Eik, who was laying out the old cases across his desk. She pulled out her chair and sat down while her downstairs neighbor informed her that he had just gone to put them down for the community garden lot.

"The house on there isn't very big," he said and generously offered to take the smaller room out back so she and Jonas could have the bedroom and the part of the living room that was screened off behind the kitchen. "There's room for an extra bed."

So all three of them in 375 square feet, Louise thought, starting to regret having let herself get carried away in her red wine buzz. She had to backpedal but really didn't feel up to it right now. He sounded so happy.

"Let's talk about it tonight," she said quickly and promised to stop by downstairs after she got home.

"I also found the case files for the two women who went missing that same summer. Check out what one of Lotte Svendsen's girlfriends said in her deposition," Eik said as soon as she put down her phone. " 'We had been hanging out all day. It was the Whitsun celebration so most of us met up early for the community breakfast down on Main Street.' "

"Give me that; I want to read it myself," she said irritably, reaching for the old report.

" 'Several of us went home to sleep for a while before meeting back up in the evening for the party in the tent. Then we rode our bikes out to Avnsø Lake and kept partying. I don't remember if Lotte went swimming, too, but she wanted to leave before the rest of us. Ole had started messing around with Helle, and so Lotte got mad and went to get her bike,' " she read out.

After skimming over the rest of the case, she determined that the deposition from Lotte Svendsen's girlfriend was the most interesting one. The other people who were interviewed hadn't even noticed that Lotte Svendsen left early to go home.

Nobody had seen her after she left the party in the woods, and it was several days before a forest worker found her bike between the trees a few hundred yards from there. No attempt had been made to hide it; it was just left there, Louise noted, which suggested to the police that she had parked it there voluntarily.

If she had been attacked that close to the others, it seemed most unlikely that nobody would have heard her calling for help. According to most of the people who had been interviewed, it was no secret that Lotte Svendsen had been deeply in love with Ole Thomsen for several years—ever since they left school, in fact, but things never really happened between the two of them. At the time, several people explained that they initially thought her disappearance might have something to do with that.

Big Thomsen had been interviewed as well but according to his deposition, he hadn't even noticed her being at the lake that evening.

What a jerk, Louise thought. That's exactly how she remembered that crowd: arrogant and indifferent.

"Would it be worth it to talk to the people who used to hang out in the woods back then?" Eik suggested, looking at her questioningly.

"Maybe," she replied, "but I think we should start by focusing on finding the consultant doctor and some of the others who worked at Eliselund back then so we can get an explanation for those death certificates." She told him about Camilla's visit to Agnete Eskildsen. "I don't like thinking about the fact that the rapist might have a connection to Mette."

Louise tipped her chin toward the phone on his desk. "You get the information on the employees," she said, "and I'll drive to Holbæk and return the two case files that you stole."

"You don't have to drive there; we'll just send them in the mail," he objected. "They don't even know that they're missing."

"I don't want to risk them getting lost in the mail," she declared. "I'm going."

She was quite happy to get away from the Rathole and from Eik, who had put the phone in his lap, tipped his chair back, and flung his boots up on the desk while punching in the number for Eliselund.

"February 1980," he repeated, and listened while nodding.

Louise was holding the case files, her bag on her shoulder, and couldn't help but smile. She had immediately picked up that Eik had Lillian Johansen—the cranky sourpuss—on the line.

"I just need to know who worked at Eliselund at the time," he continued in a deep and patient voice while shaking a cigarette from the pack with his free hand and lighting it, unconcerned with the fact that Louise was still standing in the doorway.

WHEN SHE GOT to Holbæk, Louise left the case files with the front office for the criminal police with instructions that they were to be brought to Mik's office right away. Then she slunk away before she risked running into anyone she knew. On her way back to the car, Viggo Andersen called and told her that he now intended to look for the doctor who signed the death certificates.

"I'm going to get ahold of the Division for the Care of the Mentally Retarded," he said with an air of commitment. He was showing his girls all the attention that had been withheld from them back then.

"We're already working on finding the persons responsible. Why don't we agree that I'll contact you once we get some names?" Louise said. She understood that he felt the need to act, but he would have to wait until they had had a chance to speak with those involved. Instead she suggested that he have a talk with Agnete Eskildsen, who used to work there when the girls were little. "Did you or your family have any acquaintances in the Hvalsø area? Someone who would have known the girls when they were little and knew that they grew up at Eliselund?"

A considerable amount of time passed while he pondered her question, but he finally arrived at the conclusion that they didn't.

"I was too busy working and looking after the girls to have much of a social circle," he added. "And they were mostly in their own little world and then they were just three years old when they moved away."

"No big deal, it was just a thought anyway," Louise hurried to say. "You'll hear from me after we speak with some of the old employees from Eliselund."

WHEN LOUISE REACHED the freeway exit to Hvalsø, she decided to stop by her parents' place to see if Jonas wanted to come home. She drove down the underpass and was about to take the back way around town out of habit, but then she stopped herself and continued down Main Street instead. When she reached the church, she signaled off and turned into the small parking lot. There were no other cars. She got out of the car and walked through the gate. Keeping up her pace, she continued down the path past the church and around the corner to the cemetery in the back. The cemetery was deserted aside from an older man who was watering the graves that faced out toward the inn.

She smelled the freshly cut grass from the lawn surrounding the unmarked graves. She proceeded slowly toward the rearmost paths, where she began reading the names on the headstones, an oppressive feeling growing in her chest. None of these people had died recently.

Twenty-one years had passed. Klaus was buried on September 7, 1990. It was a Friday. Louise remembered because it was exactly one week after they moved into the house. She paused for a moment to gather up courage before continuing to the rearmost path, which ran along the cemetery wall.

His grave was the third one in. The name was cut into black slate, and there was a small heart underneath.

That heart should have been from me, Louise thought sadly and squatted down.

She looked at the two small cemetery vases with fresh flowers. Everything was tidy and neat without being overly groomed, but he wouldn't have cared for that anyway. Her eyes rested on the wildflowers sown in a cluster and the two evergreen shrubs that gave his little plot a lush appearance.

Someone must come here often since the grave is so neat, she thought, reaching out to touch the fresh flowers in the vases. The leaves were still crisp. Louise let her hand linger for a moment on the stem of the flower while her thoughts traveled back, and she startled when her cell phone started ringing in her pocket.

"There's been another rape," Mik started without presenting himself. "The woman's husband found her when he came home and called an ambulance. They took her to Roskilde."

Louise stood up in a daze.

"Is she alive?"

"Yes, and it doesn't seem like she's been subjected to the same aggravated violence as we've seen in connection with the murder of the child care provider," he said, adding that he hadn't personally had a chance to speak with the victim.

"But could it be the same perpetrator?"

"Without a doubt," Mik answered.

"What do you know?"

"We know that the rapist entered the woman's home through an open patio door while she was in the bathroom."

"Where does she live?" Louise asked, feeling a jitter through her body.

"The postal code is for Hvalsø, but according to her husband, the house is inside the woods a ways," he explained. "The house has some name or other; I've got it written down somewhere. Here it is: Starling House."

"Starling House, huh?" Louise remembered it, and the large patio she had seen from the forest road.

"Yes, that's right."

"Has the victim said anything?" she asked.

"Not yet. I've got pretty much all my people out in the area so I'll have to recall one of the female officers before we can go to Roskilde to interview her," he answered. They were both well aware that the interview would be more productive with a female interviewer.

"I can go talk to her," Louise quickly suggested but then fell silent when it occurred to her that it may not be the best idea. She might not be able to go through with the interview if the rape victim turned out to be someone she knew.

"You got time?" he asked, jumping at her offer. "For now, all we need to know is whether she can describe the rapist."

"I'll talk to her." Louise made a quick decision and thought of Mette. Right now, even the smallest lead was a potential step toward finding her. She told him that she was in Hvalsø. "I can get there faster than you guys anyway."

"Thanks," he said. "I'll drive out to the house with the forensic officers then. I'll let them know that you're on your way."

Louise got in the car and threw a last glance at the cemetery, thinking that it hadn't been quite as hard as she had imagined.

She should have done it years ago.

26

WHEN SHE ARRIVED at the hospital, Louise was shown into an office next to the examination room where the woman was. She put her bag down on the floor and took off her jacket.

"How's she doing?" she asked before the nurse left. "Is it bad?"

The redheaded nurse turned around in the doorway and shrugged. "It's mostly the shock. Her injuries are superficial. But it was consummated rape and it was pretty rough," she answered, adding that the woman had locked herself in the bathroom when her husband returned home from work.

"She's barely said anything so you'll probably have to go a bit easy on her."

Louise nodded.

"Is anyone with her?"

"Her husband just left to go pick up their daughter. I found some clothes for her and he said he'll be back to pick her up after he drops off the girl with her grandparents. But go on in there," she said, following Louise into the examination room.

THE WOMAN WAS sitting in a chair by the window. A white hospital blanket was wrapped around her, and as she glanced upward, she looked like a baby bird in oversize plumage.

Louise realized immediately that she had never met the woman before. Relieved, she walked over to shake her hand.

"My name is Louise Rick." She held the woman's gaze to see if the name provoked the same response as that from the man at Pasture House.

"Bitten," the woman responded faintly, only reacting to the puffs of wind from the window, which made her pull the blanket closer around her.

Louise walked over to close the window and asked if the woman needed anything. She figured that she might be able to conjure up some coffee or a couple of sodas.

"No, thank you." Bitten looked uncertainly at Louise. Her short hair reached just below her ears, her eyebrows were plucked very thin, and a red mark from a hard blow reached from her right cheek and up around her eye.

About thirty, Louise guessed. She hadn't asked Mik what he knew about her.

"I understand that you're in a great deal of shock and that it's very uncomfortable to have to talk about what happened. But your husband reported the rape, so I have to ask you some questions. Are you okay with that?"

The woman nodded, and Louise took a seat.

"Let's start by turning back the clock," she began. "Were you at home all morning?"

Once again, the woman nodded. Then she seemed to pull herself together and cleared her throat. "I've got time off today and tomorrow. I work in the finance department with the city and I've earned some compensatory leave."

She added the last part as if her days off called for some sort of explanation. "What did you do this morning?" Louise asked in order to slowly bring the conversation to the difficult parts.

"I just puttered around. It was probably close to eleven when I went outside to sit and have a cup of coffee, and then I went in the hot tub afterward." She looked at Louise questioningly to see if that was sufficient. "We have an outdoor hot tub," she added. "After that I went back inside to take a shower."

Louise nodded and refrained from saying that she already knew about the hot tub because she had stopped by the house.

Bitten took a deep breath and closed her eyes. When she opened them again, they were dark and full of fear as if it all came crashing over her once more.

"I didn't even see him," she whispered. "I didn't notice him coming in the house."

A gleam of insecurity darted across her face as she looked at Louise.

"I don't understand how I didn't hear him. Why didn't Molly bark?"

The dog seemed only just now to cross her mind. Then she clenched her fists and covered her mouth as something occurred to her.

"Let's stick with the hot tub for a minute," Louise asked, putting aside the thought of the dead dog in the woods. "Try to remember if maybe you heard or saw anything while you were in there."

The woman shook her head. "There was no one by the house at that time. Molly was lying right next to me like she always does when I'm in there. She loves the spray of the water."

"Could someone have been watching you without you noticing?"

Bitten shrugged but then shook her head. "I'm always very aware when I get out. When I'm by myself, I never wear a bathing suit so I make sure to check if anyone's walking by. But no one was."

She fell silent, and Louise could tell that she was replaying her walk from the patio into the house. Then she shook her head again.

"He wasn't there then," she maintained. "I'm positive."

She slumped down a little.

Louise noticed that Bitten's hands had started shaking even though she was trying to keep them steady. The woman turned her face away and looked out the window, but her silence made Louise suspect she was holding something back.

Bitten took a deep breath; then she straightened herself up and squeezed her restless hands. "I didn't notice anything because my mind was elsewhere. I was getting ready," she said despairingly.

Her dark eyes seemed to penetrate Louise as if she wanted to make sure she understood.

"You were expecting company?" Louise deduced.

Bitten nodded.

"I left the patio door open when I went into the bathroom to rinse off. Maybe that was when I heard a sound from the living room—I don't remember."

Tears were in her eyes now.

"I was going into the bedroom to get my robe, and I had just opened the door when he put his hand over my mouth."

"Were you naked?" Louise asked.

Bitten nodded, looking down at the floor as if feeling ashamed that she left her own bathroom without anything on.

She squeezed her eyes tightly shut while small trembles ran through her body.

"I thought it was a friend so I was about to turn around and kiss him," she said disconsolately. "But he just held on to me and used his knee to spread my legs. He was so strong that I couldn't move at all. I couldn't…"

"Fight back?" Louise finished her sentence.

Bitten nodded and sobbed.

"He pushed me forward and thrust into me from behind," she sniffled when she had enough air to speak again. "I didn't even see him; I only felt him. It all happened so fast."

A shiver ran through her body, and she touched her neck.

"I only saw his pants. He kept them on and just unzipped them," she whispered and cleared her throat. She stared into the wall as she continued: "I could feel the fabric against my skin, and he snorted like a stallion."

"What did his pants look like?" Louise asked. "Were they light or dark?"

"Dark."

"Jeans?"

She shook her head. "The fabric was soft—and sheeny, I think."

"Did you see his shoes?"

"I don't think so."

"Try to recall if they were sneakers or regular shoes," Louise suggested.

"They were dark-colored, I think. But I'm not sure; maybe I didn't see them at all."

She straightened up.

"He grabbed my breasts," she suddenly remembered. "While

he pushed me forward and held me down with one hand, he ran his other hand all over my breasts."

She cringed and pulled her legs up under herself, curling up in the chair.

"Did you see his arms while it was happening?" Louise asked.

She shook her head.

"I completely forgot. But now it's as if I can suddenly feel his hands. He was holding on so hard. There was nothing sexual about it. It was pure violence."

She closed her eyes and Louise let her take a break.

"I think he was wearing a button-down shirt," she mumbled, still with her eyes closed. "I felt the fabric against my face."

She was quiet for a second.

"It was so brutal and it wasn't at all because he wanted me. He just... wanted," she whispered and started to cry again.

Louise left her alone while she tried to picture it: Bitten had been walking around getting ready to see her lover, and that's where her thoughts had been when the rapist grabbed her from behind.

"Was he tall?" Louise asked after they had been sitting for a little while.

She nodded. "Taller than my husband," she said, adding that he was five foot ten.

"And the guy you're seeing when your husband is out," Louise asked, "how tall is he?"

Bitten cast her eyes down again and mumbled something inaudible.

"Sorry, could you repeat that?" Louise said.

"He's almost six-three," she replied.

"And the guy from today—was he the same height?"

The woman hid her face behind her hands. "I guess he

was," she acknowledged finally, but explained that the attacker was more sinewy. "His fingers cut into my skin."

"Can you tell me anything else about him? Did you notice anything else?"

"It all happened so fast. After he finished, he shoved me into the bedroom so hard that I fell on the floor and before I could turn around, he had closed the door," she said. "I lay there and listened to him walk through the living room. He didn't run; he just walked without any rush. His shoes were loud against the floor."

She thought for a second.

"Clogs, I think. It sounded like he was wearing clogs."

"Did he leave through the patio door as well?" Louise asked.

Bitten nodded.

"Did you see him leave the property?" she wanted to know. "Did you see him in the road?"

"I wasn't looking," the woman admitted quietly, pulling the blanket around her once again. "When I was sure he had gone, I ran into the bathroom and locked the door."

Tears were streaming down her face as she bent her head again.

"He was on me; it was running down my thighs. So I turned on the water and stood there until I couldn't scrub off any more."

"What about your friend? Did he show up?"

Bitten shrugged almost imperceptibly and shook her head.

"I don't know. I hid out there and let the water run so I couldn't hear anything. Not until René came and knocked on the door. He forgot his phone and had come home to get it."

Bitten looked out the window once more.

"No matter what, things would have ended badly for me

today. So maybe it was a blessing in disguise," she said, mostly to herself, and Louise looked at her questioningly.

There was a knock at the door and a nurse poked her head in. "Your husband is back," she said.

"Just give us another minute," Louise quickly replied. "I'll bring him in once we've finished. She turned back to Bitten. "What do you mean 'blessing in disguise'?" she asked.

Bitten shook her head a little. "It would have probably been even worse if my husband had found out what was going on," she simply said. "He would never forgive me."

"What about the bruise on your cheek?" she asked, pointing to the mark below Bitten's eye.

Bitten shot a fearful glance toward the door, and that told Louise who was responsible.

"He didn't believe me," Bitten whispered, unable to look at Louise. "He wanted to know who I was seeing when he wasn't around."

"He knew?"

At first she shook her head, but then she steeled her nerves. "I suppose he's had his suspicions," she admitted. "He rushed around the house, thinking that someone was still there. At first he wouldn't listen to me at all."

She bit her knuckle and looked so ill at ease that Louise felt quite sorry for her.

"He hit me to make me say who it was. He demanded to know if it's someone he knows."

"Is it?" Louise asked.

Bitten nodded and looked down. "It was only when I told him that the man had come in through the living room that he walked over to the patio door and spotted the footprints."

She looked at Louise and started to explain: "The living room floor gets wet when I come in from the hot tub. I usually always wipe up after myself but today I didn't have the chance, and so he could see that it was dirty. The man's shoes dragged dirt all the way across the floor and on the rug in front of the couch."

She paused for a second before continuing: "You wouldn't do that, of course, if you were supposed to hide having been there."

"So the perpetrator left footprints in your living room?" Louise cut in, hoping that Bitten's husband didn't clean before the forensic officers arrived.

She nodded. "René could see that and so he started to believe me."

"Who's the man that you're seeing when your husband isn't home?"

Bitten turned her head and looked out the window, her jaw tightening.

"I need to know his name," Louise said.

No reaction. Bitten only pressed her lips together tighter and bent her head.

Louise waited as they sat in silence for a while. Finally she stood up and walked toward the door.

"Should I bring in your husband now?" she asked. "Or would you like a minute to yourself?"

"Go ahead and bring him in," Bitten mumbled, straightening herself up a little while covering her bare legs with the white hospital blanket.

Louise gave her one last chance to talk but then opened the door.

Bitten's husband was right outside, his hands in his pockets and a grim look on his face. An angry wrinkle drew a straight line across his forehead.

Louise froze in the doorway. It had been a long time since

she last saw René Gamst. He and Klaus had been classmates, and he had been part of their gang, too. He wasn't one of the worst ones back then. At least not the way Louise remembered him. She had felt a bit sorry for him sometimes, thinking that he practically lived in Big Thomsen's shadow. He was always around, but he wasn't someone that you noticed.

He took a step forward and was about to walk in when he stopped right in front of her. Louise took an insecure step backward.

At first he didn't speak; he merely contemplated her with a stony glare. Louise stood in front of him, staring back.

"If I find this bastard before you do, I'll kill him," he said and continued into his wife's room. He sank to his knees in front of her chair, pulling her close and rocking her from side to side.

Feeling shaken by the brief but intense encounter, and uncertain whether he recognized her or not, Louise hurried out into the hallway to find the nurse to let her know that the interview was over. Bitten's husband was with her.

27

C AMILLA HAD SLEPT in Jonas's room. Her head felt heavy
from all the wine and she hadn't even registered when
Louise left. It was after ten before she got up to walk Dina.
Then she sat in Louise's kitchen, staring at the wall.

She regretted the fight and all the trouble that had come
from her insisting on doing things her way. She regretted getting so angry with the workers and kicking them out before
they had finished, and that her stubbornness had caused her to
reject the minister.

She reached the conclusion that she would have to apolo-
gize. Not to the minister—no way—and not to the workers.
But to Frederik.

Rushing from Louise's house, her thoughts swirling, she got
into her car and took off. By the time she signaled off toward
Roskilde an hour later, her anger had disappeared and she was
shocked that she had gone so far as to call off the whole thing.

As she approached Boserup and caught a glimpse of the gleaming tile roof of the manor house, she slowed down. Suddenly it all seemed so difficult. She hadn't called Frederik to let him know she was on her way home, and now she was unsure of how to go about it. They had never had a falling-out before—not to the point of doors slamming.

Camilla pulled over and turned off the engine while she looked down the driveway lined with old, gnarled trees on both sides. But she couldn't pull up to the house; her hand would not turn the wheel.

It was only when she was driving down the long, straight highway past Osted that it occurred to Camilla that she might not get much out of showing up at Eliselund without an appointment. She decided to give it a try anyway, though, and turned up the radio when Beyoncé came on. She felt something unwinding inside as she began to sing along.

As she continued toward Eliselund, she finally felt like she was on home turf. If she knew anything it was how to kick down doors. She might not know how to act among the upper classes but as a journalist, she knew how to get her story and get people to talk.

"I was told that my mother worked as the director here before the institution closed," she lied effortlessly as she sat in the office across from an older lady with gray hair twenty minutes later. She hurried to explain that her parents had divorced when she was very young. "I grew up in Birmingham, England, with my father but he died last year so now I've returned to Denmark with my husband and our son."

When she had parked the car outside in the courtyard surrounded with the large, white buildings, a handicapped-accessible van had been parked there and two assistants were lifting a big boy inside while the driver folded up his wheelchair and put it in the back.

Camilla waited in the car until they drove off. There were other people in the van as well; he was the last one they put in. The two assistants waved good-bye, and it wasn't until the van left the courtyard that one of them walked over to ask if she was there to pick up Sofie.

"No," Camilla answered in confusion, but then she had quickly collected herself and asked if they were closing up for the day.

"Just about," the woman said. "The last few will be picked up within the next half hour or so and then there's always a bit of cleanup and things to take care of. But if you've come to speak with the enrollment office, that's not here, you know."

"N-no," Camilla quickly said and then took a gamble: "I'm actually here on a very private errand," she began. "A few days ago, I spoke with a woman named Agnete Eskildsen. She used to work here, and she was the one who suggested that I drive down here to see if perhaps you could help me find my mother. But maybe you're busy. Is this a bad time?"

"Oh, I don't think we're that busy," the woman had said and asked her to come along.

The other assistant had turned around in the doorway. "So, are we closing up or what?" she asked sullenly.

"It's all right, Lillian," said the gray-haired woman over-bearingly. "I can close up today. You go ahead and go home."

She put her hand on Camilla's shoulder as she directed her through the large hall to signal that she was welcome to come inside.

"Some people are such busybodies," she mumbled as she led the way to the office and held the door open for her guest. "So you know Agnete?"

She smiled and lightly nodded.

"Sure is a small world. She worked here years ago, before I started. We finished our degrees in occupational therapy together. It was her second degree, you know, and even though she's probably ten or fifteen years older than me, we always got on well."

Camilla merely smiled.

"Is her husband still alive?" the other woman asked. Camilla shook her head, hoping that there wouldn't be questions that might reveal how briefly she'd known Agnete Eskildsen.

"I'm sorry," the woman said suddenly. "I never introduced myself. My name is Lone Friis. In fact, it was Nete who suggested that I apply here back when the day center was starting up. She wasn't interested in coming back to Eliselund herself, even though a lot has changed since she was a patient care assistant here. I never really understood her aversion to the place."

She laughed warmly.

"And I've been here ever since, so I really have a lot to thank my old girlfriend for." She motioned toward the chair opposite hers by the desk. "It almost sounds like you're doing your own private version of that TV show *The Locator*," Lone Friis exclaimed after sitting down. "It's so exciting. I hope I can help. What's your mom's name?"

Camilla should have seen that coming. Of course she was going to ask that. For a moment she completely blanked as she tried desperately to remember what Agnete Eskildsen had told her about the director of the place.

"She took back her maiden name after she and my father divorced," she said, stalling for time while digging frantically for a first name. But either the former patient care assistant hadn't mentioned it, or she hadn't been paying attention.

Lone Friis was smiling patiently but the silence was beginning to seem strange.

"Her name is Parkov," Camilla said, feeling relieved that her brain was working again. "Or at least it was," she rambled on while hoping that it didn't seem too weird for her to only know her mother by her last name.

"Bodil Parkov is your mother?" the woman asked with surprise; she appeared not to register Camilla's hesitation. She cocked her head while looking at her guest with interest as if searching for recognizable features. Then she straightened herself up a little. "Well, not that I know her personally but she is a bit of a name around here, you know. She was the first female director of the institution."

"And was she here until it closed?" Camilla asked.

Lone Friis hesitated. "Close to it, at least," she said in a way that made Camilla suspect something might have happened toward the end to put her out the door before the rest of the institution staff. "It was actually only a few weeks ago that we were talking about what became of her after she left. But it shouldn't be too hard to find out."

"How come you were talking about her?" Camilla asked curiously, thinking that it definitely couldn't have been in connection with Louise's attempt to find Lisemette's family—that was too recent.

"They're looking to hire a new director at the Andersvænge center this fall, and someone brought up her name as a possible candidate. But it seems to me that she must be long retired by now."

There was a quick knock at the door and Lillian walked in wearing a light windbreaker and holding a bike helmet.

"I locked both of the back rooms and canceled the fruit

delivery for tomorrow," she said while Camilla stared straight ahead.

"Great, I'll take care of the rest then," Lone Friis replied. "But listen to this."

She motioned for her sullen colleague to come in.

"This is Bodil Parkov's daughter, who has come to learn a little about her mother from back when she was the director here at Eliselund."

Camilla tightened her grip around the armrest of the chair while she forced herself to smile and look at Lone's colleague.

Lillian tilted her head back a little as she contemplated Camilla. "You're Parkov's daughter?"

"Oh, that's right," Lone Friis exclaimed, ignoring her colleague's undisguised disapproval of her speaking with a stranger. "You were here back then. I completely forgot."

Camilla winced a little as she watched her entire fabricated story fall apart.

Lone Friis got up to go see off the last children. "What can you tell Camilla about her mother? The two of them have lost touch." Lone excused herself, leaving Lillian and Camilla alone.

"Parkov didn't have any children," Lillian snarled, still standing in the doorway. "That's how she was able to spend all of her time down here and make the rest of us do the same." She stared at Camilla. "I don't know who you are or what you've come to dig up. But I can tell you one thing that I'll stand by no matter who's asking: A lot of people would have been better off if Bodil Parkov had never set foot at Eliselund."

A car honked outside and they heard footsteps running down the hall. Lillian turned around and left, and Camilla wiped her clammy hands on the thin fabric of her skirt. She had stretched her made-up story too far.

She quickly got to her feet and grabbed her purse but stopped as Lillian stepped back into the doorway, blocking her way.

"Get in your car and leave. We're not interested in people who snoop around," she hissed.

"You knew Lise and Mette?" Camilla observed and decided to drop the story about her missing mother. "You worked here. What happened the day they died?"

Lillian turned her back to her and walked out to the courtyard where three children were throwing their bags into the trunk of the car.

"Who signed the death certificates?" Camilla called after her.

"I don't know anything about that," Lillian answered dismissively. She started walking off with her bike but just then, the car with the children drove up and she had to stop to let it through the gate first.

Camilla caught up to her and grabbed her arm.

"Tell me what happened. You must have talked about it."

"Why don't you ask Bodil Parkov? She would be the one to know."

Lillian tore herself away and pushed off with her foot to get the bike going.

"Don't mind Lillian," Lone Friis said as she walked across the courtyard. "She has a hard time with people from the outside. She gave me the silent treatment all last week because I allowed the police access to our archives. She has a hard time making the distinction between personally sensitive information and common sense."

Camilla forced herself to smile even though every fiber in her body was trembling to get going. Lone Friis did not appear to have witnessed her scene with Lillian. She had been preoccupied with getting the children sent off, Camilla thought, and started walking toward her car. There she thanked the older woman while she opened the driver's door.

"Well, I'm afraid it wasn't much help," Lone Friis lamented as the wind tussled her hair. "Wasn't your grandfather a merchant—and quite wealthy at that? At least that's what they said that one day when we were talking. It was unusual that your mother went into service at such a young age instead of finishing school since the family had money. But maybe that was all just lunchroom gossip," she apologized. "You can probably read about that in *Krak's Blue Book*," she offered, referring to the who's who of Denmark. "When we were talking about her and the job at Andersvænge, someone went and looked up your mother to find out how old she is."

"She's in the *Blue Book*?" Camilla asked, now sitting in the car with her window rolled down.

Lone Friis nodded. "But Lillian is right!" she realized. "Mrs. Tønnesen also mentioned that Parkov never had any children."

Camilla started the car just as Lone Friis took a step forward, looking at her with confusion through the rolled-down window.

She shot her a stiff smile and pushed the button to close the window.

"What did you say your name was?" Lone Friis called as Camilla started backing up.

Her heart was pounding and the dust kicked up behind the car as she sped out of the courtyard, leaving Eliselund behind in a grayish-brown fog.

28

CAMILLA SLOWED DOWN a little, her eyes darting to the rear-view mirror as she drove off down the winding dirt road. Her hands were shaking with adrenaline and her pulse rushed so rapidly that she was breathing through her mouth in sharp blows. She focused on the road and tried to take deep, calming breaths, while telling herself that it wasn't so bad.

They had seen through her lie but what did she expect?

She realized that her fingers were hurting from gripping the steering wheel so tightly and loosened her grasp. Just then her phone started ringing in her purse, but when she spotted Lillian ahead, pulling her bicycle up a hill while talking on her cell phone, she ignored it until it stopped.

Camilla watched as Lillian turned around, spotted the car, and stepped farther into the gravel road. Sweat was dripping down her back and she had no idea why she had gotten herself into this mess. She hadn't been looking for a story for the paper.

That wouldn't have been enough to make her lie like this, she thought, stopping as Lillian positioned herself in the middle of the road with her bike, blocking the way. It was solely to satisfy her own curiosity that she had gone to Eliselund—and to try to forget the mess she had made of things at home, of course.

It was more like her foot found the gas pedal than her brain actually initiated the action. Camilla proceeded slowly at first but then she sped up and put her hand on the horn, holding it there as the car continued to accelerate. Pebbles sprayed the roadside and Lillian bounded off the road when she realized that Camilla did not intend to stop. The woman waved her arms to get her attention, but Camilla kept her eyes on the potholes in the road and shot past her without looking in her direction. She could only glimpse her brightly colored windbreaker from the corner of her eye when her cell phone started ringing once again, and shortly after she heard the beep signaling a new voice mail.

The dirt road ended just a little farther ahead. Camilla glanced in her rearview mirror one more time before signaling and turning onto the highway. Lillian was nowhere to be seen. She hadn't made it over the final hilltop yet. Her heart pounding and bangs sticking to her temples, Camilla yielded to a succession of cars, her eyes continuing to dart to the mirror in case Lillian's bike helmet started coming into view.

Her cell phone started ringing again from her purse on the floor. It hadn't taken long for Lone Friis to track her down, Camilla thought, merging onto the road when a hole opened up in the line of cars snailing along now that the workday was over for most people. She had probably called up her old girl-friend to see what Agnete Eskildsen knew about Camilla or whether their connection was pure fabrication as well.

Camilla took a deep breath, cursing herself once again

for not just laying her cards on the table. This time it was a text message beeping in, and she started to wonder. The gray-haired woman was surprisingly persistent. A car honked at her when she pulled over without warning across the narrow strip of grass separating the road from the bike path. She turned off the engine and reached down for her phone.

Four missed calls and two text messages—all of them from Frederik.

The first message read: *Come to the Hotel Prindsen ASAP*; the second message merely said: *Let the front desk know when you arrive.*

Camilla stared at her phone, re-reading both messages. Then she closed her eyes.

She would have preferred to have all of Eliselund hot on her heels than to receive just one of Frederik's messages.

At a hotel, she thought, feeling the adrenaline drain suddenly from her body and leave her listless. Not even at home.

"Let the front desk know when you arrive!"

She snorted and signaled back into the road. It was as if he were summoning her to a business meeting. But then it occurred to her that this might be exactly the case. Everything had been quiet since she left their home and now he wanted to convene in a neutral location in town.

Her heart felt heavy and she cursed her temper even more. She blinked a few times as tears started welling up, blurring her vision. Her phone rang again and she answered without checking the display.

"Yes," she answered, clearing her throat as her voice cracked.

"Hello, this is Lone Friis. You were just down here at Eliselund."

"Yes," Camilla repeated. "That's correct, and it's also true that Parkov isn't my mom. I made up that story to find out who was the director of the place when it closed down." The words came tumbling out. "I want to find her to ask how someone could have signed a death certificate for a person who isn't dead. And why…"

She fell silent, her voice faltering as she looked in the direction of the riding academy located just before the town of Osted. One of her girlfriends once had a horse down there.

"I just wanted to say that you forgot your sweater."

Camilla was barely listening. Now she had admitted to her story, and lying hadn't done her one damn bit of good. Lone Friis had every right to be angry.

It was the older woman's turn to clear her throat. "It wasn't your mother…or Bodil Parkov," she corrected herself. "I just went and checked. She quit and left at the end of February the same year that Eliselund closed down, but at that time the deputy director had taken over the management."

Camilla was now fully attentive once again and looked around for a place to pull over. She knew there would be a bus stop a little way ahead. This time she signaled well in advance.

"I got out the old registers. We don't use those anymore, of course, but they're still stored in the old superintendent's office. I got curious after you ran off like that. I heard what you said to Lillian and of course I can put two and two together since the police came down here as well, asking about the same girls."

"What did it say?" Camilla interrupted her, staring at the dashboard of the car without really seeing it.

"It says that the sisters died from pneumonia. They were admitted for three days before they passed away, and were under the care of the same doctor who later signed the death certificates."

"What was his name?"

"Hmmm…" It sounded like Lone Friis was reading. "Dr. Ernst Holsted."

"How is it possible that nobody reacted to their deaths coming so close together?" Camilla asked.

"It would appear that the doctor didn't quite live up to his responsibilities. From what it says here, it looks like he didn't attend to his two patients as often as he should have considering the fatal development of the situation for the girls."

"But the girls didn't die," Camilla insisted—*or at least one of them didn't*, she thought. "So how did the death certificates get issued?"

"That does sound very strange," Lone Friis conceded.

"I suppose it's possible that nobody at Eliselund proceeded any further because someone was trying to protect themselves against accusations of medical malpractice and subsequent lawsuits. Maybe the former consultant doctor can offer you an explanation."

I'll definitely see what he has to say, Camilla decided. She inquired curiously to how Lone Friis had been able to track down her number.

"You had some business cards in the pocket of your sweater so it wasn't really that difficult." Then she asked Camilla to refrain from mentioning that the source of her information was the old register.

"Of course," Camilla promised and thanked Lone Friis for her offer to mail the sweater back to her.

SHE WAS JUST about to put her cell phone down when Markus called.

"Hi, honey!" she said.

"Mom, can you come get me from August's house? I'm too tired to walk home and Frederik isn't answering his phone."

"Aren't you with Dad?"

"No, I didn't want to go there after school so I went home with August."

Markus hadn't bothered to say hi or ask how she'd been these past few days. He just expected her to be at his disposal when he needed her, and that infuriated Camilla.

"No way. You're old enough to walk the two miles to get home," she answered briefly and turned off her phone.

Markus had always had the chores she deemed necessary for him to build a sense of responsibility, but since they had been living at the manor house, he tended to just forget things. And maybe she did, too, she thought as she drove through Osted. Maybe that's why she lost her touch...and her focus.

Something inside her had gone missing lately, something that used to be important to her. She felt terribly lost and disconnected. As the small-town scenery rolled by outside, she realized that she needed to find herself again. To reignite her passion; to relocate her personal touch. If not, she feared she'd wither away.

Come to think of it, that was probably why she'd gotten so out of hand at Eliselund. Apparently she needed a story to devote herself to if she was to stand being around herself.

It was another six miles to Roskilde when she called her old executive editor, Terkel Høyer, at the morning paper to find out why he had contacted her. He picked up on the second ring and apparently he still had her number in his phone.

"Hey, Lind!"

"You called me?"

"Well, yeah—but that was just to remind you that you still need to turn in your key card to the front gate."

"I need to get back to work," Camilla said. "Please let me know if you've got something for me. I miss writing. Freelance would be fine, too."

"I don't suppose you need the money," he teased in a snide

tone that she hadn't heard from him before. Maybe she had made a mistake in calling. And she certainly wasn't going to say that she may end up needing the money now more than ever if she was going to have to support herself and Markus on an unstable freelancer's pay.

"Just give me a call if you need something," she said, already on the retreat. "And I'll be in touch if I think of any ideas that might be interesting to you."

"All right, that's settled then," Høyer said, sounding pleased. He hadn't promised anything. Camilla recognized his rejection. She had heard him say the same thing to scores of freelance journalists trying to sell their stories. "That's settled then," he would always say, and then that was the last of it.

She turned off her phone, regretting having made the call. Just then she saw the blue lights flashing in her side-view mirror. She hadn't noticed the police car following her while she talked on her cell phone. Now it pulled forward a little and signaled for her to pull over.

"Fuck!" she exclaimed and signaled off, throwing her cell phone down on the passenger seat.

"That's going to be an expensive call," the officer opened after she rolled down her window.

"Yes." Camilla went to get her driver's license out.

"Because you know it's illegal to talk on the phone like that while driving."

"Yes," Camilla snapped, handing him her license.

"I see you have a hands-free phone device installed," he said, leaning forward to look inside the car. "If you had used it, you could have avoided the ticket I'm about to write."

Camilla turned in her seat and looked at him. "My day can't get much worse so you just go ahead and write up that ticket. Or two of them—I really don't care," she hissed.

"But it might be nice if you learned a little from the ticket," he mumbled. "It's because it's dangerous to talk on the phone while driving, you know."

Camilla just managed to bite her tongue before her temper got the best of her. Mustering all her strength she attempted to smile at him, hoping it didn't look quite as forced as it felt.

"Of course," she said. "Of course one should take it seriously and learn something."

For one, she was definitely going to have to learn to control her temper, she thought, and angelically accepted the ticket that the officer handed her.

"Have a nice day," she said as he was about to return to his car.

"You too." He shot her an awkward smile. "Sounds like it can only get better."

She stayed parked until after they left.

Unfortunately, the officer was wrong. Her day could get much worse. She still had to go to the hotel and see Frederik.

29

L OUISE BOUGHT A sandwich from the hospital cafeteria and finished her Sprite before getting up from the bench. She considered going back to the ward to make another attempt to speak with Bitten, but obviously the woman wasn't going to cough up the name of her lover as long as her husband was there. She would wait to try again when Bitten was back home.

She'd just left the large parking lot when Eik called to tell her that he had been working on the list of previous employees at Eliselund and had made an appointment with the consultant doctor's widow.

"It was her husband that signed the death certificates," he said and told her that he was meeting her in Solrød at 7 p.m. "I thought you might like to come?"

That was in an hour. Louise glanced at her watch and told him that she'd just finished up in Roskilde.

"I could meet you down there," he suggested. "Or I can talk to Birte Holsted alone."

"I'll be there," Louise said quickly, surprised that Eik was even still at work. She had called when she left Hvalsø to assist the Holbæk police with the interview, and it had sounded like he was running out of steam looking for the previous employees at Eliselund. But it suited her just fine because it would give her an excuse to put off her talk with Melvin. She wasn't looking forward to disappointing him by backing out of the community garden project.

EIK WAS STANDING by the curb in front of a yellow single-family house when she turned the corner onto the residential street behind the Solrød train station. He stepped on his cigarette to put it out and walked in front of her up the driveway, where an elderly lady was waiting to receive them, a crutch under her one arm and an unwelcoming look on her face.

"We'll sit in here," said the widow, who explained she needed the crutch because of recent hip surgery.

She showed them into the living room, where a wide patio door was open, the evening sun casting a blanket of light on the floor. For once, Louise had hoped that there would be coffee waiting on the table, but there was nothing to suggest that the former consultant doctor's widow had any intention of serving them anything.

And she didn't point toward the comfortable couch when she asked them to have a seat.

"Here you go," she said, pulling out a high-backed chair by the dining table instead before hobbling to the head of the table herself. "You know, I have no idea why you suddenly want to talk about Ernst. It's been so long since we buried him that even our grandchildren have had babies in the meantime."

"I understand your surprise," Eik said, taking off his leather jacket before edging down onto the hard chair. "But as I said on the phone, this is really more about Eliselund than it is about your late husband."

Louise watched him while he talked. His voice was deep and pleasant, confidential, she thought. He folded his hands on the table and smiled disarmingly at the widow.

"We're working on an old missing person case and in that connection, we're trying to locate some of the people who worked at the institution in the time before it closed down," he continued. "And during that time, your husband was still working down there."

"My husband killed himself while working down there," the widow corrected him.

"What do you mean?" Louise cut in.

Birte Holsted slowly looked at her.

"He committed suicide," she merely said. "He ruined our lives." Her lips were tight and her gaze lingered somewhere above their heads.

"When did it happen?" Louise moved forward in her seat a little.

The widow grabbed on to her crutch, which was about to slide down from the back of the chair. "They cut him down on March sixteen, 1980," she said, her face impassive, and put the crutch on the floor. "I knew for a long time that some things were going on down there. I could feel him pulling away from us. He became increasingly pressured and shut himself off. It was only after his death that I heard about the case."

"The case?" Louise asked.

"A disciplinary case had been launched against him. He was under suspicion of gross medical misconduct but they never got to the bottom of it," she told them. Then she straightened up and looked at them.

"My husband was weak and unable to set boundaries," she said.

"Can you be a little more specific?" Eik asked patiently.

"There was a director at the place who caught him making a mistake," she told them, "and then he was caught in her snares. Finally, the pressure became too much. And even though it was hard at the time, I'll readily admit that what happened was probably for the best."

"His death?" asked Louise, and the widow nodded. "What happened?"

"They claimed that a patient died of pneumonia because my husband didn't start treatment in time."

"Was it a young woman who died?" Louise asked, leaning in over the table.

The widow looked at her and shook her head.

"It was a young, mentally retarded boy," she replied as if that made it insignificant. "It wasn't until after his death that I learned there was another case against him, one that was far more serious and would have led to his dismissal as well as a prison sentence if he hadn't prevented that himself."

"What was it concerning?" Eik quickly asked.

The widow sighed heavily. "You'd be better off asking Bodil Parkov what went on at Eliselund back then. She was the director down there, and if anyone knows it would be her."

The look she shot in Louise's direction held many years' worth of bitterness.

"Did your husband issue death certificates for a pair of

seventeen-year-old twin sisters before his death? Did you ever hear about them?"

Louise couldn't be sure but she thought she saw a twitch across the widow's wrinkled forehead before she shook her head and pressed her lips together.

"One of the twins was just buried," Louise said. "She didn't actually die back then, and we need to know if the other one is still alive, too, and how the two sisters disappeared from Eliselund."

"I couldn't tell you," Birte Holsted said, slumping. "I never heard about any twins."

She suddenly looked tired. Even if she had reacted to the question about the forged death certificates, she now seemed to be telling the truth in saying that she didn't know anything about Lisemette.

"Perhaps you can help us with the names of some of the others who worked at Eliselund at the same time as your husband?" Eik tried, ignoring the fact that Louise had gotten up from her chair.

"I didn't know any of them," the widow answered quietly. "My husband didn't talk about the patients or the employees once he was finally home. And we were quite thankful for that, really."

She bent down and picked her crutch up from the floor, preparing to walk them out.

"We'll show ourselves out," Louise quickly said as Eik got up and thanked her for the conversation.

"That's enough to make you want a drink," Eik moaned as they were standing on the sidewalk once again. "What a life. Do you suppose she's been sitting in there feeling resentful for the past thirty years?"

Louise shrugged and began walking toward the car. "It certainly doesn't seem like the two of them had the ideal relationship," she conceded and asked where he had parked.

"The train was faster," he said, jumping at Louise's offer to drive around Sydhavnen to drop him off.

When they pulled up in front of Ulla's, Eik gave it another shot.

"Come on, just one," he coaxed. "I'm buying."

"PATIENTS DIED BECAUSE he neglected his work," Louise said after Ulla had stopped by their table, placing two beers in front of them.

The room was smoky; behind their table, four men were playing pool. Louise leaned forward in an attempt to make herself heard above the jukebox.

"But you can't exactly call it neglect when a person manages to survive their own death certificate," she said, shaking her head. "What the heck did he have to gain from writing Lisemette out of the system? And what did the widow mean when she said that he was caught in the director's snares?"

Eik threw back a shot and raised his glass to let Ulla know that he was ready for another.

"It also sends a strong message that he chose to take his own life down here," he said and put his cigarettes on the table. "Do you mind if I smoke?"

Louise laughed and shook her head. She looked around. "Thanks for asking, but everyone is smoking in here."

"So, he killed himself at Eliselund because he wanted to make sure that everyone saw him take the consequences of his mistakes," Eik said, getting back on point.

"And why was that important to him?" Louise asked,

looking down at the table when a dark-haired man with a beer belly and leather vest leaned on her chair and asked if she wanted to dance.

"Jønne, get lost," Eik said, waving him off.

There were only eight or nine patrons at Ulla's. Aside from the ones playing pool, the rest were hanging out by the bar where Ulla herself was holding court with her meaty arms on the counter and eyes that regularly wandered to Eik and Louise's table.

"Because something was over," he continued. "He took the consequences of something that had happened."

"Something to do with Lisemette?" Louise suggested. When he asked if she wanted to share one last beer, she agreed.

30

E VERY PART OF Louise's body ached when she was woken by her phone. She had passed out on the couch the night before after a taxi had dropped her off in Frederiksberg around 11 p.m. The one last beer had turned into many. She had found out that Eik Nordstrøm had only black clothes in his wardrobe because he couldn't care less about clothes and it was just easier when everything looked the same and he could buy a stack at a time. That piece of information had cost her a beer but in return, he had bought a round when he revealed that he took a dip off the pier in Sydhavnen every morning come rain or shine. Louise had tried asking a few questions about his personal life but he clammed up. She did the same when he wanted to know about her old boyfriend and Big Thomsen.

The phone was still ringing, and Louise swore out loud when her dog poked its wet nose in her face, thrilled to finally see signs of life.

"I'm getting married," Camilla sang when Louise finally answered the phone.

"Hmmm," she answered, pushing Dina away a little. "Were you able to appease the minister?"

"God, no!" Camilla laughed. "I'm getting married today—at eleven thirty at city hall. Frederik made all the arrangements."

Louise sat up.

"I don't think I'll be able to make it," she exclaimed, worried that her friend might expect her to turn up with flowers and champagne.

"Well, you're not invited. We're going to celebrate our wedding day in bed with plenty of champagne." Camilla laughed again.

"Are you drunk?" Louise asked with confusion as she got up. "Where are you?"

"I'm at Hotel Prindsen. Frederik rented the suite, and he had scattered red rose petals all across the room before I got there."

"This morning?" Louise asked, checking the time on her phone. She was suddenly worried that she was the one who had overslept. But it was only seven oh four . . .

"No, we've been here since yesterday."

"Well, I'm glad you guys made up," she said, yawning. "What about Markus; where is he?"

"He doesn't know anything. The last time I talked to him was yesterday afternoon when I was on my way home from Eliselund." Camilla snorted. "The kid called me because he didn't feel up to walking home from a friend's house, so he got to stay there and spend the night but we'll pick him up after we've been to city hall."

Louise sat up straight. "You were at Eliselund yesterday?" she asked as she heard Frederik's voice and a door closing. "What were you doing there?"

"Back when the death certificates were signed, the director of the place was someone named Parkov."

"I know that," Louise cut in irritably.

"After Eliselund, she worked at Avnstrup until that closed down, too, but as far as I can tell she still lives out in the woods," she went on. "I had actually planned to go talk to her myself, but…you know…something more important has kind of come up." She laughed, adding that she and Frederik had agreed that she would start working again after the wedding. "Apparently I get completely impossible if I don't have a story to keep me busy."

"Could you stop talking for a second?" Louise cut through while she could hear the clatter of plates and silverware in the hotel room. "How do you know that she lives by Avnstrup?"

"Because I looked her up in the *Blue Book* and then ran a search for her. She lives on Bukkeskov Road."

"Is it Bodil from the gamekeeper's house?"

"How would I know what the place is called?"

Louise tried to focus her thoughts.

"She was at Eliselund when the twins died," Camilla added. "But then she left shortly after. Lillian was there at the time as well."

"Well, I'll be damned," Louise said and stood up.

It was one thing that Bodil had not recognized the photograph of Lisemette. But she should at least be able to tell them how the twins had left Eliselund.

"WE'RE GOING TO see Bodil," Louise said breathlessly when she got into the office. Dina had run off in Frederiksberg Park because Louise had gambled on finishing up their morning walk faster by letting her off the leash. But the dog didn't return when Louise called her; it wasn't until fifteen minutes later, when she spotted the yellow Lab on the grass with a chocolate counterpart, that she had succeeded in calling her dog over.

She removed her sunglasses from her hair, which had air-dried during her bike ride. She could tell from the look on Eik's face that he expected her to elaborate.

"And then we need to have a talk with Lillian Johansen, who still works at Eliselund," she said, telling him about Camilla's visit to the day center.

"Last night was fun," Eik said, his voice raspy, and it was only then that Louise got a good look at him.

"Jesus!" she blurted out. "What happened to you?" The bags under his eyes made them look small and screwed-up and he had a large scrape across his left temple.

"I didn't do as good a job as you going home," he said, rubbing his wound. "And then this morning I misjudged the distance to the wharf when I jumped in the water."

"You look like hell. What about the car? Did you drive here?"

"Yes. We can take my car; it's parked down there," he said and added that first he would like to go by the cafeteria to get something to eat. "Do you want anything?"

Louise hadn't had time for breakfast or tea before dashing out the door, so she nodded as he got up. At least he didn't smell like booze, she thought as he walked by her.

While Eik was getting them food, Louise went to inform Rønholt that they were driving out to Hvalsø.

"You look nice!" Hanne said appreciatively and pointed to Louise's hair, which was still hanging down. Confused, Louise stopped for a second in the doorway before Hanne nodded to signal that it was okay for her to go in. "He's not busy."

"Take a look at this," Rønholt said when he saw her. He

waved her over to his window and pointed to a large yellow-and-brown flower.

"We're going to Hvalsø," she said and began to retreat toward the door.

"It's a lady's slipper," he said lovingly, "the largest and rarest type of orchid in all of Europe. It only blooms for two weeks. Isn't it beautiful?"

Orchids had never been Louise's strong suit but she nodded. It did look pretty with its heavy flowers.

"By the way, they called from Holbæk to say that they were very happy with your interview."

"Thanks," said Louise, her hand on the door handle. "I'm glad to hear it. They've got plenty on their plates right now with the murder in the woods and the runner who's still missing."

"In fact, it sounded like there would probably be a spot for you up there if this agency doesn't work out," he said, letting go of the plant.

"That won't be necessary," she cut in tartly. "The new agency will work out, and there's no way I'm going to Holbæk."

She stopped in the hallway and thought that it was pretty darn soon for Rønholt to start airing his doubts about the new special agency. She watched Eik walk down the hall holding two small bottles of 1 percent milk and a couple of cut sandwich rolls, which he balanced on a paper plate.

"We're bringing it, right?" he asked, gesturing toward the food.

Louise pulled herself together and walked with him toward the office while thinking that maybe it was quite normal to be less affected by hangovers if you kept up your state of intoxication on a regular basis.

"Yup," she said and picked up her bag. "Let's get going."

31

Jørgen was hunched over, completely focused on raking the pebbles in the courtyard as Louise and Eik pulled up in front of the white gate. He stopped in mid-motion and looked at them hesitantly. He wore a cap pulled down to his ears and wiped his hands meticulously on his blue work overalls before straightening up and folding his arms, resting them on the rake handle. He watched them carefully as they got out of the car.

He didn't walk down to open the gate for them, but he also didn't react when Louise walked over and depressed the handle.

"Hey, Jørgen—is Bodil home?" she asked before pushing the gate open.

"Bodil," he said, pointing toward the house.

He dropped the rake onto the pebbles and shuffled toward the front door while Louise remained standing just inside the courtyard. Eik stayed by the car, waiting for them to be invited inside.

Jørgen returned with Bodil, a big smile on his face.

He was holding her hand and looked as pleased as if he had just gone inside to bring out his favorite doll.

"Are you here about the van?" Bodil asked after they said hello. "Jørgen saw it yesterday. This time it came driving from the woods." She tipped her head toward Avnsø Lake and the road to Starling House.

"The white Toyota?" Eik asked, walking over to them. Jørgen eagerly headed outside to look at the black Jeep Cherokee.

"Yes. We thought that we'd better call you," she continued.

"When did you see it?" Louise asked and thought about the rape that had taken place the previous morning.

"It was around five or six, I think. We were just about to have dinner. Jørgen was hungry so we ate a little earlier than usual."

Bodil's husband had walked all the way around the car and was now admiring its wide bumper.

"He's just crazy about cars," Bodil smiled.

The courtyard was peaceful, with the branches of the large chestnut tree swaying in the breeze. Louise didn't particularly feel like bringing up what they had come there to talk about.

"You didn't leave the key in there, did you?" Bodil asked nervously. "Not that he knows how to drive, but he's not always aware of his own limitations."

"I've got it right here," Eik reassured her, waving his key ring before stuffing it back into the pocket of his black jeans.

"Bodil, there's something that we wanted to talk to you about," Louise started. "Can we step inside?"

She had brought the pictures of Lise in the bag, which she carried on her shoulder. Clouds were gathering over the tree-tops of the forest and the wind was picking up. It looked like it might rain soon. Louise looked at her watch. Camilla would be getting married at Roskilde City Hall in an hour and a half. Bodil pointed toward the house and asked them to go on in while she closed a window in the barn.

Louise followed Eik, who was holding the door for her. His cheeks had picked up a bit more color, but he still looked tired and worn-out. It was kind of her fault, she thought, as she slipped past him.

Stacks of hand-painted plates were lined up on the coffee table, and Louise admired the delicate floral motifs. Eik stayed in the hallway where the walls were lined with perfectly polished brass hunting horns all the way around the ceiling. For a moment her eyes rested on his back, his muscular shoulders underneath the black T-shirt and his narrow hips that made his pants sag.

"Jørgen collects them," Bodil told her as she walked into the living room. "He finds the flowers that he wants and then I paint a plate for him. But we try to avoid duplicates so last night we were going through all of the ones we already have."

She smiled and asked if they wanted coffee.

"No, thanks," Eik said quickly from the hallway, and Louise guessed that he would prefer to get this visit over with soon.

"I would, please," she said, catching his eye.

Eik shook his head at her before pointing to the hunting horns and asking Bodil where they came from.

"My father used to hunt," she smiled. "He had a large hunting lodge up by Jægerspris and the way I remember it, he would be gone from the first day of hunting season until it ended. I'm sure that's not quite true; he was just rarely home because he worked so much. But he was always in the best mood when he left the house with his rifles." Her smile turned a little sad. She asked them to come into the kitchen with her and got out two coffee cups.

"Would you prefer tea?" she asked, looking at Eik while pointing to a box of tea bags.

He put up his hands and politely declined.

"What did you want to talk about?" Bodil went on while putting on the kettle and bringing out instant coffee and a couple of spoons.

Louise brought out the picture of Lise from her bag. "The last time we were here, we asked if you had seen this woman." She held out the photo.

Bodil accepted it and walked over to the window, studying it for a second before returning to the table and putting it down.

"I don't recall seeing her," she said and went to get the kettle of boiling water. "Do you take milk?"

Louise shook her head. "I've been told that you were the director at Eliselund until shortly before the old institution closed down," she continued, watching as Bodil raised her eyebrows in surprise and then nodded.

"Yes," she said. "That's right; I worked down there from 1973 until 1980."

"Lise Andersen and her sister, Mette, grew up at the institution and lived there during that period," Eik offered, pulling out a chair when Bodil returned to the table to sit down.

"The twins." Bodil reached for the picture to look at it again.

For a minute she seemed lost in her own thoughts while regarding Lise's face. Then she looked at Louise and hesitated briefly before speaking.

"I do remember the twin sisters. Back then, all of our residents had numbers. Theirs were fifty-one and fifty-two. But they both died."

"Were you at work the day they died?" Louise asked.

Bodil was still staring straight ahead until she slowly started shaking her head. "It happened the day before I left Eliselund," she began. "It's been so long that I barely remember the course of events. I believe the girls were admitted to the sick ward a few days earlier. They both had a high fever and had already been bedridden for a couple of days."

"What happened on the day they died?" Louise asked. Bodil looked at the door as Jørgen called her from the hallway.

"Excuse me," she said, getting up to go talk to him. A minute later she returned with two yellow roses, which she held out for Louise. "He picked these for you."

Louise thanked her and put the flowers down on the table, asking Bodil once again to tell them what happened on the day that Lisemette disappeared from the sick ward.

"I was packing up my things," she said hesitantly, as if the memory had to be brought out from the very back of her mind. She told them that she had lived in a small director's apartment in the main building, which she needed to pack up to get ready for the movers, who were coming to pick up her belongings the following morning. "When I left the place the next day, they were flying the flag at half-mast. They must have died the previous evening, or perhaps it happened overnight. I don't recall."

"There was a consultant doctor there back then," Louise continued. "He was the one who signed the death certificates. What do you know about him?"

"He's dead."

"We know that," Louise quickly cut in. "But to me, it sounds implausible that two sisters should die just one minute apart. You were there when it happened. How is something like that possible?"

Bodil folded her hands in front of her and looked down at the table before turning her eyes toward Louise.

"We had several unfortunate incidents with that doctor,"

she finally said, clearing her throat. "Perhaps what really happened was that one of them died some time before the other one, and he was the one who neglected to get the paperwork done and then later entered both of them at the same time. I can't say."

Bodil sat for a moment as if considering how much she could tell them.

"There were more errors back then. Today you would call it medical malpractice and it would be reported to the National Agency for Patients' Rights and Complaints, but..." She sighed heavily. "Back then, the public didn't give the same attention to homes for the mentally deficient—and certainly not in those cases where the patients had no next of kin. So medical errors were easy to hide with a death certificate."

"But she didn't die," Louise said.

"The consultant doctor hung himself, and there was probably a good reason for that," Bodil said. She apologized for being unable to answer Louise's questions.

Deeply frustrated, Louise finished her instant coffee and exhaled loudly. She was preparing to leave when Eik asked whether Bodil had always cared for Jørgen herself.

She nodded briefly. "Luckily, I've been able to."

Louise got up, and Eik got the message. Bodil walked with them to the courtyard. When they reached the car, they saw Jørgen sitting behind the wheel, looking focused as if he were driving.

"We need to clear up what happened in the sick ward at Eliselund on February twenty-seven, 1980," Louise said as she was standing one-on-one with Bodil. "We have to find the other twin. Do you remember anyone who used to work down there back then?"

"It's been thirty years," Bodil reminded her. "And I'm not good with names."

"What about Lillian; do you know her?"

"Lillian..." Bodil repeated reflectively. "We had a couple of student nurses. I guess she might have been one of them."

She shuddered slightly before looking up at Louise with a small, apologetic smile. "The end of my time at Eliselund wasn't the best," she admitted. "I wasn't really in touch with my coworkers. They thought I was too tough, and they were opposed to our continued practice of tying down those residents who were unable to feed themselves so that we could feed them without any trouble. Back then, we cut up their sandwiches into small bites in a bowl, and then we poured tea over it to make it easy to mix with a spoon. It turned into a terrible mess if they were too unsettled."

She shook her head a little.

"A few staff members also objected to the fact that the employees ate a more varied diet than the residents but I never took to that, because the sandwiches that we mixed in with their tea had liver pâté and salami as well as herring."

"Not all three at the same time, I hope?" Louise said.

Bodil looked at her uncomprehendingly; then she nodded. "Yes. They were supposed to eat both fish and meat, and they did. But toward the end it seemed like more and more conflicts arose between us, and so I chose to put in my resignation."

Bodil took Jørgen's hand when he got out of the car. As Louise was backing out, she noticed in her side-view mirror how the old couple walked back to the house hand in hand.

The tenderness was lovely, but Louise suspected their relationship wasn't always that uncomplicated. *They never were,* she thought.

32

M IK CALLED JUST as Eik had rolled down the window and lit a cigarette. Louise pulled over in front of the entrance to the old sawmill.

"I have to ask you for a favor," he started off. "We can't get Bitten Gamst to cough up the name of her lover but we need to get ahold of him to find out if he saw the rapist in or around the house when he came to visit her."

"So you want me to give it another try?" Louise asked.

"We also need to get her husband to talk and tell us if he knows who drives the white van," he continued. He added that a couple of his people had caught René that same morning walking around the woods with a loaded shotgun. "Of course he denied looking for the rapist but I don't want him roaming around out there. And I feel certain that he and his wife are covering for someone who frequents the woods."

"Did the forensic officers get anything out of searching the scene?"

"There were some pretty nice footprints by the door. Right now we're working on sorting out which fingerprints belong to the people who usually visit the house so we can exclude them."

"You're not going to exclude them just like that?" Louise blurted out.

"No, of course not." Mik told her that Bitten and her husband didn't appear to have much of a social life. "It's limited to her mother and two other couples. Those are the only people who have been to the house in the past month."

"And her lover," Louise added. She promised to see what she could get out of them.

"TA-DAH!" CAMILLA EXULTED when she called back a minute later. "You may now call me Mrs. Sachs-Smith."

"Congratulations," Louise said, holding the phone away from her ear a little. "That's wonderful news. Listen, I want to hear everything, but I'm in the middle of something serious here. I promise to call as soon as I'm done. Enjoy each other— I'm so happy for you."

"We can go by there on our way home and have a toast with them," Eik suggested, looking quite serious.

Louise quickly shook her head. "I don't think they're at all interested in having company. It seems like they've got more than enough in each other," she said. "And I was actually going to ask if you would mind stopping by my parents' house and picking up Jonas after we talk to Bitten."

Louise had given a lot of thought to her meeting with René at the hospital. If he didn't recognize her when they saw each other in the doorway, he had bigger things on his mind. But now that he had had some time to think, something might start to ring a bell. Of course, he might well have known exactly who she was. The whole thing was unsettling, but she'd decided that she would have to ignore whatever may come. That idea had felt sensible then, but now that they were approaching the Starling House, her chest started tightening.

She turned Eik's massive vehicle into the narrow driveway to the thatched house and pulled the emergency brake.

"Does this thing work?" she asked worriedly as the car rolled forward a little.

"It's not razor-sharp but it works." He spit out his chewing gum in the tall grass as he got out.

Every door and window of the house was closed; the place was completely quiet, and there was no sign of life. Aside from a car parked right by the road, there was no indication that anybody was home.

They walked together along the uneven stone path to the door at the end of the old forest guard's house. The small-paned windows were lined up close together all the way along the side of the old farmhouse. Hollyhocks climbed up the white, lime-washed timber frame, their top flowers bending down like swans when they reached the bottom edge of the thatched roof.

Louise walked over and knocked on a low stable door, which seemed to be the original one, still on the house. It was so low that she would risk bumping her head walking through. On the opposite end of the house was the patio where the hot tub was set up. It faced the closed-off part of the property; a dense thicket of beech marked the division between yard and forest. There was no sign of the forensic officers, who had long finished in the house, except for a small piece of barrier tape used for preventing passage through the area around the patio door.

Louise didn't hear anyone coming until the door opened, and she instinctively took a step back when she saw Bitten. The slight woman had a large, bluish-black mark around one eye, which was completely swollen shut. She wore a white robe, and her hair was rumpled and flat on one side as if she had lain down with it still wet.

"Are you alone?" Louise asked while Eik stayed in the background.

Bitten shook her head a little. "Come in."

"How are you doing?" Louise asked, leaving the door open for Eik while she followed Bitten into the living room, which had been renovated with a floor made from ship's planks—a remarkably poor decorating choice for the old house. All in all, René and Bitten had a nautical theme going on with both furniture and paintings in shades of blue and green. At one end of the living room, a large, built-in aquarium ran all the way behind the sofa set to the patio door. At least the style was consistent, Louise thought, but it seemed completely out of place in the middle of the forest. There was neither sea nor a harbor nearby. The closest thing to a body of water was Avnsø Lake.

"I'm okay," Bitten answered, her voice like that of a little girl. Louise had enough experience to register that what was missing from her voice was her dignity.

"Where's your husband?"

Louise followed Bitten's gaze out into the yard. "He's putting a cross on the dog's grave." Bitten sank onto the wide couch, her eyes shiny. "Our daughter insisted."

Mik had told them that they had found the dog in the yard next to the toolshed, its neck broken and upper body crushed. "It wasn't a pretty sight," he had added.

"My daughter and I didn't get to see her, so we haven't even had a chance to say good-bye," she sniffled. "René buried her this morning and now there's going to be a cross on there."

Louise leaned in very close. "Did he hit you again?"

She looked at the woman's swollen eye. Although swelling always took some time, she would almost swear that it wasn't the injuries from the day before that made Bitten's face look like that.

The woman shook her head and clasped her hands while biting her lip.

"Then who did it?" Louise pushed. "I can tell that something happened since I last saw you."

The woman turned her head away without responding.

"Damn it, Bitten!" Louise changed tactics. "You have to tell me what's going on. Who are you having an affair with? We're going to find him anyway, and you can save us a lot of trouble and yourself a lot of discomfort by telling us."

A tear rolled down her cheek and she folded her slender hands in front of her mouth, biting her knuckle.

"We might not even have to tell your husband," Louise finally said, uncomfortable about making that kind of promise.

"He already knows," Bitten whispered, leaning forward a little while casting a quick, sidelong glance at Louise without turning her head. "When we got home from the hospital, Ole was suddenly at the door. He had seen the police cars and wanted to know what happened earlier that day and whether I had said anything about him."

She wiped her face.

"Ole Thomsen?" Louise whispered even though they were alone in the room. "Please tell me that's not who you were waiting for?"

Bitten twitched and nodded so slightly, it was difficult to see.

"And René knows?"

"He does now. He didn't understand how Ole knew that I'd

had the day off. I didn't have time to think of a lie while they were both standing there so I told the truth."

She swallowed and bent her head, her chin touching her chest.

"What did your husband say?" Louise asked.

Bitten gave a small scoff as she straightened herself up. "What do you think?" she said with sarcasm and looked at Louise while shaking her head, making her short hair fall in front of her ear. "He didn't say anything; he didn't dare, just like I knew he wouldn't. Nobody tells Big Thomsen no. If they do, they lose either their job or their business. Their car gets stolen or their house burns down. And of course he's never the one who stands to take the fall for it. So you'd be a fool to try to stop him if there's something he wants."

"And he wanted you," Louise concluded sympathetically.

Bitten nodded. "I didn't really have a choice once René started working for him."

"In the woods?" Louise asked.

"No, he's a driver. He just goes to the woods to laze around. He's got three trucks on the side; that's how he makes his money. Two of them carry gravel from the gravel pit—that's what René does—and the third one carries freight. That's the one the new guy from Pasture House drives—Thomsen's cousin."

Louise took a deep breath. That explained the man's behavior the other day.

"So what happened once it was just the two of you?" she asked.

"At first he was angry, but I think that was mostly because he was hurt. I guess he thought his friend had enough respect for him to keep his hands to himself, and now he's running around the woods searching for the rapist, maybe mostly to convince himself that he won't stand for another man touching his wife."

In a way it didn't surprise her, Louise thought. She could just picture Big Thomsen slinking in to see his friend's wife.

She imagined him sneaking up in his lumberjack getup, hiding the old Land Cruiser between the trees in order to take the back way through the yard and in between Bitten's legs.

Come to think of it, she wasn't sure that Ole Thomsen would even bother to hide his car when he came around to visit. He probably parked right in the driveway.

It was no wonder that René had freaked out. Just then, he appeared at the doorway, having come in from the yard, where Eik was talking with his and Bitten's young daughter.

"Did you find him?" René asked

René Gamst needed a haircut, Louise observed as she moved to an armchair to let him take a seat on the couch next to his wife. He put his arm around Bitten's shoulder and pulled her close.

"I want you to find out who came into my house and raped my wife."

As he sat there, aggrieved in so many ways, Louise suddenly felt sorry for him. His friend screwed his wife and a stranger had entered his home and done the same. He had been robbed of his dignity and manhood.

"I promise we'll find out," she said, meaning it.

"Please don't say that unless you really believe it," he said.

Louise leaned in a little. "I do. We'll find him," she repeated.

"If you don't, I will."

"Please stop it, René," Bitten pleaded.

Louise could tell that though he stopped himself from making a pointed reply, he was frustrated and upset. His face red, his eyes shifting back and forth, he pressed his lips together and remained silent.

She leaned back in her chair.

"Have either of you seen a white van in the woods or by the Stokkebo Road parking area?" she asked.

Bitten quickly shook her head but looked at René, who averted his eyes.

"You've seen it," Louise concluded. "Who's the driver?"

His face twitched. He gave a small sniffle and folded his hands but still didn't answer.

From the corner of her eye, she sensed Bitten straightening up and holding her breath.

Louise got out the picture of Lise Andersen and placed it on the table. "Do you know anything about this woman?"

They both looked at the photograph, then shook their heads. Eik came back into the house and sat down in the chair next to Louise.

"Please. Tell us who drives the white van," she urged.

But this time René didn't react. Bitten was no longer holding her breath, but she was still as a mouse.

Louise got so angry that she jumped out of her chair. She grabbed René by the shoulders and shook him, holding on firmly.

"Why the hell should I lift a finger to find out who was in your house when you don't even want to help?" she yelled.

Looking startled, Bitten had moved all the way to the opposite end of the couch.

Louise shook him again. "Several women have gone missing, one has been murdered, and your own wife has been raped. Now, you're going to tell me who drives that van!"

She released her hold on him, letting him drop back down on the couch. She avoided looking at Eik as she walked back to her chair.

"If we can rule out that this person is connected to the ongoing cases, then we can eliminate the van from the equation and stop wasting our time on it," she said in a more subdued tone of voice.

"It's Ole," René finally disclosed.

"Ole Thomsen?" she asked in surprise. "I thought he drove an old Land Cruiser?"

"Not when he's selling meat."

"Shut your mouth, René!" Bitten shouted angrily and kicked him.

Louise ignored her, keeping René's eyes locked. "Meat?" she asked.

He looked down at the table.

"Tell me what you know about that van," she demanded. "It's been spotted in the woods on several occasions and it might be connected to the attacks that have occurred out there. It was last seen yesterday, driving out from the woods."

"That's because he was here after I picked up Bitten from the hospital," René admitted at last. "The woods were crawling with police so he came over here instead to find out what we knew."

"Be quiet, René," Bitten whispered without looking at her husband.

"Keep talking," Louise commanded. "What's with the meat?"

"Just that he goes and parks in the parking lot twice a week to sell it."

Louise shook her head, not understanding what it was all about.

"Off the books, for crying out loud," René blurted out, gesticulating. "Whatever the butcher doesn't sell in the shop goes out the back door."

"And gets sold off the books," Eik concluded. René nodded.

"Lars Frandsen's shop," Louise guessed.

Another one of the guys from the old gang, he had taken over the butcher shop after his dad.

"René, please stop it now!" his wife begged. "We're not supposed to say anything. You know what will happen. And we've never seen it, either."

That last part was a lie, Louise thought. She was willing to bet that they bought the cheap meat as well.

René's eyes wandered. "That was a mistake," he stammered. "Bitten is right. I don't know anything."

"But you know that Big Thomsen drives the van?"

He had started sweating, and his eyes were suddenly frightened as he turned toward them.

"Please don't tell him what I said," he pleaded. "It was a mistake."

Bitten sat behind him, curling herself up while she kept shaking her head.

Louise shrugged. It was sad to see the degree to which they were subjected to the hierarchy that had been built up while they were still in school. She could hardly believe that this kind of thing could last all the way into adulthood. It had to be more than friendship tying that gang together, she thought as she got up.

René and Bitten stayed seated and watched them leave when they offered to show themselves out.

"That was hot!" Eik said approvingly as they walked toward the car. "I like it when you get mad."

"Shut up," she snapped, getting into the car. The couple were genuinely scared senseless at the thought that they were the ones to reveal that Ole Thomsen and Frandsen the butcher were doing business under the table together.

They were driving down the forest road toward Lerbjerg when Louise suggested that she had better call Mik and tell him to check up on Big Thomsen.

"So that's why nobody knows anything about that van," she said. "He's got everyone under his thumb so they won't say anything that might provoke him. I never understood how he managed to build up that position. It seems like he's got something on everyone so they have to yield to him."

She shook her head and got her cell phone from her bag.

"Could he be our guy?" Eik asked as they drove through the last intersection before Lerbjerg. "He was around the area in 1991 as well."

"Then it had to be Big Thomsen who raped Bitten, even though she was there waiting for him," Louise said, but then she nodded a second later. "It's not impossible, I guess. He's clearly in touch with his inner primitive beast."

Louise had to go through the switchboard before being transferred to Mik and she briefly regretted not opting to call his cell phone. She still had his number on speed dial.

"Mik Rasmussen," he answered, sounding rushed.

"Ole Thomsen is the one who drives the white van," she began. "He's also Bitten's lover so it's a double bonus. The vehicle may be registered under the name of Lars Frandsen, the butcher." She told him about the illegal meat sales.

"We've already spoken with the butcher. It's his car but he flatout denies that it's been in the woods. He says it's a company car."

Louise sighed. *Cocky as always*, she thought.

"Ole Thomsen is the driver. So he's the one you need to talk to, and he needs to be busted for the meat thing along with Frandsen."

She nodded to Eik, who signaled that he wanted to get out of the car. They had pulled into her parents' courtyard.

"We've already got our sights on him," Mik said. "It appears that he's been sleeping his way through half of central Zealand. At least his alibis for the times that we're interested in were provided by several different women. But I'm not buying those stories. Something is very wrong here."

33

Louise waved to Jonas as he appeared by the kitchen door. She hadn't had a chance to call and let him know that she would be by to pick him up. She had missed him.

"Hey!" she called out and smiled when her son walked out into the courtyard to say hello to Eik. He was such a great kid. Louise walked over to give him a hug.

"Do you feel like going home?" she asked before greeting her father, who came around the corner from the backyard.

"You have to come in the house and listen to what the boy's been doing with his time while he's been laid up," he said and beckoned them inside. "It's just amazing what these young kids can do with their computers."

"We'll probably have to listen to it some other time, Dad," Louise cut in, shooting Eik an apologetic smile. "We have to get back to the city."

Her father turned and gave her a stern look. "It'll just take a second, and of course you have the time to listen to what Jonas can do," he said, taking it for granted that they would follow him. "He's very gifted, you know."

Jonas shrugged a little, looking self-conscious.

"It's nothing, really," he whispered. "But Grandpa seems to think I'm some sort of musical genius."

"That's grandparents, I guess," Eik said, good-humoredly following Louise's father. In the living room he walked over and introduced himself to her mother and immediately accepted her offer of coffee.

Louise was still standing in the doorway. The inside of the old timber-frame house had been completely renovated, the walls covered with grayish wood and tile on the floor. The living room opened up into the kitchen where Louise's mother had insisted on leaving the old woodstove even though she used a new gas stove for cooking.

Her mother walked over to the cupboard, and of course she got out the mugs she herself had thrown and fired. Before Louise knew it, Eik was following her mother outside to the wing that had been set up as a pottery. As the door closed behind them, she heard him inquiring with interest about the things her mother made out there.

"All right, I'm ready," said Jonas, coming out of the guest room after gathering his stuff.

"No," Louise hurried to say. "I want to hear what you've made."

Not that she expected to be able to tell it apart from what she had listened to through the door to his room, but she wanted to show that she cared about his interests.

He opened his computer on the dining table and asked her if she was ready.

Louise nodded and sat down as he turned up the music. Just then, her mother and Eik walked in through the kitchen door, Eik carrying a small green vase that she'd apparently given him.

He put down the vase and listened for a minute before nodding appreciatively.

"That's good stuff," he said and closed his eyes as if tasting the notes. "It's got kind of a Nick Cave sound but then not really—it's more contemporary. Who made it?"

"The kid did, of course," Louise's father boasted. "That's his music."

Eik raised one bushy eyebrow and didn't seem to understand.

"Jonas makes music," Louise pitched in. "He's got several songs on YouTube, and they get played all the time."

Jonas nodded shyly.

"What do you call yourself again?" Louise's father asked.

"Joe H," he answered quietly. "And the song is called 'Back to Normal.'"

"As in Jonas Holm," her father enthused with a big smile.

"Well, I'll be," Eik exclaimed, sounding impressed.

"One of his pieces is on the list of the most popular songs on YouTube," her father went on.

Jonas smiled a little more confidently.

"It's what?" Louise exclaimed with surprise and took a step back.

"I told you the boy is on to something," her father said.

"Did you think I was kidding when I said I wanted to play at Roskilde Festival?" Jonas asked Louise.

"Honestly, yes," she admitted. She asked him to play the song again.

"I told him we need to talk to Kjær," her father grumbled.

Kjær was the old family lawyer. "All the stuff about copyright and those kinds of things needs to be looked over by someone who knows about it."

"Okay, Grandpa," Jonas laughed. "We'll take a look at it."

It wasn't that long ago that the boy had started calling Louise's parents Grandma and Grandpa. It wasn't something they had talked about. Louise had just suddenly realized that he was saying it and that it sounded natural. She was pleased.

"Come on then, superstar. Let's get back to the city," she said, swatting at him.

34

"Where are you?" Camilla yelled into the phone as Louise sat squeezed in with Jonas in the front seat of the big four-wheeler. Eik had insisted that his blood alcohol level from the previous night had long since dropped and had gotten behind the wheel.

"On our way home from Hvalsø. How are things with you guys?"

"Why don't you come and have dinner with us?" she asked. "Markus was disappointed, to put it lightly, that we got married without him and now he insists that we at least go and have a nice dinner and invite you along."

Jonas shoved his cell phone in Louise's face.

"Markus just texted me," he mimed, pointing to the phone display. "He wants to know if I can make it."

"What time were you thinking?" Louise asked, feeling a bit overwhelmed by the thought.

"Right now!" Camilla laughed excitedly. "We'll drink champagne and have a lovely dinner. Frederik made arrangements for a menu with Danish lobster at Restaurant Raadhuskælderen."

Louise sighed. It did feel strange not to be part of celebrating her friend's big day.

"I'm not the one driving," she said. "Jonas and I are riding with Eik."

"Just bring him along," Camilla bubbled happily. "That'll make it an even number for our table."

"He probably has other plans?" Louise mumbled and realized that Jonas was already including their chauffeur in the invitation.

"But we need to go home and get changed first," Louise objected after Jonas and Eik had both made it clear that they were game for an impromptu wedding dinner.

"Don't be silly; just come as you are. After all, the whole idea is to keep it informal. They're setting up a special table for us in a corner of the back garden. Just come in from the Stendertorv Square side."

Louise was familiar with the restaurant in the basement of the old city hall. She just wasn't in the mood for razzle and celebration. They still needed to get ahold of Lillian down at Eliselund, but of course she was gone for the day so they would have to wait until morning anyway.

She closed her eyes for a second to get a grip and settle herself. Her demons were circling. It wasn't the sorrow or the feeling of guilt. She had put those behind her—at least for a while, she thought. It was Big Thomsen that worried her. It was always like that. She had always been able to avoid him, but now he kept showing up everywhere and it had her rattled.

She had seen the same insecurity in René's eyes, but Bitten had been difficult to read. She had found only emptiness when she attempted to see behind her glazed-over eyes. Louise had no doubt that her anger had been real when René started giving too much away about the white van. But she didn't have the chance to register if Bitten was angry that he'd exposed Big Thomsen or if her reaction was caused by fear.

"What should we bring them?" Eik asked as they approached Roskilde.

Louise shrugged. Flowers didn't seem right now that she knew that the hotel room had been covered with a truckload of rose petals the previous night, and they didn't need champagne, either.

She shook her head, unable to think of anything, and felt a chill coming on from exhaustion.

"I know!" she burst out, suddenly hitting on an idea as they drove toward the square. She turned to look at Jonas. "We need to go somewhere with an Internet connection—maybe they've got Wi-Fi at the café. And then we need to download a song to your computer."

She pointed ahead and instructed Eik to drive in and park on Stendertorv Square.

"Camilla always said that she would only get married if Big Fat Snake played at her wedding. I want you to find 'Bonsoir Madame.'"

"All right," Jonas mumbled. "Then we'll have to go to the café because I don't have that one."

She noticed a smile twitching at the corner of Eik's mouth and thought that he was probably much more in tune with the boy's taste in music than hers.

SMALL TORCHES HAD been lit on the sidewalk, and the archway leading into the back garden was decorated with flowers.

Louise stopped to breathe in the smell of the white lilies.

"How many guests are invited?" Eik asked, pulling down on his T-shirt a little although it didn't seem to otherwise bother him that he wasn't dressed for a fancy wedding dinner. He had stopped by the corner store to buy an extra pack of cigarettes while they downloaded the music.

"I think it's just us," Louise answered doubtfully, kicking herself for not having picked a more presentable outfit for work that day.

She ran her fingers through her long hair, tousling it a bit.

"Shall we?" Eik offered her his arm. She accepted somewhat hesitantly, resting her hand on his arm while Jonas led the way through the gate in the old red-brick wall.

Louise stopped in surprise as they stepped onto the cobblestone. To the right at the back of the garden, a light canvas was suspended above two tables that had been pushed together. Torches were lit all the way around, screening off the private party from the other tables, and the tables were set with white tablecloths and tall candelabras. There were no other guests yet in the garden but several tables had small, white reservation cards.

"It doesn't look like anyone else was invited but us," Jonas said before looking up at a pair of speakers mounted in each corner of the back garden. "I'm just going to run inside to see if I can set up the music."

"Holy moly," Louise mumbled. The setup was impressive, but standing there with Eik felt a little awkward; neither really knew what to do with themselves until the host couple showed up.

Just then they heard the sound of horseshoes on the pavement, and a carriage came around the corner. When Jonas came back outside, he gave a quick nod to signal that it was all under control. Louise felt Eik's hand on her back as the carriage drawn by neighing horses stopped in front of them and they saw Camilla, smiling and waving with flowers in her hair and holding a large bouquet.

Markus was quick. He chivalrously jumped down from his seat next to the driver and walked around to open the door for his mother and Frederik.

"Congratulations!" they all shouted in unison.

Louise had brought the two yellow roses that Jørgen had picked for her and she now passed them on to the newlyweds. Jonas had stolen a lily from the decoration, which he held out for Camilla, who repaid him with a kiss and asked them to come inside.

"WELL, I'VE HEARD that you're married now. And I've heard that you don't fool around," the voice of singer Anders Blichfeldt sounded from the speakers just as Frederik and Camilla walked into the back garden, and two waiters came up the stairs from the restaurant with champagne and glasses.

"...Bonsoir Madame. I know who you are, Madame. You used to be a Mademoiselle, I know you too well..."

Louise couldn't help but laugh when she saw her friend kick off her high heels and dance around barefoot with her arms over her head while singing along. Then she surrendered and forgot all about Bitten and Big Thomsen when Eik grabbed her and started swinging her around.

"Is this a private party?" a younger couple asked, looking somewhat timidly at the four of them dancing in the otherwise empty back garden.

"No, come on in," Camilla shouted while Frederik asked the waiters to get more glasses.

After the song was finished, they made their way to the table beneath the canvas where candles had now been lit.

"I'd like to propose a toast to my beautiful wife," Frederik opened once they were all seated. He looked at Jonas and Markus and toasted in Louise and Eik's direction. "Thank you for dropping everything you were doing in order to celebrate this evening with us. I've come to realize that I'd better get used to acting quickly now that Camilla has come into my life." He gazed at her lovingly. "And so that's what I did today."

"We've had the most amazing day," Camilla said after they toasted. She also gestured toward the young couple, who had picked a table as far from the wedding party as possible. "We picked up Markus after school and then we went sailing on the bay."

"You've both been acting like a pair of loonies," her son interjected. "It was so embarrassing when you came into my school wearing that and with flowers in your hair. What do you think my friends are gonna say?"

Camilla shrugged and suggested that maybe they would tell him how nice it was that he had a happy mother.

"What have you guys been up to?" she asked, leaning forward with curiosity.

"We went to see Bodil Parkov and her husband," Eik said, asking for a draft beer instead of champagne.

Louise put her foot on top of his and pushed down, making him turn toward her in surprise. He didn't know Camilla, and she hadn't had a chance to instruct him on which things not to talk about around her friend. It had taken her years to establish watertight dividers between the things they could talk about and what she needed to hold back when they would get together privately.

"Yes," Louise hurried to say. "It's been a busy day but then we were able to pick up Jonas on the way so that worked out well."

She was about to talk about Jonas's song when Camilla interrupted her. "Her husband?" she exclaimed. "Bodil Parkov isn't married!"

Louise looked at her quizzically.

"Uhh, yes, she is," she replied, annoyed. "She's been married to Jørgen for as long as I can recall."

Camilla put down her silverware and leaned forward. "The Bodil Parkov who worked as director of Eliselund until March 1980 was unwed. Otherwise she wouldn't even have been eligible for the position. The job required that you be single and live at the institution."

"I guess she had a secret then!" Eik interjected, leaning in toward Louise when the waiter arrived to switch out his empty glass. "But then that might be understandable considering the guy she's got hanging around at home."

"Hey, now," Louise snapped at him irritably.

"Bodil Parkov was a spinster," Camilla said, "and they said at Eliselund that she had dedicated her entire life to working with the mentally disabled because her family had been personally affected."

"Yes," said Louise. "Her husband was in a work accident and suffered a brain injury."

"According to the *Blue Book*, she's single," Camilla maintained, but then she clapped her hands and gave Frederik a big kiss as the two waiters brought in large plates of lobster just then. "I sold the story about Eliselund to *Roskilde Tidende*, by the way," she said once the lobster was on the table. "It sounded like they were interested in entering into a freelance agreement with me."

"So you're going to start working as a journalist again?"

Louise leaned toward Eik to make room as a small glass bowl with a slice of lemon was placed next to her plate.

"They were looking for people for the crime section," Camilla said, smiling as she broke a claw off her lobster. "They just laid off the entire editorial office and now they only want freelancers in order to keep the costs down."

Louise wasn't really paying attention. She noticed that Eik had put his hand on her back. It tickled as he ran his thumb down her spine, and she realized that her foot was still on his boot. She wrapped it around his ankle and kept leaning toward him even though the waiter had already gone.

"EIK..." SHE MUMBLED the following morning when she woke up with her lips against his naked chest. "That's not a very common name. Were you named after someone?"

He had his arm around her, his fingers tangled through her long hair. After the wedding dinner, the party had moved to Frederik and Camilla's house. In her champagne buzz Louise had granted Jonas a skip day since he had been ill. So they had stayed the night out there.

Jonas slept in Markus's room, and Eik had followed Louise when she went to make up a bed in one of the guest rooms down the hall.

"There was a musician once by the name of Eik Skaløe. Do you remember him?" he asked, pushing down the covers a little. It was warm in the room even though Louise had gotten up at some point in the night to open a window. "If I got anything from someone else, it's probably a remnant of his soul."

"He disappeared, didn't he?" Louise asked, propping herself up on her elbow to look down at his furrowed face. "He was the lead singer of that band, Steppeulvene, and quite young."

Eik opened his eyes and looked at her. "He was twenty-five when he committed suicide somewhere between India and Pakistan."

"Is it his musical part that's inside you?" she asked, running her hand down his chest.

"Hmm," he mumbled. "I used to think maybe it was the desire to let go. I've often thought that it would be a relief, but I've never had the courage, which probably means I don't want it enough after all."

He pulled her down toward him.

"What do you want to get away from?"

Louise kept looking at him even though he had turned his face away and was looking out at the early-morning sun and the hazy blue skies. He grumbled a little, and she tugged on him.

"What do you want to get away from?" she repeated and put her hands around his face.

Finally he turned his head and looked at her with pain in his eyes and a dry laugh.

"Me," he said. "It's completely trivial. A lonely heart and pain and something that never heals."

He had closed his eyes again while speaking.

"I had a girlfriend who disappeared from a boat in the Mediterranean. The boat was found drifting around outside a small harbor, and the two she had been sailing with washed ashore the very next day. But she never turned up."

"So she drowned?"

At first he didn't answer; then he inhaled deeply.

"I don't know. When they searched the boat, they found the other two people's possessions, but all her things were missing."

"So you think she ran off?" Louise whispered.

He shrugged. "I don't know and I probably never will."

The silence grew heavy between them.

"I had sailed with them to Rome but then we had a fight and I took off. I went out and got drunk and when I came back, they had sailed on. I stayed in Italy for a few days before I began to hitchhike home, and it wasn't until I got back to Denmark that I heard the news of what had happened."

He reached for the cigarettes, which sat on the nightstand along with his keys and the spare change from his pocket.

The smoke rose in a spiral, drifting toward the open window.

Louise closed her eyes. She felt for him; she understood his anguish only too well. He, too, was torn up inside with sorrow. She hated that he suffered, but she now felt closer to him, and somehow less lonely. She reached out and touched his face, and was about to get up when he put out his cigarette in a glass of water and pulled her down on top of him.

35

Goodness!" Hanne exclaimed when they arrived at the department. "You're radiating red."

Rønholt's secretary was watering the plants in the hallway windows.

"Red is the aura of eroticism."

Hanne cocked her head and contemplated them as if they were enveloped in one big speech bubble that was telling her everything about the night they had spent together.

"Passion and eroticism."

Jonas had stayed in Roskilde, and Eik had dropped off Louise in Frederiksberg before driving to Sydhavnen himself. He had returned an hour later, his hair wet and clothes clean, to chivalrously pick her up and drive her to the department.

Louise didn't know what it was that Hanne had spotted—maybe it was all the kissing that had made her chin flush. She looked down while Eik merely laughed as if he didn't mind getting found out one bit.

"You spend too much time on crystals and all of your spiritual bullshit, Hanne," he said.

"This has nothing to do with spirituality," she objected. "It's about aura and energy. And right now, you're both emitting red and I know what that means."

As Louise turned on her computer, she couldn't help but smile. She would have a hard time keeping certain details out of her head. Like the fact that her new partner did not wear underpants, a habit he had adopted during the years he spent traveling around Asia and India. And that he refused to send text messages.

She wasn't really mad at herself; she just felt overwhelmed at the thought of them working together so closely all day. Apparently she was never going to learn. It had been the same story with Mik—awkward.

On the other hand, her prospects of sex were minimal if it wasn't going to be with a colleague, because she never met anyone else.

"Do you want anything from the cafeteria?" Eik asked from the doorway.

Louise shook her head absentmindedly without taking her eyes off the screen as she re-read the first few lines once more.

When he returned and flopped down across from her, she had logged on to CPR, the police access to the Civil Registration System, and finding Bodil Parkov on Bukkeskov Road in Hvalsø had not been difficult in the least. Louise wrote down the names of her late parents and looked through the rest of the personal data one more time.

"Camilla was right," she pronounced. "Bodil isn't married."

Eik pulled his legs off the table and walked over to stand behind her chair. He ran a finger down her back, making her contract her shoulder blades.

"Jørgen is her brother," she said and looked up at him.

"Then please explain to me why she's going around telling people that he's her husband?" he asked, slurping from his cup. "Incest?"

He looked at her.

Louise shrugged, thinking back for a minute. Maybe she was the one who had misunderstood about them being husband and wife, she thought, but then she shook her head. Bodil had always referred to Jørgen as her husband.

"But that doesn't make sense," she moaned, looking out the window while thinking it over. "What does she stand to gain from telling people that they're married?"

She couldn't think of anything. She said, "I could kind of see it if it were the other way around; if you were trying to fool social services, so you made up a story that the person you're living with is your brother."

She looked questioningly at Eik. When he didn't react, she added: "Some people do that kind of thing to be able to collect higher benefits." She rested her chin on her hands, her head feeling tired. Too much champagne and not enough sleep. "They're renting their house but she probably doesn't get any subsidies," she went on.

"Well, they've obviously wanted to trick someone," Eik determined. "Why else would you lie about something like that?"

She nodded. "Yes, why?" she repeated dully.

"What do you know about them?" he asked, filling his cup from the white thermos that he had brought in.

"Nothing," Louise admitted, considering the question. "Aside from the fact that they've lived out there for many years. They keep to themselves, and they're part of the area."

Louise moaned and tried to ignore a suffocating smell of fried onions. It was as if the cooking odors from the kitchen below seeped through every crack and opening. With small beads of sweat on her forehead, she got up to open a window but quickly shut it again when she realized that the outlet for the range hood was right underneath.

"Hold on a second," she excused herself. She needed some cold water on her face to keep the nausea from taking over. She was about to close the restroom door when Eik slid up behind her and pushed his way in there as well.

She gasped for breath as he pressed her up against the wall and kissed her. Louise felt the weight of his body as he leaned in against her, and she gave in when he fumbled for the button on her jeans and clumsily pulled them down over her hips while someone pushed down the door handle, pulling on the locked door.

Louise insisted that Eik leave the restroom before her. Once he was out, she leaned in over the sink and gave herself a quick wash-down with the industrial soap from the dispenser. She attempted to comb out her long hair with her fingers but had to abandon the idea, gathering it in a loose braid without an elastic band instead. Once she felt fairly certain that all tracks had been covered, she opened the door and stepped right into the arms of Olle, who had been patiently waiting for the restroom to become available.

For a second they just stood there staring at each other while Louise tried feverishly to think of something to say. She could tell from his expression that he had been standing there when Eik had come out as well, and she had to resist an instinctive urge to run away with her tail between her legs. Instead she raised her head and smiled at him before walking back toward the Rathole as straight as a ramrod.

"Could you get me the brother's civil registration number?" Eik asked after she sat back down.

He appeared unaffected by the situation. Either he was used to morning quickies at the office or the lusts of the flesh were simply as natural to him as not wearing underpants.

"Then I'll run him through the Central Crime Register."

Louise was uncomfortable with handing over Jørgen and Bodil like that just because Bodil happened to have been a part of the twins' life at one point in the distant past. And she probably ought to call Viggo Andersen, she thought. But what would she say to him? There was no news, after all.

"Jørgen Parkov," she read aloud and then the number while Eik entered the digits.

Louise watched him as his eyes moved down the lines and lingered on his pronounced cheekbones and angular chin. She felt flushed and cast down her eyes.

"There's nothing on him," he said, shaking his head. "Aside from a remark that there's an old police report on him but it dates so far back that we would have to go to the National Archives to find it."

"Then I'll go to the National Archives," she decided.

"But is it of interest?" he objected, washing down two Tylenols with his black coffee before getting up. On the way to the waste-basket, he stopped to caress the back of her neck. "Wouldn't we be better off having a talk with the strict Lillian?"

Louise tried to remain calm and focused as she entered Bodil Parkov's civil registration number into the Central Crime

Register. She wasn't sure what she was looking for but she needed to do something while the heat from his fingers sent surges of electricity through her.

"You think Parkov knows what happened to the twins," he guessed, reading along on her screen. It showed zero results on her search.

Louise shrugged. "I don't know what I think," she answered honestly.

He let go of her when they heard a knock at the door but not quickly enough for Hanne to miss the intimate touch as she came to inform Louise that she had put her name on her cubbyhole and put the agenda for the next managers' meeting in there.

"Thanks, Hanne," Louise said, flustered, and stood up. She suddenly felt like she was suffocating. The office walls were closing in on her.

"Why don't you set up an appointment with Lillian? I'll be back in an hour," she said to Eik as she grabbed her jacket.

She needed to get some air and get away from what they had set in motion. She avoided his gaze as she left the office, embarrassed to be fleeing like that.

SHE LEANED HER head against the wall and dozed while waiting for the young archivist at the National Archives to return. She had no idea if he had been gone for two or twenty minutes, and she startled when he put his hand on her shoulder and lightly shook her.

"No luck, I'm afraid," he apologized. "We don't have anything on him or Bodil Parkov. Just this old police report, which the neighbor retracted soon after."

"Can I see it?" Louise asked, straightening herself up.

"It doesn't say much. It's from 1958 and no charges were ever filed."

"Does it have the name of the informer?" she asked, reaching for the file.

Louise pulled a piece of paper from the faded brown folder. As she tried to decipher the old police report, she realized that she needed to seriously consider whether it might be time for her to get some reading glasses.

She got up and walked over to the window, but the archivist was right: The case had been retracted just five days after the neighbor, Rosen, filed the report against the Parkov family. And then it was closed and archived.

Louise dug around her bag for a notepad, cursing when she concluded that she had forgotten to bring one when she left the office in such a rush.

Eik was in every fiber of her body. Her skin burned whenever she thought of him, and she longed for the dark of the night and his warm breath.

"Can I make a copy?" Louise asked when she returned to the counter where the young guy was having an apple and some juice.

He tipped his head toward an open door next to him. "It's in there," he said without getting up. Apparently it was self-service while he was "on lunch."

She was putting the photocopies in her bag when Eik called.

"I've tracked down an old medical file for Jørgen Parkov," he began. "We need a court order to have it turned over to us but I just got an oral summary. You'd better hurry back."

"Sexual abnormality," Eik said, reading from his notes when Louise walked back into the office. "As a result of the injury to his frontal lobes, Jørgen Parkov is unable to restrain his natural urges."

He looked at her gravely. Every hint of eroticism and flirtation had gone from his eyes.

"Hunger, desire," he listed. "The body's natural need for full strength."

Louise listened dumbfounded while she pulled out her chair and sat down.

"The file covers a four-year period during which he was placed in a mental home," he continued.

"How old was he at the time?" she broke in.

He looked at her seriously.

"He was fourteen when he was placed under the Care Division."

"So what about the work accident? That never happened?" Louise asked in confusion.

"Apparently not," Eik said. "While he was at the home, he assaulted the other boys. According to the consultant doctor's summary, the boy's mother, Gerda Parkov, wouldn't face how bad things were with her son. Throughout the years that Jørgen was placed in the men's isolation facility, he was medicated to curb his urges and allow the doctors to control him. As a natural step in the course of treatment, a castration was planned for a later date."

"And that never happened?" Louise asked.

Eik shook his head. "His treatment was interrupted when his mother objected to her son being forcibly castrated."

"What about the medication?"

He shrugged.

"When did all of this take place?"

"He was placed at the institution in 1958," he said. "He was just a teenager then. He was discharged in 1962."

"But then what happened?" she asked, noting that 1958 was the same year the neighbor had filed the police report.

They sat for a minute, letting it all sink in. Shaken, Louise then turned around to the computer on her desk to see what she could find on Parkov's old neighbor.

EDITH ROSEN LIVED in a summer house in a town called Horneby in northern Zealand. According to Louise's search, she was the only living person who could be traced back to Rungsted, where the family had lived next door to the merchant Parkov ages ago. Louise learned from the national register database that they had moved from the address in 1962—the same year that Jørgen was discharged.

Edith Rosen's parents were long gone. Their daughter was an only child, and Louise worked out that she must have just turned sixty-seven.

"I'm driving up to northern Zealand to speak with the old neighbor," she told Eik. "And maybe you can try charming your way to an interview with cranky Lillian in the meantime?"

He smiled at her.

"I can charm anyone."

FROM THE ROAD, the summer house looked like a dark cigar box with tiny windows. It was situated on a large, natural plot facing out to a field where a herd of Icelandic horses walked around, swatting their tails to keep away the flies.

As she walked through the gate, Louise saw a figure dressed in blue at the back of the large yard.

"Hello," she called, walking down the garden path toward the house. She had to call out a couple of times before the lady turned and hesitantly walked toward her with a basket in hand.

Louise had gone through a McDonald's drive-through on the way there. A Coke and two cheeseburgers had settled her stomach, and she was slowly regaining her inner balance as well.

"My name is Louise Rick," she said, holding out her hand and explaining who she was. In the same breath, she apologized for interrupting Edith Rosen's gardening.

The woman had pulled her almost white hair back into a ponytail, which hung limply down the back of her loose dress.

"But I wasn't expecting anyone at all," she said apologetically, running her hand somewhat feverishly down her old dress, which was stained from dirt and green sap.

"It's perfectly all right. I should have called," Louise hurried to say. She knew very well that information was never given quite as freely if people had time to prepare for the conversation. "Growing up, you lived with your parents in a villa in Rungsted?"

Edith Rosen nodded uncertainly, clearly unable to figure out where the police officer was trying to go with that. "Yes," she answered hesitantly. "That was the house where I was born."

"Do you remember the Parkovs who lived in the house next door?"

"I remember them," she acknowledged.

"There was an incident with their son, Jørgen, which made your father file a police report," Louise continued. Then she fell silent as she saw the color drain from Edith Rosen's face.

"Let's go inside, shall we?" the older lady asked. "I need to sit down."

Louise supported her as they walked toward the door together. A cat slipped out as they opened the door and stepped into a small kitchen with flowered wallpaper and laundry in the sink.

They sat down and Louise went straight to the point. "Did he assault you?" she asked.

The woman's eyes were shiny. She nodded quickly and then looked away when Louise asked her to tell her about the incident.

"It wasn't an incident," she finally said, working herself up to look at Louise.

"No, I can see that the report was retracted..."

"It was the beginning of the nightmare of my life," the woman continued, her voice cracking, her shoulders starting to shake.

Her crying sounded like the whimper of a small child. The eerie, long sounds of lament sent shivers down Louise's spine, and she moved her chair closer to the table, placing her hand over the woman's. They sat like that for a little while before Edith Rosen cleared her throat and looked up.

"Will you tell me what happened?" Louise asked. "I need to know."

She could tell that Edith Rosen was trying, but then the eerie wailing started again. The sound was like a knife to the heart, and Louise was shocked at the still-intense reaction to something that had happened more than fifty years ago. She tried once again to comfort the woman, thinking that she had obviously never been able to put the incident behind her, even though her father had apparently regretted going to the police.

Louise got up and got a glass, which she filled from the tap and placed on the table.

"Please, have a drink," she suggested.

The older woman's lungs whistled and Louise worried for a

second that she couldn't breathe or that perhaps she was having a heart attack. But then Edith Rosen straightened herself up, holding on to the tabletop as if she needed a fixed point. She wiped her face on her dress sleeve and drank a little water.

"I always knew it would come out one day," she whispered and looked at Louise with despairing eyes. "Something like that haunts you for the rest of your life."

"What happened?" Louise asked, but she could tell that Edith Rosen wasn't listening.

"I wonder whatever happened to Bodil?" she mumbled quietly.

"She and Jørgen are living together by a forest down on central Zealand."

"That's not possible!" Edith Rosen exclaimed, with aggression.

Louise jumped, surprised at the fierce outburst, and tried to interpret the woman's facial expression now that her eyes had finally come back to life.

"Why wouldn't they be?" she asked calmly.

"Bodil would never do that," she answered firmly. "Never." They looked at each other for a minute.

"So he's still alive then," Edith Rosen concluded.

Then she folded her hands in front of her, suddenly sad.

"Poor Bodil had her life ruined as well."

Her voice rose and fell as if pulled from the fog of the past. Louise shivered.

"They're really living together?"

Louise nodded.

"You know what evil is?" Edith Rosen whispered, looking at some point above Louise's head. "It's when fate corrupts and destroys a relationship between two people, and then forces them to live together."

"If I'm to understand a word of what you're saying, you'll

have to tell me what happened back then," Louise cut in matter-of-factly.

"And he's still alive?" Edith Rosen repeated, holding Louise's gaze.

She nodded patiently and repeated that so was Bodil.

"No," Edith Rosen broke in, suddenly short-tempered. "The Bodil that I knew is no longer alive."

"Please just tell me what happened," Louise asked. She was beginning to doubt whether the woman was all there.

Edith Rosen's hands fluttered around a little as she tried to collect herself.

"When Bodil was nine years old, her brother was five," she began at last, staring straight ahead, focusing. "Bodil would pick him up from preschool on her way home from school."

She spoke more calmly now, but her hands were still in motion.

"I attended the same preschool, and some days she would bring me along with them when my mother was at the hairdresser's or shopping. We had to cross two residential streets. It wasn't a very long walk but one day Jørgen outpaced her. He loved cars—there weren't that many of them back then—and he had spotted one that he wanted to see before it disappeared."

Louise let her be as she fell silent and got lost in her own thoughts.

"Bodil didn't have a chance to stop him before he stepped into the road," she went on. "Just then, another car came around the corner and hit him."

"It was a traffic accident?" Louise exclaimed in surprise. She could tell from the look on Edith Rosen's face that she didn't know what Louise was referring to.

"It was so frightening," Edith Rosen whispered. "None of us kids understood how a boy that we all knew could get picked up by an ambulance and then come back from the hospital a completely different person."

She shook her head.

"It didn't look like he was really hurt. There wasn't even any blood," she explained. "He just fell down when the car hit him but it didn't run him over."

"He must have been hit in a very unlucky way," Louise said, aware that it took very little to damage the frontal lobes.

Edith Rosen got up and walked to a kitchen cupboard, where she got out a bottle with a patent stopper. She seemed to be slowly regaining her composure, and Louise accepted her offer of a glass of homemade elderflower juice.

"I can't tell you exactly when the nightmare began," Edith Rosen admitted when they were seated across from each other once again. "I guess Jørgen was fourteen back then so Bodil must have been eighteen. But one day she was suddenly gone. She left school even though she was a straight-A student. People said that their mother knew what went on and she had told Bodil that she ought to be thankful that she wasn't the one who had been hit by the car. I guess it was a teacher who helped her secure a maid's position through the city with a doctor at Ebberødgård in Birkerød. But by then Jørgen had already been next door to see me, so I knew what her homeroom teacher had saved her from."

She pressed her lips together. Her mouth was thin as both corners twitched, but she didn't succeed in holding back the tears.

"I was afraid to tell anyone," she whispered. "But my parents found out and went to see the merchant. My father also went to the police and he demanded that Jørgen be sent away since his parents were unable to control him."

"But later he retracted the report?" Louise asked.

Edith Rosen nodded. "That was part of the deal that my

father made with the merchant. If they sent Jørgen away, the report would be retracted."

"What about Bodil; did she come back home then?"

"I never saw her again. I don't even know if she had the chance to see her father again. The merchant died four years later, and then his wife brought Jørgen home."

Her chin quivered.

"It started again the very next day after he returned," she stammered, trying to keep her head high.

Louise's breath caught. Afraid she would stutter, she took a moment to compose her thoughts before speaking. "And then you moved?" she asked.

Edith Rosen nodded. "And then we moved," she repeated.

When Louise's cell phone started ringing in her bag, she realized she'd been sitting in Edith Rosen's kitchen for two hours. She took Eik's call.

"Lillian Johansen is here, eager to tell us what went on at Eliselund. It turns out that the twins disappeared while she was on duty."

"Why did you bring her in?" Louise asked quietly. She could tell that Eik had walked out into the hallway.

"Because I had to arrest her and threaten to charge her with withholding information of significant importance to the investigation."

"Eik, damn it!" Louise exclaimed. "You're running the risk of a liability suit."

She sighed and smiled apologetically to Edith Rosen.

"I'll just wrap things up here and then I'll head back," she told Eik.

36

LOUISE WAITED IMPATIENTLY in the traffic jam on the freeway by Hørsholm. She cursed rush-hour traffic, and the
way back from Horneby suddenly seemed very long. She also
felt guilty about Edith Rosen. She had thanked her for their
conversation and apologized for raking up the past, but she had
left her with wounds that were unlikely to ever heal.

Considering what she had learned, she was inclined to
agree with the former neighbor that it seemed unlikely that
Bodil would choose to live with her brother of her own free
will. Louise could think of only one thing that could tie the
two siblings together: Bodil feeling enough guilt at not having
looked after her younger brother well enough when walking
him home from preschool.

Louise noted that Melvin had called a couple of times while
she had been sitting in the flowered kitchen. She might as well

take advantage of the traffic standstill to tackle the conversation that she had put off a bit too long.

"The sales contract is all ready to go," said her downstairs neighbor, sounding so pleased that the objections caught in Louise's throat.

"You bought it?" she said instead.

"No, *we* bought a community garden lot," he corrected her, explaining that she just needed to sign the papers as well. "I've got it all right here. I promised Jonas that we'll go take a look at the 'mansion' tonight. He just got back from Roskilde."

Louise took a deep breath. She hadn't even had a chance to see the garden yet. But it was her own fault that she had not backed out in time.

"There's new wiring and a new bathroom," Melvin said, adding that they would probably need to paint the kitchen and living room. "But that's up to you."

His enthusiasm made her smile.

"And the garden is amazing," he continued dreamily. "There are berries and potatoes and herbs…"

"I hope there's a bit of grass, too?" Louise interjected, suddenly worried that there might not be any room for her sunbed.

"Plenty of grass," he reassured her. "And it's positioned perfectly so there's sun all day and even in the evening."

"I can't wait to see it," Louise said, catching his excitement, and thought: Why shouldn't she have a community garden? She pulled into the passing lane once traffic finally started moving again and told him that she would sign it as soon as she got home.

"Just go ahead and bring Jonas out there. I'll probably be home kind of late today."

*   *   *

WHEN LOUISE WALKED into the Rathole, Lillian Johansen was sitting on a chair, pressed up against the wall. It was quite obvious that she hadn't the slightest desire to speak with the police. Eik sat by his desk, his hands folded in front of him.

They had clearly been waiting for her, so Louise quickly pulled off her sweater and said hello to the woman who had been so unsympathetic the first time she called Eliselund.

"Lillian worked down there the last year that the twins lived there, and she just told me that she looked after them while they were admitted to the sick ward for pneumonia in February."

Eik turned his attention to the sullen woman in the guest chair.

"Could you please repeat what happened the last evening?"

He had turned the blinds to let in only a thin stripe of daylight. In front of Lillian was an untouched coffee cup and a glass of water.

The heavyset woman folded her arms across her chest with obvious animosity.

"There was nothing that you could have done differently," Eik helped out. "You were only a student at the time."

She still didn't say anything; just sat there quietly, staring straight ahead.

They waited for a while for her to start talking, until Eik ran out of patience.

"Before you got here," he began, "Lillian told me that she found it odd that the girls had been admitted to the section of the sick ward that was isolated in the basement. Because neither of them seemed particularly affected by pneumonia. They had neither symptoms nor a temperature and when she pointed this out to Bodil Parkov, she was told to leave the basement and take over the restroom task in the men's wing instead, making sure that the worst-off patients got to use the restroom."

Louise reached for an empty cup and poured herself some coffee. "Do you want some?" she asked, offering it to Lillian.

The woman shook her head and looked down at the table.

"The night that the twins died, the sick ward in the basement was locked up. Nobody aside from Parkov and the consultant doctor had access, which meant that they took the night shift themselves. The next morning, the flag was flying at half-mast and nobody saw the twins again. They didn't see them leave the place, either."

"Eik," Louise cut in. "Why don't we let Lillian tell us what happened now?"

He fell silent and shot her an annoyed look. Then he nodded to Lillian, signaling for her to go on, but still nothing happened and so they waited once again. Eik made an approach to break the silence several times but Louise shut him up with a stern look.

They sat like that for nine minutes, in complete silence. Louise picked at her frayed cuticles, occasionally shooting a quick glance at Lillian until she noticed that tears had started rolling down the woman's plump cheeks. She looked quickly at Eik, who was leaning back; his hands folded behind his head. He looked like he might have dozed off.

"At first I didn't know what went on when they locked up the section down there," Lillian began flatly. "And I couldn't tell you how long the others had known about it. In any event, they stayed away when the door was barred."

Louise leaned in and Eik reached for his notepad. *Maybe he hadn't been asleep after all,* she thought.

"One evening I had gone down there to find the case file for a patient who was being transferred to the University Hospital of Copenhagen the next day," she said.

"While the twins were admitted?" Louise asked, afraid to interrupt.

"No," Lillian answered, wringing her hands. "This was long before that."

For a moment it looked like she might stall again but then suddenly she continued, her words almost like a burst of anger as she looked up.

"They were walking down the hall with him," she said. "Parkov and the doctor held him between them as they came out of the bathroom. He was naked and they led him to the rearmost sickroom, which we called the epidemic room."

She seemed ill at ease as she looked away, working herself up to continue.

"In all my time, that room was never in use. It was always empty, reserved for emergency situations. I was so shocked because I had never seen him before even though I was on the permanent day shift in the men's section."

"Who was it?" Eik asked, placing a match between his teeth.

"Well, I didn't know this at the time but later I was told that it was Parkov's brother. She let him live down there, and the consultant doctor treated him. At first it was all very hush-hush and nobody dared say anything but then we got used to it. We never saw him; he had his meals brought down there and didn't mingle with the other residents, but we heard the sounds."

She closed her eyes and her face contracted. It looked as if it was all coming back to her, and she started rocking from side to side in torment.

"They let him in with the girls who were ill. The ones who were admitted to the sick ward," she whispered and took a heavy breath. "If you had an evening shift in the hospital wing, you could sometimes hear the sounds. But we never said anything. We didn't dare—not even the more senior staff. So it remained an unspoken thing."

She straightened herself up.

"And it should stay that way," she said.

"Why?" Eik exclaimed. The angry line across his forehead made it clear that he disagreed.

Lillian Johansen turned toward him. "Because we were all to blame. Bodil Parkov was a tough leader but we knew what went on and should have stepped in. This made us party to the crimes that took place. And you shouldn't start exposing someone after so many years."

"You all turned a blind eye," Eik declared, indignantly spitting out his match. "Maybe because you knew that the mentally handicapped girls wouldn't tell. Or was it because they had no next of kin to file a complaint?"

"Stop," Louise cut him off sternly and thought about sending him out of the room.

"It's been over thirty years," Lillian said, defending herself. "Things were different back then, and the consultant doctor objected to the charges that were raised against Parkov. He denied that the assaults happened. And then in the end her brother was removed."

"When was that?" Louise asked.

"It was just before the thing with the twins. Maybe a week or two earlier."

"So you mean to say that Bodil Parkov's brother was staying at Eliselund all the time until she quit and subsequently left the place?"

Lillian nodded.

"And on the day that she quit, the girls disappeared?" Eik took over, already standing up.

Lillian Johansen sat motionless, her eyes following him as he put on his leather jacket and grabbed his car keys. "Maybe we should have pursued it after the doctor killed himself but he was the one responsible for the sick ward, so the case was allowed to die with him."

"And nobody cared to know what had become of Lise and Mette?" Louise concluded.

Then she picked up her sweater to follow Eik out the door.

"The forgotten girls were left to their own devices from the beginning anyway so what were we supposed to do?" Lillian mumbled.

Louise spun around in the doorway, only barely stopping herself from yelling at her.

"That's where you're mistaken," she said angrily. "Those two girls were not forgotten from the beginning. Their father was urged to forget them. He was told to stay away, and that was apparently the case with many of the children and adults who had no contact with their families. They were left to their own devices because they were different and were stowed away in a place where the only concern was how to make it easy to look after them. But you were the ones who were supposed to take an interest in them. Because they didn't have anyone else…"

The words and the anger bubbled up inside, and she struggled to keep from exploding. Instead she turned her back on Lillian and left the office.

37

This time Louise didn't notice the old sawmill or the other houses because Eik was driving so fast down Bukkeskov Road that rocks sprayed from underneath the car. She had her eyes fixed on the tall chestnut trees around the gamekeeper's house.

Louise had called Mik from the car to briefly update him on their interview with Lillian Johansen and share the information that they had dug up on Jørgen Parkov and the family's background.

"He lived here back when the first series of rapes happened as well," she pointed out.

But she had been unable to answer one of Mik's questions:

"What about the intervening twenty years?" he had asked. "Doesn't it seem unlikely that he would take that long a break and then pick back up where he left off?"

When they pulled up in front of the gamekeeper's house,

the gate in the fence as well as the front door were both wide open.

"Something is not right," Louise said to Eik when she noticed Jørgen's rake in the middle of the courtyard.

She tore off her headset and hurried toward the house while calling Bodil's name. The place was eerily quiet. The only sound was from a bird, which flushed from the thatched roof. Her heart was beating fast as she placed her hand on her gun and slowly stepped into the hallway. There was no one in the living room and not a sound to be heard from the rest of the house. She nodded to Eik, signaling for him to proceed to the living room while she headed for the kitchen.

Empty. Two used dishes were left on the table along with an empty milk glass. There were crumbs on the table still, and the butter had not been put away.

Louise continued slowly toward the door to the room behind the kitchen; then she quietly pressed down the handle and opened it.

THE ROOM WAS shaded by a large tree in the yard and a cool, faintly perfumed scent hit her nostrils as she stepped into Bodil's bedroom.

Bodil was sitting in a rocking chair between the two windows facing the garden. She was holding a heavy piece of knitting, a pair of large headphones covering her ears while she rocked mechanically back and forward.

Louise registered her tense breathing and loosened her grip on her pistol while she watched the older woman's focused work with the knitting needles. She called her name a couple of times before walking over to position herself in front of the rocking chair.

Bodil gave a little start. She looked up and as she removed her headphones, Louise could hear the classical music that had filled her ears. She didn't speak. She only stared up at Louise with sad eyes while her hands stopped and then dropped limply into her lap.

Louise squatted down in front of her.

"Where's Jørgen?" she asked.

The woman pressed her lips together and shook her head.

"Bodil," Louise said, this time a little more sharply. "I need to speak with him and it would probably be best if you were there, too."

Bodil's chin quivered and her lips trembled.

"He's not home," she said almost inaudibly.

Louise placed a hand on the armrest of the rocking chair and stopped its movement.

"Where is he?"

"In the woods. I told him he had to bring back the lady."

"Which lady?" Louise asked, standing back up.

"The one he brought home."

"Who's that?"

"The one from the woods that everyone is looking for," Bodil answered without meeting Louise's eye.

"The runner?" Louise asked. "Has he been keeping her here?"

"Yes. Down in his room."

LOUISE SPRINTED OUT of the bedroom, through the kitchen, and into the living room. She registered Bodil following her to the small hallway leading out to the back of the house, where a solid oak door separated Jørgen's section from the rest of the house. Louise contemplated the heavy bolt at the top of the door. The bolt was unlocked, and the door was open now.

The front room was Jørgen's bedroom. It was larger than Bodil's, and one wall was lined with long shelves on which small cars were neatly displayed. Not just Matchbox cars but real collector's items.

Louise quickly continued toward the small room in the back but stopped abruptly when the stench hit her. Both windows were open yet the smell was nauseating and acrid. The only object in the dark chamber was a bed, and on it was a crumpled sheet soiled with urine and feces. For a second she felt completely paralyzed as she let the impression sink in; then she walked to the bed and picked up a rope from the floor. It was tied to the headboard.

"Has he been keeping her tied to the bed?" she asked without turning around.

"Jørgen was always good at knots," Bodil answered. She walked over to the mattress and started folding up the sheet. "That smell will probably be hard to get out, don't you think?"

Louise bent down and looked under the bed. There were more ropes and rope snippets but nothing else.

"Jesus," she whispered, straightening herself up. Through the open windows, she heard Eik's swift footsteps moving across the gravel of the courtyard; a second later he was by the door.

"You've got to come over here really quick. There's something you need to see," Eik said, his voice sounding grim.

38

LOUISE SPRINTED AFTER Eik toward the barn, which was attached to the main house at an angle. The black double barn door was open, and from the courtyard she could see the bars in front of a horse pen.

Eik grabbed her and put a finger to his lips. He held on to her arm as they stepped inside the barn. It was dark in there and the air felt cool. The only source of light came from two crescent-shaped barn windows facing the courtyard.

"She's in there," he whispered.

They walked together to the two horse pens located side by side. Both doors were decorated with hand-painted signs that said LISEMETTE.

Louise looked inside the one that Eik pointed to and gasped.

She estimated that the pen was about six by ten feet. The woman lay on a bed pushed up against the partition wall to the other pen.

They stood there quietly and watched her. She lay motionless, her eyes closed, and next to her on the pillow was a doll with blond hair. The only part of her that was visible was her severely battered face, which was swollen and bloodstained. Next to the simple bed was a small nightstand with a rose in a tall water glass. Against the brick wall on the opposite side was an old grandfather clock and a low table with an embroidered table mat. Two flower plaques hung on the wall along with a heavy painting in a gilded frame. Louise figured that the decor probably came from the old merchant's villa in Rungsted.

Louise grabbed the lock on the door to the horse pen and carefully slid it open. She slowly opened the door and waited to see if the woman would react. She didn't stir.

Louise didn't say anything as she tiptoed toward the bed and looked down at the woman's closed eyes and the large wounds on her forehead. Eik stayed in the barn corridor.

"Don't wake her," Bodil said behind them. She was standing in the doorway, her hands on her hips.

"What's been going on in here?" Eik asked, turning to look at her.

"Jørgen's girls live out here."

Apparently she won't try to hide anything, Louise thought. She seemed to be aware that the game was up and now merely waited to see what was about to happen.

"I've had to give her some of Jørgen's medicine to keep her at rest so she wouldn't keep harming herself."

"Have they been living out here in the barn since 1980?" Louise asked, appalled, and retreated from the pen.

"Yes," was Bodil's only reply.

Louise was conflicted. While the mother in her wanted to protect Viggo Andersen, she had promised to keep him involved and aware of every bit of movement in the case as it pertained to his daughters. He'd been through so much, and wanted only the truth now. And he deserved that respect. Already holding her cell phone, Louise walked into the courtyard to call him, leaving it to Eik to contact Mik.

"We found your daughter," she began and quickly added: "She's alive, I can tell you that. But that's all I can say for now. Do you want to come?"

He did. She gave him the address, explaining that the house was right by the woods.

"Bukkeskov Road," she repeated, figuring that it should take him about fifteen or twenty minutes to get there. It was eerie to think that he and his children had been that close to each other through all those years.

"Did you write the twins out of the system so your brother would have something to screw after he couldn't get his needs met at Eliselund anymore?" Eik asked, standing by the barn door, each word vibrating with anger. "And so you could escape his assaults?"

Bodil looked at him with puzzlement.

"Yes, but we always took good care of them. They've had it better here than they ever did at Eliselund." His anger seemed completely lost on her.

"Was it your brother who raped and killed the child care provider in the woods?" Eik continued, breaking the filter off a cigarette before lighting it.

Finally he got a reaction. Bodil's eyes wandered and she started pulling away, but Eik grabbed hold of her.

"Why did he take the runner?" Louise asked, walking over to them. "Mette was still here after all."

"He never laid a hand on her; she's just a child. It was always just the other one," Bodil answered as if that made perfect sense. She told them that it was like the time many years ago

283

when Lisemette had some feminine trouble and was bleeding all the time. "That summer I worked the night shift at the Saint Hans psychiatric center during the weekends, which was lucky because that way I was able to bring home antibiotics for her."

"The summer of 1991?" Louise asked.

Bodil nodded. "He would steal out into the woods in the morning before I got home. Even though I told him not to."

"And then he raped the women he came across," Louise said.

Bodil's eyes shifted once again before she looked away.

"So how come Mette is in such a state?" Eik asked, gesturing toward the pen. "What did you do to her?"

"She has been difficult ever since her sister disappeared," Bodil answered, looking at them again. "Unless someone is standing over her, she'll hit her head against the wall, and she refuses to eat or drink. But that's what they do when they miss someone."

"How did her sister get away?"

"Jørgen must have forgotten to close the door. I'm always on him about it because they're not used to being outside. But when he's raking, he sometimes opens up the door."

Louise looked inside the empty pen where the comforter was smoothed neatly across the narrow bed. On top of the white linen were two yellow roses like the ones Jørgen had cut for her on their last visit to the gamekeeper's house.

The pen was decorated the same as Mette's with simple antiques and things from Bodil and Jørgen's childhood home. It was a stark contrast with the rough brickwork of the barn and the peeling wood boards of the horse pens—but the furnishing was undoubtedly well intentioned, Louise thought. At the end of the corridor was an old saddle rack and on the wall behind it were bridles, which must have been there when Bodil and her brother took over the old farm.

She walked back in to see Mette, who was still lying motionless on the bed, and squatted down next to her. She looked like her sister with the same long, dark hair. Her age did not seem to be taking a toll on her yet. From what Louise could tell, her features were as delicate as her sister's beneath the bloodied wounds and the swelling that distorted the shape of her head.

Louise checked the woman's pulse: weak. Then, as she was about to stand up, Mette suddenly started thrashing her head around as if invisible forces were pulling at her from every direction. Her eyes were still closed but her entire body was twitching.

A car pulled into the courtyard. Louise had overheard Eik calling an ambulance and the Holbæk Police Department, but she thought it most likely that Lisemette's father would be the first to arrive. She went outside to greet him.

Viggo Andersen had left his house so quickly that he was still wearing his slippers.

"Your daughter is in there," she said, showing him into the barn. "I'm afraid I have to warn you that she has caused herself quite a bit of injury."

He followed her hesitantly without asking questions, staying tentatively behind Louise as they walked to the horse pen.

"She's asleep, but I think she might be waking up."

Just then some restless sounds rose from the bed. Mette thrashed her head to the side again, hitting it hard against the wooden planks of the partition wall. Her arms jerked under the comforter and she emitted a series of mournful sounds as her head fell back once more, her long hair covering her face.

"We've already called for an ambulance, and it's on its way,"

Louise said quietly. She stepped aside when Viggo Andersen asked if he could go in.

His eyes were full of tenderness as he laboriously knelt down next to his restless daughter and put a hand on her shoulder. Softly he started to sing:

"Twinkle, twinkle, little star, How I wonder what you are."

He gently stroked his thumb over the fabric of the yellowish nightshirt that Mette was wearing. Her chest rose with heavy breaths before she flung her head against the wall yet again.

"Up above the world so high, like a diamond in the sky."

From where Louise was standing, it looked as if her breathing was becoming somewhat calmer. She didn't want to get any closer and risk ruining the father's attempt at soothing his daughter.

"Twinkle, twinkle, little star, how I wonder what you are."

It was as if sleep embraced Mette once more. Her tense body settled into the mattress a little deeper, and her cheek rested on the pillow.

The father's smile was heartbreaking as he told Louise he always used to sing that song to the girls at bedtime.

"You found her," he said and looked down at his daughter again. His hand was still on her shoulder as he quietly started to cry. He let his eyes wander across the clock and the small table. "Someone has been taking care of them."

Louise swallowed an outburst; this was not the time to share with the father what his two girls had lived through in the past thirty-one years. She realized that the horse pens at the game-keeper's house probably seemed like a preferable alternative to death. She could tell that Viggo Andersen had yet to notice that a similar box had been furnished next door, and so she decided to wait to tell him more. He would know soon enough what had happened to his two little girls after they were erased from history.

"The ambulance is here," Eik said from the doorway.

Louise heard footsteps in the gravel and someone opening the tailgate. Soon after, one of the paramedics stepped into the barn.

"She's in here," she said, pointing into the pen. The young man opened his eyes wide and dropped his jaw but Louise stopped his outburst by shaking her head sternly and putting a finger to her lips.

Outside in the courtyard more cars were arriving. She made room as they carried the stretcher across the uneven concrete floor of the barn corridor and indicated to Viggo Andersen to do the same.

"Has she been conscious in the time that you've been here?" the young paramedic asked when Louise came back into the barn.

"She's sedated at the moment," she explained. "But when she wakes up, you'll need to be aware that she can get quite restless and..."

"My daughter is severely disabled," Viggo Andersen took over. "As a child, she would always react very strongly to any situation that felt unfamiliar or unsafe to her. I'd like to ride along with her if that's possible?"

The young guy was unfolding a blanket, and his older colleague nodded. "Of course," he said. "Just get in the back next to her."

The two men wheeled in the stretcher next to the bed and very carefully lifted Mette onto it. She was slight, almost bony, Louise noted when her legs were uncovered. Her body was devoid of muscle tone, atrophied like that of a patient who'd been bedridden for a long time.

As they were about to edge the stretcher back out of the pen, she started moving about restlessly again. The sound that rose from her throat sounded like an angry growl. The young paramedic shot a startled look at the father, who stepped forward and put a hand on his daughter's arm. Louise was standing right next to them when Mette opened her eyes and started screaming. Her eyes were darting around the room and she balled up her hands in front of her chest.

Her father started mumbling soothingly, but she swatted at his hands and thrashed her head while the screaming continued.

"Let's get her in," the older paramedic announced firmly. He asked Viggo Andersen to step back a little while they pushed the stretcher into the ambulance.

"I'll strap her in," said the young paramedic and jumped into the back.

Mette was flailing and her sounds were angry and rejecting. Two long safety belts were fastened around her on the stretcher.

"What medication has she been given and how much?" the older paramedic asked Louise.

"I don't know."

She looked around for Eik and spotted Mik.

"Mik," she called. "We need to know when Mette received her last dose of medication and what it was."

After they put Mette in the ambulance, she heard Mik inform the driver about the medication. Viggo Andersen had settled in the low seat next to the stretcher. He appeared unaffected by her violent behavior. He gazed unwaveringly at his daughter's face as he started to sing to her again.

Louise leaned against the timber frame of the barn and watched thirty-one years of captivity come to an end. Behind the father, an IV was being prepared and the young paramedic struggled to place an oxygen mask across Mette's nose and mouth. They closed the back, and soon after the ambulance pulled out of the courtyard and left.

* * *

Mɪᴋ ᴡᴀs ɢɪᴠɪɴɢ the group of police officers a quick briefing by the white fence. Louise made eye contact with Eik before he walked over to tell them what they knew about Jørgen Parkov.

"We have confirmation that he was keeping the female runner here until just a few hours ago, when he brought her into the woods. She was alive when they left the gamekeeper's house but she's probably in pretty bad shape."

"We've already warned the residents of the woods against Jørgen Parkov and asked them to contact us if they see the young woman," Mik said, taking over. "And you need to be aware that René Gamst is most likely somewhere out there with a loaded firearm. So be sure to identify yourselves clearly whenever you run into anyone."

39

Louise stood for a minute and watched them as they disappeared into the woods. Then she slowly started walking toward the main house. She had seen Bodil's back as a female officer led her, and knew that the most difficult interrogation of her life was waiting for her inside.

She stopped on the stairs and closed her eyes for a second. How many times had she driven by the house? She had sat in their large yard, drinking lemonade. And all that time, Lise and Mette had been in the barn. Louise tried to shake it off but it was too surreal; too devastating to accept.

Then she went inside, closing the front door behind her. They were sitting in the living room, the officer in an armchair and Bodil on the couch.

Louise didn't know what to say as she pulled up a chair at the head of the coffee table and noted that the police officer from Holbæk had gotten out her Dictaphone. She suddenly had difficulty thinking of an opening and was grateful when the female officer started to read Bodil's rights to her while Louise got herself situated.

"Do you want to proceed?" the officer asked and turned toward Louise.

"Yes." She looked at Bodil, who focused on her, waiting for her to speak.

"You'll probably have to take me back in time, Bodil, if I am to try to make sense of some of the things I've seen out here today," she began. "I've spoken with your old neighbor, Edith Rosen, who told me about what happened to Jørgen when he was a child."

"What I did to him." Bodil corrected her without flinching. "Mother was right. I should have watched out for him better."

Louise tried to hide her disgust. Their speculation about Bodil was right. Looking into her eyes, she continued. "Edith Rosen also told me what happened in 1958. Were your parents aware of what your brother did to you?"

Bodil nodded and her eyes darkened. It took her a minute before she was ready.

"The first time, I cried so hard that I accidentally ran to Mother's room. My father wasn't home," she started. "I was frightened and I tried to stop him, but I couldn't. My mother just said that I was lucky to have a life. And she told me not to mention it to my father because it was my own fault that Jørgen turned out that way."

"She couldn't possibly have meant that you should continue to be victimized because he couldn't control himself," Louise objected.

"We didn't really talk about that. I knew he couldn't help it. He became like that when he hurt his head. It wasn't that he wanted to hurt me."

"What about your father?" Louise asked. "Didn't he ever find out?"

"Yes," she said. "But that wasn't until later."

"Your mother didn't say anything to him?"

Bodil shook her head. "Father never blamed me for the accident, and when he realized what was going on, he and one of my teachers arranged for me to go into service as a maid for a doctor at Ebberødgård. I saw my father now and then but even once Jørgen was gone, after our neighbor complained, I couldn't come home because Mother couldn't come to terms with him being sent away."

She paused for a second, staring into the wall across the room.

"Then when my father died, she brought Jørgen back home. And I've often thought that things probably weren't easy for her, either, in the subsequent years."

Silence descended. The ticking from the wall clock boomed.

"When Mother fell ill and was on her deathbed, I received a letter from her, asking me to come," Bodil continued quietly. "She wanted me to promise that I would take care of Jørgen after she was gone, and that I would never put him in a home. If I didn't agree, she would disown me. But her threats were unnecessary because I always knew that one day it would be my turn to take care of him. So I was prepared. By that time I was working at Eliselund, and the consultant doctor and I had come to an agreement that my brother could secretly move into the basement when the time came."

"We spoke with Lillian Johansen. She told us how you used to let him use the girls at Eliselund," Louise said. "But she couldn't explain how you managed to remove the twins from the institution."

Bodil looked at her quizzically as if she didn't quite understand.

"We drove them, of course," she said with a sweeping gesture. "Ernst had a car. We always used it when we wanted to get away together for a bit."

"Together?" said Louise. "Were you and the doctor having an affair?"

Bodil folded her hands back in her lap. "I guess you could call it that. We benefited from each other in various ways. He helped me with my brother and I was there for him. But I broke it off after we moved out here with Jørgen's girls. He became very angry and accused me of abandoning him."

"Did he take his own life because of the breakup?"

"I don't believe so," she said dismissively. "He was never good at standing on his own two feet. But he probably also realized that things were bound to get difficult when his paperwork was reviewed in connection with them closing down Eliselund."

Louise was dumbfounded at how easily Bodil had sacrificed the consultant doctor.

"Weren't you worried that he would reveal your secret?"

"No," Bodil answered, "why would I be? He was the one who put his name on the death certificates. And besides, he knew just as well as I did that they would be better off here," she went on. "After Eliselund closed down, the residents were to be transferred to other institutions. Who knows how things would have been for them, or if they would have been allowed to stay together?"

She was quiet for a moment before continuing in the same neutral voice.

"We've always been able to offer them security and stability. These people just function best like that, and as long as Jørgen gets his psychological and physical needs met, he is a picture of good nature. Just the way you know him."

Louise opened her mouth to say something but didn't have the chance before Bodil went on.

"Mette never progressed past being a little girl, and my brother always took good care of her. After he finished with the other one, he always went to sit with Mette and would brush her long hair. He was always so gentle, making sure that he didn't hurt her. They got along well, the three of them."

"He never touched Mette?" Louise asked.

Bodil shook her head.

"She wasn't a woman. She didn't arouse the urge in him."

"Not even after Lise disappeared?"

"He didn't see her that way. He would never go after a child."

"But he could have gone to you?" Louise said, checking that the Dictaphone light was still on. The female officer was gazing out the window. It was impossible to tell if she was even paying attention.

Bodil bent her head without answering, so Louise continued.

"Was that why you didn't intervene when he brought home the female runner?" she pushed. "So you could avoid it?"

It was a little while before Bodil finally nodded, and despite all of Louise's disgust she suddenly felt sorry for the woman. It wasn't just Jørgen's life that was ruined that day when the car hit him. It was Bodil's life as well. She'd had to shoulder a responsibility that she was much too young for, and their mother did her part to remind her of her guilt. There had never been any room for a normal life and normal emotions.

"What about the time when Jørgen lived with your mother?" she asked instead of digging deeper.

"Mother covered all of his needs," she answered briefly. "She would never run the risk of him helping himself outside the home. She was very good at nurturing his gentle side.

Just look at the flowers—that was something the two of them shared. They would pick flowers from the garden and then sit and enjoy the sight of them. It was a diversion for him to help take the focus off the other things. It's the same thing when we paint the plates."

Louise thought of the two yellow roses that Jørgen had cut for her that ended up as a table decoration at Camilla's wedding dinner. Now she wished she'd thrown them away.

"Didn't Lise and Mette ever try to get away from here?"

Bodil looked at her in surprise.

"No, why would they?"

"Because nobody wants to live in a barn."

"But they couldn't stay in here," she exclaimed. "I sometimes lock off Jørgen's section after dinner. Evening time is when he becomes most restless and then it's better to keep your distance."

Louise was aware that injuries to the frontal lobes could also result in a violent level of aggression, but she didn't realize how severely it had affected Bodil's brother.

"We spent our days together," Bodil continued. "It was never my impression, though, that the girls didn't like living here. In the winter we would put heaters out there so it didn't get too cold. Jørgen doesn't like that, either, when he goes over there."

"So he would just go to the horse pen whenever he felt the urge?" Louise asked, feeling provoked by how Bodil tried to portray their everyday life.

"That was most practical. Whenever the urge came over him, it was best if it was addressed quickly."

Bodil fell silent for a second before adding: "And I didn't want it going on in the house."

"But the runner was in his room," Louise interjected.

"That was only because he got so angry when I told him to

put her in the barn. That was their place and the one from the woods was a different story."

Bodil seemed genuinely sad.

"The last week since the one went missing has been hard on him. I went looking for her in the woods but then when I heard that they found a dead woman, I figured it was probably her. I didn't say anything to Jørgen even though he kept asking if she would be home soon. I don't know if he'll ever really calm back down again. And what happens now?"

Louise couldn't think of what to say. She just sat there, speechless and deeply shaken by hearing Bodil speak of the twins as if they were objects. And as if she genuinely believed that she and her brother had given them a good life.

"Why did you make us all believe that Jørgen was your husband?" she asked instead.

Bodil gave a quick laugh as she straightened herself up. "When siblings live together at our age, people tend to gossip. I wanted to avoid too many questions being raised. That's why I came up with the little story about the work accident. That's the kind of thing that evokes sympathy because it could happen to anyone."

Louise suddenly couldn't stand to hear another word. They had another interrogation to get through anyway, so this had to be enough for now.

"Do you have anything further to add?" she asked.

Bodil began to shake her head then stopped. "There are the two of them out in the yard, of course. You'd better take those with you as well."

"What's that supposed to mean?"

"Well, I didn't know where else to put them. If I had said anything then Jørgen wouldn't have been allowed to stay here."

"Who are we talking about?" the officer asked in confusion.

"He was probably a little too rough with them," Bodil admitted without answering the question. "But you have to understand that he was never a cruel person. He is just so strong that when the urge comes over him, it's best not to fight back."

For a moment her eyes turned glossy and she was quiet.

"It might be Lotte Svendsen from Hvalsø and another young woman from Espergærde," Louise guessed. "They disappeared the same summer that the first series of rapes took place in the woods. And their bodies were never found."

THEY BOTH FOLLOWED Bodil to the patio door leading out to the yard.

"Now, I don't remember the exact spot," she said, looking around as they stood on the large lawn. "It's down here in the back somewhere by the herb garden."

She led them toward the woods' edge where a large area had been cleared and turned into a vegetable garden.

"You buried them here?" the female officer asked.

"Yes. Jørgen did the digging. He's good at that sort of thing."

"We'll have the dogs search the yard when they get back from the woods," Louise decided and signaled that they could go back inside. "Did you get Bodil and Jørgen's personal data for the file?" she asked the officer from Holbæk, who would soon be the one left with the case.

She shook her head. "We'll go inside and take care of that now."

Louise nodded. She didn't feel like going back inside. Right now she needed to distance herself as much as possible from what she'd just heard, and so she walked around the house toward the courtyard to wait for the others. Her interest in putting her name down for the gamekeeper's house had vanished completely.

She thought of the young, pregnant runner who had been locked up and tied to a bed while she had been drinking coffee in the kitchen. She knew that it would be naive to hope that Jørgen hadn't hurt her; even if her physical injuries healed, she would have to live with the nightmare for the rest of her life— just like Edith Rosen had.

And what about the baby? Louise thought, walking in to take one last look inside the barn.

Silence had descended on the cool livestock wing. The only sound came from the tall grandfather clock with its rhythmic moving hands. She looked at the bed, then walked over and pulled out a drawer from the small dresser. It contained the same type of smock-like dresses that Lise had been wearing. There were two of them, neatly folded, and next to them a few pairs of socks and underwear. That was it.

Louise had just closed the drawer when she heard footsteps in the gravel outside. She pushed the door to the horse pen shut and when she turned around, he was standing in the barn doorway.

40

H<small>E WAS SWEATING</small>, his thin hair sticking to his forehead, and his lumberjack shirt had come untucked. For a minute he stood transfixed, staring through the bars into the empty pen. Then he turned his gaze toward Louise, and his eyes lit up as he held out his hand.

"Jørgen," she said, her back against the pen.

She only took one step sideways before she felt his hands on her face. He ran his fingers down her cheeks. She pressed her arm against her body and felt her shoulder holster but didn't have a chance to react when he suddenly grabbed her and pulled her toward him.

"Jørgen. Let me go," she demanded angrily and tried to wrench free of him but he brutally tightened his grip and she lost her breath. When she made another attempt, he squeezed her so hard that an intense pain shot behind her left lung as a couple of her ribs cracked.

Louise gasped for breath as he pushed her farther down the barn corridor, his one arm still locked around her. Yet she still tried to resist when he pulled off her sweater and yanked the gun holster over her head, the sharp leather straps cutting into her skin.

Don't fight back, she suddenly thought, remembering Bodil's words.

She registered a new sound behind her—footsteps on the concrete floors. She wanted to turn her head but fell against the wall when Jørgen tore her blouse and pulled it off her, panting and snorting. With a single jerk, he tore her bra and started roughly fondling her breasts.

It hurt. His hands were rough against her skin. Louise closed her eyes, unable to look at his face. She felt his heavy breathing very close to her neck and then against her cheek as he stuffed a piece of her torn blouse into her mouth.

Using his entire body weight, he pressed her forward until she was doubled over across the saddle rack. The old grain sacks, heavy with dust, scratched her face as he pushed both hands down inside the waistband of her jeans to pull them down. The grit on the barn corridor crunched beneath her feet as he tugged on her pants one more time so the button fell off, enabling him to shove them all the way down.

The steps behind her came closer. Louise lifted her head to see the barn door and the twilight hitting the corridor from the doorway. At first she could only make out the outline of a person behind Jørgen's broad body but as it came closer, she recognized René Gamst standing there holding his shotgun.

Relief rushed through her as they made eye contact, but then he moved his eyes to her exposed lower body and Louise noticed the bulge in his pants.

Jørgen was right behind her. She could feel the fabric of his pants against her naked buttocks. The pain was burning in her chest, and her breathing was wheezy. His breath was like hard blows as she heard him undo his zipper. Louise closed her eyes and looked away from the barn door.

Then the first shot fell, and Jørgen's body jerked violently. Another shot followed a second later.

LOUISE FELT THE warmth spreading across her naked torso as the blood from Jørgen's torn veins pumped onto her skin, and he slumped over heavily on top of her.

As his grasp around her slackened, she grabbed onto the end of the saddle rack and started pulling herself out from beneath the weight of his large body. She gasped for breath as a bloody splodge from his head landed on her shoulder.

She tumbled into the corridor and pulled up her jeans while Jørgen's body was left slumped, his arms dangling limply over the floor. Louise breathed in sharp blows after pulling the rag out of her mouth.

René was still holding the gun with both hands.

"You could have hit me," she whispered, covering her breasts with what was left of her blouse.

"That was a risk I was willing to take."

She watched a speck of dust floating in the light from the window and heard the sound of Jørgen's blood dripping onto the floor.

"Why didn't you shoot him right away?"

She couldn't bear to look at him while asking.

"Because you liked it," he answered scornfully. "If only Klaus could have seen how little you fought it."

"I'll kill you," Louise snarled at him, her heart starting to pound. She could feel her pulse beating in her neck, and her chest getting tight. He had recognized her after all. Determined not to lose control entirely, she breathed in and out, dug her nails into her palm, and stared directly into his eyes. "Leave Klaus out of this," she said through her teeth. "No wonder he didn't want to hang out with you guys anymore."

"You!" he snorted. "You don't understand a damn thing. You never did, not now and not then."

"What do you mean?" Louise asked him, straightening up so the pain from her broken ribs stabbed inside her chest.

"Thomsen was right. You were so gullible."

Despite her agonizing pain, she got up before he had a chance to react, kicked the weapon out of his hands, and twisted his arm around so hard that he doubled over.

René Gamst moaned.

"Tell me what happened!" she yelled, pulling on his arm.

"Your boyfriend was a pussy," he gasped. "He didn't have the fucking guts to put the noose around his own neck."

His words made everything go black as she pushed him down the barn corridor in an armlock. She pressed him against the ground as she bent down, pulling out two plastic strips from her shoulder holster on the floor.

He screamed when she tightened one of them around his hands before using the other strip to fasten his wrist to a bar in front of the horse pen. Then she left the barn without looking back just as the door to the main house swung open and the female officer came running out.

"Did you hear the shots?" she shouted. "It was right nearby. I called Mik. They're on their—"

She stopped abruptly as if she only just then really noticed Louise.

"What...?" she exclaimed, stunned, and walked toward her.

Louise brushed her aside and crumpled up in the small

pebbles. She pulled her shirt together around her naked chest and leaned back against the black-tarred plinth before closing her eyes.

She heard René calling from the barn and soon after the sound of running steps approaching. Someone stopped next to her but she didn't open her eyes, and then she heard him continue into the barn. He returned a minute later and fell to his knees next to her. When he said her name, she recognized Mik's voice.

"I think he broke a couple of my ribs," she said quietly and opened her eyes.

Others came running as well. Louise registered that the female runner had been found not far from there. She was alive but in bad shape. Nobody mentioned the baby in her belly. More footsteps and more voices but she couldn't take part in it. Ambulances had been called, and someone put a blanket around her.

Eik was wheezing as he stumbled into the courtyard, out of breath. With a cry of shock, he dropped down on the rocks next to her, reaching his hand out for her soiled face.

EIK WAS STILL sitting there when two ambulances pulled into the courtyard. She could smell his leather jacket and hear him breathing but she couldn't see him.

Someone reached a hand down to her and she managed to get up while pain shot through her entire body. She slowly shook her head when he asked if she wanted him to ride along.

"When you head out together, you go home together," he tried.

"Not today," she mumbled, pulling the blanket closer around her body as she walked to the ambulance.

Over by the barn René was about to be put into the back-seat of a police car. Louise turned her eyes away quickly but not quickly enough to avoid his scornful look and the twitching at the corner of his mouth.

She nodded when the ambulance driver asked if she would prefer to lie down. He asked about her condition and where it hurt but by then Louise had already turned her face away and closed her eyes.

She heard the police car drive off with René before they closed the back of the ambulance. She could feel his eyes on her naked body again before the shot was fired. She had thought he would help her. But in that gang, they only helped each other.

The potholes in the gravel road made the first-aid kit in the back of the ambulance rattle as they drove away.

EPILOGUE

Jonas and Melvin raced to the hospital as soon as they heard. Louise's concerned parents were already there, sitting by their daughter's side, reassuring her it was only broken ribs. She was tough. She'd weathered far worse, and would be fine. If they only knew, Louise thought. Her ribs and bruises, with their accompanying aches and pains, were the least of her wounds.

Before discharging her, Louise's doctors urged her to consult a psychiatrist. She thanked them for taking care of her and going to the trouble, promised to make some calls sooner rather than later, and then balled up and tossed the paper they'd handed her with the list of referrals into the trash can in the hospital parking lot.

She was mentally and physically exhausted. She knew full well she needed to heal and regroup, but was going to do it her own way. Not by talking and telling her sob stories, puffy-eyed, nose red and running, with soggy tissues in hand, to a highly trained stranger. No. She needed to get away. She needed a break. And time to sort it all through.

Two DAYS LATER Louise headed up to her attic, in search of an old suitcase. Inside were so many scattered but profound items and keepsakes, all pieces of her history. She was terrified by what she might rediscover there, but fought the urge to run back downstairs, away from the mementos and records that she had carefully ignored and left untouched for so long. René Gamst's final taunt lingered in her mind. *He didn't have the guts to put the noose around his own neck.* Louise knew it was time. The past couldn't wait any longer.

In all the years since Klaus had died, she'd struggled to forget—to bury her memories and grief along with his body and their love. She'd been going through the motions for years, but had ultimately outsmarted herself. *You don't understand a thing*, René had said. *You never did, not now and not then.* Louise had to focus. She wouldn't give in to despair. She owed at least that much to Jonas.

She didn't have to haggle or get lost in red tape and doctor's notes for time off; a medical leave of absence from the force was a given. And though she did not have to worry about job security, Louise stressed over the impact on the department. She'd only just started and had so much responsibility resting on her shoulders. Eik would have to carry the heavy load until she was ready to return. But she knew he could handle it. Besides, the one thing of which she was certain was that she was no good to her colleagues in her current state.

Her mind made up, Louise packed up the car, her treasured old suitcase safely at the bottom of the pile of randomly chosen clothes. She would lay hands on the truth, no matter how shattering. If Klaus hadn't tethered that rope around his own neck, she would find out who had.

With her son, their dog, and promises from Melvin to visit, Louise got behind the wheel of her car. She drove toward their modest, tiny, but welcoming weekend cottage, only steps from the ocean. Jonas seemed to understand that this getaway was crucial to his mother's recovery, and chatted, at first, with great enthusiasm about working on his music at the beach, and getting Dina out to run on the sand and paddle through the water. When things got suddenly quiet between them, and then stayed that way for miles, Louise stole sideways glances at Jonas, who looked deep in thought. And newly serious.

"What's up? Are you okay?" she asked, trying not to push.

"I know you love your job," he started, a minute or two later. "What will you do if you get fired?"

"Oh no, Jonas. My work will be fine." Louise tried to reassure him. "My boss wants me to be okay; he's counting on it. Everyone there wants me to get better. They know I need this break and totally support it. And me. Please don't worry about me. Spending time with you will be the best possible medicine." She reached over and ruffled his hair, smiling and hoping to convince him she was going to be all right.

THEY DROVE ON. As the sun began its descent, Louise and Jonas talked about the changes to the little houses that dotted the road, with their small but well-tended gardens and Danish flags in front. They talked about dinner.

Pulling up to the cottage, she didn't bother to properly park. Following Jonas's excited lead, she jumped out of the car and breathed in the salty air. An uphill battle awaited her. It would take time to heal what was broken. But looking at her smiling child, this lovely young man whom she needed and would do anything for, Louise exhaled. And then walked with her family to the shore.

A NOTE FROM THE AUTHOR

The Forgotten Girls is a work of fiction, and I have liberally changed and adapted reality to fit into my story.

Some parts are based on actual events that took place at the old mental institutions around the country. Most, though, are figments of my imagination—just as none of the characters in this novel are based on real people.

Likewise, I have taken a casual approach to the geography of the area around Hvalsø, which was the setting of my own youth. Most of the places are real but many have moved around a little in this book. Eliselund, however, exists only in my mind.

Finally, I would like to extend a big thank-you to everyone who so openly and kindly took the time to help me in my research for this book. My special thanks to Charlotte, Steen Holger, Tom, Lotte, and Christine.

—Sara Blaedel

ABOUT THE AUTHOR

Sara Blaedel's interest in stories, writing, and especially crime fiction was nurtured from a young age, long before Scandinavian crime fiction took the world by storm. Today she is Denmark's "Queen of Crime," and her series featuring police detective Louise Rick is adored the world over.

The daughter of a renowned Danish journalist and an actress whose career included roles in theater, radio, TV, and movies, Sara grew up surrounded by a constant flow of professional writers and performers visiting the Blaedel home. Despite a struggle with dyslexia, Sara found in books a world in which to escape when her introverted nature demanded an exit from the hustle and bustle of life.

She tried a number of careers, from a restaurant apprenticeship to graphic design, before she started a publishing company called Sara B, where she published Danish translations of American crime fiction.

Publishing ultimately led Sara to journalism, and she covered a wide range of stories, from criminal trials to the premiere of *Star Wars*: *Episode I The Phantom Menace*. It was during this time—and while skiing in Norway—that Sara started brewing the ideas for her first novel. In 2004 Louise and Camilla were introduced in *Grønt Støv* (*Green Dust*), and Sara won the Danish Academy for Crime Fiction's debut prize.

Today Sara lives north of Copenhagen with her family. She has always loved animals; she still enjoys horseback riding and shares her home with her cat and golden retriever. When she isn't busy committing brutal murders on the page, she is an ambassador with Save the Children and serves on the jury of a documentary film competition.